CRAIG PRIESTLEY

WATCHERS

Copyright © 2020 Craig Priestley

All rights reserved. No part of this book may be used or reproduced in any manner whatsoever without written permission except in the case of brief quotations embodied in critical articles or reviews.

This is a work of fiction. Names, characters, businesses, organisations, places, events and incidents either are the product of the author's imagination or are used fictitiously. Any resemblance to actual persons, living or dead, events, or locales is entirely coincidental.

Cover design by Sarah Carter

Second Edition, 2020

10 9 8 7 6 5 4 3 2

ISBN: 9781653726059

1

Her hair skipped as she collected glasses from behind the bar - each golden strand taking a life of its own: a ripple of anticipation, the slow dance of infatuation.

Something about her held Charlie's attention. It wasn't her beauty. There was something strange about the way she held herself, something almost too rigid and perfect. She seemed like a puzzle piece that didn't quite seem to fit.

It was the distraction he needed, though. He moved his attention from the delicate dimple in her chin to the curvature in her top lip, from her small button nose to her ferociously piercing eyes. On the faintest of occasions when he had managed to catch her glance, it had felt like a lifetime - yet he had not gathered the courage to talk to her. Instead, he sat alone with his first beer at the end of a long week.

Charlie took a long, self-medicating sip as he encouraged the carbonated lager to swirl around his mouth before he swallowed. But not even the revitalising effect of the drink that sat before him could hold his attention. Instead, his head swam with rising anxiety that sat heavily on his mind. But when he looked at her, it was as if everything faded: a bubbling pot of life that simmered until only the barmaid and he remained.

Charlie Taylor was not a hopeless romantic, but he did think of himself as reasonably old-fashioned when it came to dating. There had been the occasional fling in his past, but the vast majority of his experience with the opposite sex had happened in a relationship that had long left him.

At almost thirty years old, dating was the last thing on Charlie's mind. The London dating scene filled him with dread, and he couldn't let another person in. Not yet.

He had tried online dating for a while, mostly out of sheer pressure from his friends and old work colleagues, but it had never led anywhere. Charlie didn't think he was a bad looking guy: when he looked in the mirror, he saw a strong jaw, gentle eyes and a welcoming smile. But his appearance meant little to him.

When the right person came along, if that were to happen, he needed to be in a better place. Romance was at the bottom of his priority list. But deep down, he still held a hope for catching someone's eye across a crowded room.

"Charlie!" a voice boomed, breaking the spell of the bartender prematurely. "Care if I join you?"

Steve was of a similar age to Charlie. He dressed in louder clothes and, despite being shorter, held himself so that he appeared a good inch or two taller. He pounded across the bar; his drink splashed from side to side as droplet after cloudy yellow droplet landed on unexpectant inhabitants of the local establishment. Steve seemed far too preoccupied with his internal excitement and self-assuredness to care.

Charlie pushed the chair that sat opposite out from under the table with his foot, inviting Steve to take a seat. However, his level of excitement did not quite match that of his friend.

"Charlie! It's so good to see you, mate," Steve accepted the invitation to sit down, placing his now partially empty drink atop the table. "It's been what, a month?"

"Yeah, how are you doing?" Charlie asked.

"Can't complain. Pretty reasonable crowd tonight."

Charlie first met Steve in their media studies class at college. Steve had caught him staring with a little too much interest at Mrs Camberwell as she bent over to pick up a suspiciously placed pen on the floor. During her retrieval, her blouse found itself unable to protect her bosom for the entirety of the collection. Steve had given Charlie a cheeky smile, Charlie laughed, and their hormone-riddled youth had provided the building blocks for their friendship. That was at the tender age of eighteen.

Despite his attraction towards the barmaid, Charlie's appetite for gazing at women had subsided slightly over the past decade, whereas Steve's had only flourished.

"Anyway," Steve continued. "Did I tell you about last weekend?"

"How can I forget; a stunner with legs that went on forever, right?"

"Ah, so I did tell you."

Charlie nodded. He found the strength to refrain from a remark along the lines of 'no shit, Sherlock!'

"She was that and much, much more my friend," Steve bragged, reaching over and playfully punching Charlie's arm. "Any luck your end?"

"You know me," Charlie answered, hoping the closed response would move them on to the next subject.

"I do know you," Steve took a long gulp of his beer and eyed the bar before returning his attention to Charlie. "And I know that you need a kick up the arse when it comes to the fairer sex."

Steve rose to and walked around the table behind Charlie. He grabbed the back of his chair to force him to his feet gently. Steve nodded towards a couple of women at another table.

"Let's go."

"But you've just sat down," Charlie sighed, running his fingers through the front of his scruffy, hazel hair.

Charlie was about to make a break for it, but before he got the chance, Steve placed a hand on his arm.

"I thought we'd just catch up and, you know, shoot the shit like old times," Charlie complained.

Steve grinned widely. It was at that moment that Charlie could see there would be no convincing him otherwise.

"This will be much better," Steve explained.

Before Charlie had time to argue, he was being dragged against his will into a situation that would either end in awkward conversation, or the very best-case scenario, a night of meaningless sex - that would then lead to another awkward conversation. Some might say that Charlie was a glass half empty kind of guy, but he often wondered, why not just use a smaller glass?

"Ladies, this is my good friend Charlie, and you can call me Stevie B," Steve took the time to over-emphasise each syllable in his name.

"Would you mind if we joined you for a drink?"

Charlie's friend had already begun to sit down as the girls looked awkwardly at each other. In the end, they nodded and smiled.

Steve encouraged Charlie into a chair next to him.

"So then, what do we call you?"

"I'm Rachel, and this is Jenny," the more confident of the two replied.

They can, of course, be wrong, but first impressions were important to Charlie and more often than not, he would find them to be justified. He believed that everybody made a conscious or subconscious judgement in one way or another, so he always allowed his thoughts to drift to the front of his mind. Charlie's first impression of Rachel was something in line with a loud and sassy caricature from a reality television show.

As he observed Rachel, he noticed that her skin was a slight shade of orange from what he was sure was more than a mild overuse of fake tan. He glanced at her eyes and, in his mind, imagined a scenario where her eyelashes would cause a small breeze if she happened to blink hard enough. He also couldn't help but notice the way that she crossed her arms to hoist her cleavage - possibly to welcome attention from his friend.

Steve continued.

"Nice to meet you. Can I ask you girls something?"

"Sure," Rachel replied, taking a sip of her wine.

"My friend here, he's a good-looking guy, right?" Steve glanced cheekily in Charlie's direction, giving him a wink in the process. Charlie stared stoically in Steve's direction before moving his attention back to his pint of solace.

Rachel stroked her chin for a moment, seeming to revel in the power bestowed upon her. Charlie did not enjoy the spotlight quite as much.

"I think so," Jenny interrupted, peering over a wall of shyness.

Steve slapped Charlie on the back - hard enough to encourage a little of the drink to escape from his lips.

"There we go. Jenny, was it? You seem like a smart girl," Steve moved his hand from Charlie's back and began ruffling his hair playfully.

"Why don't the two of you get better acquainted, and I'll go and get us all another drink? Wine, is it?"

The ladies nodded as Charlie shuffled uncomfortably.

"It's fine mate. You don't have to."

Steve grinned and gently pinched Charlie's cheek before heading to the bar. The resulting red mark spread across Charlie's face in-line with his embarrassment.

Apart from being slightly uncomfortable with the overly touchy nature of his friend, and being in the company of two strange women, the only thing on Charlie's mind was the barmaid. His mind wandered. Did she have any hobbies? What music did she like? Was she as crazy about sweet things as he was? Did she think that he was attractive? In those solitary moments, he lost all concentration on his surroundings.

The common question that he had was one that he contemplated multiple times – just what was it was about her that monopolised his attention?

Rachel and Jenny glanced at each other a few times as Charlie regained his focus on the conversation at hand. He tried to think of an engaging subject matter that would be appropriate to discuss with someone he had just met in a bar.

"So, what do the two of you do?" was the best he could muster.

Jenny answered first, the more eager of the two to form conversation.

"I'm a waitress at the moment, but I want to be an actress. I'm just working at a café until something comes along. You know, that stereotypical waitress waiting for her big break type of thing."

"You'll get there, doll," Rachel encouraged her friend, before responding to Charlie. "I'm a hairdresser. It's such a good job. I love it."

Rachel took a deep, long mouthful of her wine and continued.

"You get to talk to people all day and hear loads of gossip; it's just like reading Heat all day. The people you get coming in, they have so much chat - and they all know that I'm the best hairdresser you can get north of the river."

Charlie's attention wavered; he hoped that second impressions could also be wrong.

"That sounds nice," Charlie responded as sincerely as possible, doubting any insincerity would have been picked up on.

"Yeah, like this old bird Maggie who came in today, she's worried that her husband has been cheating on her, but she's not said anything yet. She was thinking whether to like burn his clothes and kick him out, or whether to, you know, talk to him about it."

"And?"

"I gave her a lighter."

Steve, where are you? Charlie wondered.

Almost on cue, Steve re-entered the scene and placed two glasses of wine down on the table.

"So then ladies, what are your plans on this fine evening?" Steve asked with no apparent fear of rejection.

"We're just here for a quick one, and then I'm off to meet my boyfriend," Rachel smirked in Steve's direction. She finished the rest of her old glass of wine and swapped the now empty glass with the full one that he had just brought over.

"You could have told me that before I got you a drink," Steve exclaimed.

"Well, you didn't ask," Rachel winked in reply.

"I don't have any plans," Jenny smiled in Charlie's direction, curling a section of her dark hair with her right index finger. The wall of shyness almost toppled.

"Just call me the matchmaker," Steve stood up. "Well, I'll leave you to it. It has been a pleasure - expensive for a quick hello, but a pleasure none the less. Rachel if you want some real fun then come find me. I'm sure you can do better."

Rachel flicked her hair and stuck two fingers up at Steve in a playful gesture.

"And Jenny, take care of my boy here."

"I will," Jenny replied with a cheeky grin.

Steve picked up his beer, patted Charlie on the shoulder and headed towards his next victim standing by herself at the bar.

"Your mate is a bit of a dick," Rachel observed.

Charlie tried his best to contain a smirk, only partially succeeding. "No arguments there."

Despite calling him a dick, Rachel stared in Steve's direction. Steve had already found himself in the throes of a conversation with someone else.

"What kind of acting do you want to do?" Charlie was intrigued to find out more about the person who had seemingly taken an interest in him.

"Rachel thinks I should try out for Hollyoaks."

Charlie nodded slowly.

"Don't worry, I'm not going to," Jenny giggled. "It's nice to know how you truly feel, though."

"I'm sorry, I just…"

"I want to act on stage, in the West End," Jenny interrupted.

"That is pretty interesting," Charlie admitted. His interest piqued.

Of course, he felt guilty for judging someone on the basis of their likes and dislikes, but this was the 21st century and the age of disposable dating - the era where people chose whether to talk to someone based on a picture. The time where people dated based on the back of a three-minute speed date, a few words, or even an emoji or two.

If Romeo and Juliet were alive today, they wouldn't have even made it to the first date.

"I'm currently in theatre school, and work in town to pay the bills."

"Tell me more about your acting."

"At the moment I'm going to as many auditions as I can, I'm just looking for someone to take that chance on me."

"Someone will, babes," Rachel added.

Jenny continued to talk about her hopes of finding her next role and becoming a successful actress when the barmaid appeared in Charlie's eye-line over her shoulder. Of what Charlie heard, he could not recollect a thing.

The barmaid stared in their direction. Not at Charlie, but Jenny.

"I've got to go," Charlie stumbled into the table as he shot up from his seat. "Nice meeting you."

Before either girl had the chance to reply, Charlie was out of his chair and halfway across the room. He scurried away from the conversation, leaving the barmaid behind.

Charlie regained his composure a few steps away from his favourite drinking hole. Was the barmaid jealous? Charlie wondered to himself. He quickly dismissed the notion, but couldn't shake off the look in her eye. Something was questioning. Something felt familiar.

He decided to walk home. The pub wasn't too far from his small one-bedroom flat in Kentish Town, and he needed some time to think.

Charlie wouldn't argue if someone said that he thought too much - he knew that was accurate, but he could feel something significant happening. A part of his mind whirred as he tried to process the situation, but alas, to no effect.

Charlie breathed in the last of the day's late-summer sun as he unsuccessfully attempted to take his mind from the barmaid. Typical Charlie: someone who seemed nice finally showed some interest, and he blew it for this imaginary, far-away possibility. He wondered for a moment whether he should go back and apologise, but concluded that they probably thought he was a bit weird for running away mid-sentence. And who'd blame them? No, Charlie would go home, watch some television and quieten his mind from the commotion that accompanied his restless thoughts.

It was just past seven-thirty on a Friday. He doubted there would be anything on TV, so he would probably spend his evening watching episodes of shows that he'd seen multiple times before. If nothing more, it offered comfort and familiarity.

At least it was the end of the week; Charlie thought, as he walked past rows of trees in blossom.

***

The following morning Charlie woke in a daze, not necessarily from the two pints of beer consumed the night before, but more likely due to clouded thoughts and troubled sleep.

As a modern-day twenty-something going-on thirty-something, one of the first things Charlie did upon waking was to check his phone. Today was no different: two text messages.

'I knew Rachel would come around.'

He scrolled to the next message.

'I've had like 2 hours sleep. Where did you go m8?'

Charlie wondered if his inability to find someone to share his life with wasn't because of some inept ability to talk to women, but instead because he wasn't a complete and utter arsehole. Regardless, after waking, the internal chatter had lessened, leaving only one voice that still spoke to him: the barmaid.

2

Why did weekends exist? Charlie pondered the question internally as he walked through a series of winding roads from Kentish Town to Highgate.

Partying was one option that didn't sit right with him, hanging out with friends a more viable possibility, as was going to watch football or rugby. Still, for Charlie, Saturday would always involve family - and today was no different.

As he walked towards the house where he was born and raised, childhood memories swarmed inside his head. The specific one that came to the forefront was of a fourteen-year-old Charlie in his bedroom, stealing his first kiss from his school friend Samantha. They were in his bedroom to study for a geography exam but, to his delight, she showed more of an interest in him than tectonic plates. The two of them remained friends for a while afterwards. They spent a lot of time with each other, but nothing romantic ever occurred beyond that other than the occasional flirt and neglected opportunity.

As most people did, Samantha faded from his life. When she turned sixteen, she dated a more popular boy from school, and there was no place in her life for a male friend who was that little bit too close.

Charlie walked along the small garden pathway, noticing that the garden needed a trim - a vast understatement for the behemoth of entanglement created by wild thickets and forgotten shrubbery.

Memories of his mother were fleeting.

His knuckles landed on the old, wooden door. Particles of dust jumped from the surface with each rap. There was no answer: it was a good thing he had remembered his spare key.

As he placed the key in the lock, it turned with slight resistance. With an audible creak, the door opened. The musty smell from the house flooded out into the world outside.

"Mum?"

Silence welcomed him.

"Mum?" he tried for a second time.

Charlie entered the house; the smell of damp wood filled his lungs.

As he walked through the hallway towards the dining room, a bright light flickered and filled the house.

"Oh, sorry darling, I was just setting the table for lunch," the voice of his mother greeted him.

The smell in the air shifted from one of dampness to fresh food that was cooking on the stove. All it had taken were those few words to alter perception.

Charlie and his mother met in a tight embrace. For a woman who has a son pushing thirty, she didn't look a day over forty.

"How are you Mum?" he asked as she planted a kiss on his cheek.

"Fantastic. I've missed you so much."

Charlie mimicked her thoughts.

"I've made your favourite." his mother stalled, either to create suspense or perhaps illicit a response. He let her continue. "Mac and cheese, with bacon bits."

"It might have been my favourite when I was fifteen." Charlie countered.

"I know it's still your favourite."

Aren't mothers always right? Even though mac and cheese was a somewhat dull, not to mention high-carb meal, it reminded Charlie of a simpler time - a time when, despite a truckload of teenage angst, he would sit down to a home-cooked meal and a loving mother. Plus, bacon; everything was better with bacon.

The thought slowed his heart and calmed his mind.

"So how are things going, darling?" his mother asked with a loving smile.

"It's okay, but I'm still waiting for a new role. The last one ended a while back."

"Do you need any-"

"No, I'm fine," Charlie interrupted. "Thanks, Mum, but I am fine. I still have enough money to pay the rent, eat Chinese and have a beer or two."

"Good," his mother's cheery face changed into one of unease. "I do worry about you."

"I know," Charlie noticed the transformation of his mother's expression and changed the subject. "How is everything with you?" he asked, turning the line of fire away from one of self-reflection.

"I'm waiting to hear back about a job, but no rush."

"How long have you been out of work now, Mum?"

"Oh, it's been a while love," his mother admitted. "But we're doing alright, so I don't need to go back."

Charlie's father had passed away when he was a child, but he had a life insurance policy that left his mother well covered. She hadn't used much of it, apart from a bit here and there to help out Charlie with his tuition fees. And, despite being an emergency bank for Charlie, his mother had waited to tell him about the money left from his father; she wanted to help him with a deposit and pay for a wedding should he meet the right partner. Charlie agreed and respected her decision, but his mind often drifted to the idea of lying on the beach in the Caribbean, drinking from a coconut without a worry in the world. That would do for a few months at least.

"Have you met a nice girl yet?"

The word 'yet' grated at Charlie's ego slightly. He knew that it had been a while since his last girlfriend, but life was like a dodgeball game - the only way to survive was to duck and dodge until the right catch came along.

"I'm working on it."

"I'm sure she's just around the corner."

The cooker alarm chimed.

"Why don't you go and turn on the TV? I'll give you a call when everything's dished up."

Charlie gave her another quick hug and proceeded to the couch.

As Charlie entered the living room, there was a flash. Not a burst of brightness, but darkness and shadow. A flash of something distressing. A flash of an empty and decaying home.

Charlie saw a picture of his life that was not as he saw it. The room was bare and cold, with dust and cobwebs growing in occupancy.

Charlie turned on the television, causing the darkness to disappear as quickly as it had arrived. It was not long until he had drifted away into a world of bright colours and flashing images, where sleep found him.

***

Charlie floated from his childhood bed, through the ceiling of the house, until he was hovering above the street. He wore the blue and white striped pyjamas that he used to wear as a child, like a kooky 'walking in the air' tribute act.

He floated from his house towards the street.

The tarmac below turned to gold, each section forming in turn to create a yellow-bricked road. Charlie followed the golden path and, on each side of the street, he noticed bright and vibrant colours being painted on objects as he passed.

Doors transformed from dull brown and white to dazzling ruby reds, pinks and blues. Windows became painted in green, violet walls appeared, and bricks turned to orange and blue as colour circulated all around.

Each building was painted differently to the one before it, which created a magical rainbow effect in a vivid world of colour.

He floated along the middle of the multi-coloured street and realised that he recognised below.

To the left was his high school English teacher, Mr Hinchcliffe, who was the first person that made him feel excited about reading outside of school. Just up ahead on his right was Charlie's first boss from the supermarket, where he worked to save enough money to go out drinking with friends at the tender age of seventeen.

Various people from the past appeared as he floated by and, after he reached the end of the street, he looped back around from where he came. He waved to the people from his past, no matter how distant a memory. He approached his mother's house again.

The smell of mac and cheese became more prominent, tantalising his taste buds from afar.

The warmth and happiness created by familiar faces brought a feeling of safety. Yet the forgotten connections began to introduce an element of distress.

His mother waved as Charlie approached; just a few metres away. A dark flash.

Something dragged his mother violently into the house. The door slammed shut, and all colour around him disappeared.

The light turned off.

***

"Darling. Dinner's ready," a voice boomed, pulling Charlie from his dream.

Disorientated and tired, all he could manage was a perplexed grunt.

"You fell asleep dear," his mother stood over him. "Dinner's ready."

Being an only child, Charlie and his mother shared a secure connection; however, she often blurred the lines between parent and want-to-be-best-pal.

One would imagine the average eighteenth birthday party would involve a lot of friends giving a middle finger to the oppressive puppet masters that had ruled their lives to that point. Charlie's eighteenth celebrations included being mothered in front of a few of his best friends and going to a local restaurant for a very awkward meal.

A proud mother sat alongside four eighteen-year-olds, or soon to be, who wanted to go out on the town, get drunk and have as wild a time as possible on a twenty-five-pound budget. It was adolescence at its purest.

Charlie thought back to the day when he went on a bar crawl around the town's taverns and bars, joined by his mother. On the odd occasion, he'd catch her nudging his friends, complimenting the size of a few of the women's breasts - as they sat in silence.

At the time it was excruciating but, looking back, it made Charlie proud to know that she cared for him enough to put herself in some extraordinary situations. It had taken him a while to realise that he wouldn't want it any other way.

Charlie sat down at the dinner table as his mother placed a generous portion on to his plate. He lifted a sizeable forkful of the mac and cheese to his mouth. It tasted just as good as he remembered - if not even better, creating a warming sensation to wash over him.

Every worry that Charlie had left him.

Charlie wolfed down dinner by himself, as his mother politely refused to join him. Instead, she started the washing up. He continued to use only his fork to shovel the pasta, hot cheese and salty bacon bits into his mouth as quickly as humanly possible.

With thoughts fresh in his mind of the past, he decided it was time to reach out to an old friend.

"Can I be excused?" Charlie asked, finding his words through a mouthful.

"Of course, dear."

Charlie left the table and sat down in the living room. He took his phone from his pocket to talk to a friend he hadn't spoken to in over a year. He hoped the phone number still worked.

He looked through his contact list and clicked dial. After a few rings, his friend answered.

"Yo, Paulos, how's it hanging?" Charlie reverted to a less mature tone, as he spoke to his friend. "What's going on?"

Paul - sometimes referred to by the not-so-inventive childhood nickname of Paulos, had settled down with a wife and child. Charlie never thought that he would be the type to marry at a young age, but as with the rest of his friends, whether they were loners or philanthropists, almost all of them had met that someone special and started a family.

Without wanting to feel too selfish, Paul was one of the few people Charlie could rely on to stop him from feeling quite so bad about his own life. It's not that there was anything wrong with Paul's life; more like a void in Charlie's.

Misery loves company, so they say.

Speaking to Paul stirred feelings of immaturity and lead to Charlie's second-guessing of his life choices. He wondered if he should have stayed with his ex-girlfriend of four years. Maybe she had been the one. Perhaps they were too young to see it, and perhaps the cracks could have been fixed.

Yet they continued, talking about old times and the new.

"Maria is pregnant, again!" was the news from the other end of the phone. They were expecting their second child. Charlie attempted to dust off his feelings of regret and loneliness.

As often happened after two people went in different directions, Charlie and Paul had drifted entirely apart. They had different lives, different responsibilities. Heck, Charlie hadn't even met his friend's first child, and now there was another one on the way. Strange how life can appear to move so slowly, yet pass so quickly by.

"I'll come up to see you and the little one soon," Charlie promised, speaking truthfully at the time, but knowing full well that he'd most likely manufacture a reason for putting it off further.

Babies were not in his area of comfort and as a slightly socially awkward human being that relied somewhat on the effects of beer to get through nights out, he questioned how he would fare against an entity that pooped and cried all the time. Maybe it would be simple, as long as he didn't have to change the diaper.

"How are you coping?" Paul asked, with a tentative edge to his voice.

Charlie noticed the tone and wondered what he might be referring to. He thought back to his last Facebook update. Was it about looking for work? He thought so and told Paul he was sure something would come along soon. He felt a need to turn the conversation into a validation of sorts that his life wasn't entirely off the rails, and so he told him about the barmaid.

"So, what's her name?"

Quite possibly, what was the main driving force in his life right now, had no name. No solidity. She was a fleeting moment of infatuation that had felt like so much more.

He'd dated, he'd been in love, but this was different. Or at least he thought so.

"I'll give you all the details when I see you," Charlie changed the subject back on to Paul and his wife. It's incredible how much joy can be conveyed in someone's voice by a simple thing such as bath time; the stories he told about the difficulties of parenthood he recited with laughter. Paul even shared vivid stories of poo flying all over the place during a diaper change, which left Charlie with a thought. If he ever had a baby, he would always wear dark clothes.

After a while, the void in Charlie's life dissipated. They continued to share stories from the past, as well as discuss Paul's plans for the future. The only thought that lingered was how strange it was that two people at the same age, with the same upbringing, to be in such different places in their lives.

It was useful for Charlie to talk. However, the mere thought of his childhood friends growing up and leaving him behind left a bitter taste, and that was something he promised himself never to be. He needed to be positive, even in his own, curious way.

Watchers

There was only one thing for it. Charlie would be positive. He would drown the conversation in his head, and try to push away the feelings of worry and angst.

Tonight, he would face his fears and talk to the barmaid.

Charlie wondered why bar staff often received attention from the opposite sex. Was it because they were always open to conversation and tended to offer a friendly greeting? Or was it because they provided a mood-enhancing substance that conditioned an attraction? Charlie knew that his fascination for the barmaid was different. He'd never spoken to her, let alone received a beer from her. There was something about her that he still couldn't put his finger on.

Charlie leant forward on the armrests, pushed himself out of the chair and went into the kitchen. He was greeted only by darkness.

The smell of mac and cheese waivered. The kitchen appeared lifeless and unkempt. Charlie knew what was true, but could not admit it. Not to himself, not again.

His senses became overwhelmed as light flooded from behind him. His mother appeared over his shoulder, brushing the hair away from his forehead.

"Don't worry dear. I'll see you next week."

Charlie turned to an empty living room as the house took its true form.

He turned from the darkness to face his mother; the look on her face flickered unnaturally between one of happiness and despair.

The tray of the leftover mac and cheese sat in her hand in one moment, yet with a single blink, her hands appeared empty.

"I'll see you next week," she said again as the light and darkness fought for control.

"See you next week, Mum."

Charlie left the dining room before his mind asked questions. He rushed down the hallway and, without looking back, he unlocked the door to the world outside.

***

Interior bar. Evening. Destiny.

Charlie wasn't overly comfortable approaching the barmaid entirely alone, so he decided to invite a friend: even though Steve was crude, he was one of his only friends who were available for this type of mission.

Steve entered the bar as if he was starring in an aftershave commercial, one of those where the man that had sprayed himself became suddenly irresistible to women.

The two friends sat down at the same table as the night before.

The self-acclaimed 'woman magnet' rubbed his stubble. "I'm intrigued about your message," Steve continued, putting on a slightly upper-class British accent to mock Charlie as he quoted the text message. "Meet me at the bar. Tonight is the night," he eased off the impression. "The 'P.S. free beer' bit at the end was definitely the clincher, though."

Charlie dug into his wallet and removed a tattered £10 note.

"Go crazy. Mine's an Amstel."

Steve tipped his proverbial hat and headed to the bar.

His friend ordered the drinks, giving Charlie time to plan his first move.

Initiating contact was easy; when they finished their drinks, he would go to the bar, make sure that she served him and then introduce himself. What came next was the tricky part. The only thing in his heart that he desired to do was confess his attraction, which was so strong that he'd not been able to stop thinking about her. He wanted to tell her that it wasn't merely a physical crush, but that there was something about her and he felt a need to be with her - a need so strong that it was driving him insane.

"Maybe a little too forward," Charlie mumbled to himself.

He thought that if Steve's track record was anything to go by then perhaps he should tell her that even though she's not that pretty, that there was something about her he just could not put his finger on. It was a putdown hidden within a compliment. Steve was an asshole, but it worked, well, sometimes, but Charlie wouldn't do that. Instead, he planned to go with the whole 'be yourself' advice that multiple people had given him: it either worked or perhaps they didn't have any real guidance.

"Here you go, mate," Steve returned from the bar, beers in hand. "Amstel for you and I've gone for one of the craft ales, Hoppy Ending."

"You're kidding me?"

Steve showed off the bottle of ale. The beer was indeed called Hoppy Ending, complete with an illustration of a scantily clad woman giving a hop a massage. Now that was top drawer marketing.

As always, the very first sip of lager was refreshing. Charlie enjoyed a drink two or three times a week, often using it as a crutch.

"So, what are we doing here, then? Well, apart from enjoying each other's fine company, of course."

"I've decided to ask someone out."

"That's brilliant mate, who's the victim?" Steve gave him no chance to answer. "Oh, Jenny of course, yeah she's nice. We could go on double dates together. Might give me another chance to get in with Rachel."

"No… what happened with Rachel?"

"What do you think? In and out. No survivors. You know the drill by now."

Charlie laughed but felt a stab of sadness inside. Is this what his life was to become?

Moments of reflection passed.

"She was actually alright," Steve admitted.

"Then, why?"

"I don't know. You know me. It'd just end badly."

Charlie was intrigued by Steve's momentary display of vulnerability regarding the fairer sex, but it was something he decided to park and bring up later. He needed to focus on the nerve-shattering task that lay ahead.

After relaxing and enjoying their drinks for a few moments, Charlie was first to break the silence.

"So, the girl I wanted to ask out," Charlie paused dramatically.

"Come on; it's not The X Factor."

"Alright. Well, it's the barmaid."

"Ah dude, barmaids are no good. I mean, think about it. How many sleazeballs go to the bar on a daily basis? You've got to think if she's the least bit hot, which, if you're breaking your duck to ask her out, I'm guessing she must be pretty damn hot, she will have guys swarming all over her."

He had a point: a fundamentally primitive and chauvinistic point, but a point nonetheless.

"She doesn't seem the type to want a lot of attention. I don't think I've ever seen her chatting to a guy."

"So, she works in a bar, full of guys who want a drink, and she doesn't chat with them? Okay, mate, sure."

"Well, all the more reason to speak to her sooner rather than later, right?"

Steve shrugged and then nodded. "Go and get her squire. I doff my hat to thee."

After a few more minutes of back and forth jokes around potential chatup lines, Charlie finished his drink. His heart pumped blood through his veins quicker and harder than he had felt in years. It was a countdown to a moment he'd only known was possible for a short amount of time, but somehow felt like destiny; as cheesy as that seemed.

He finished his pint in record time and marched over to the bar.

The middle-class, British pub had high ceilings, top-shelf whisky, and a small range of over-priced beers. It was Charlie's local establishment and after he'd seen the barmaid here a few weeks ago, he'd either been coming in or at least walking by, every evening since.

An attentive barman approached, but Charlie waved him away. Yes, he walked to the bar. Yes, he had an empty pint glass in his hand, but no, he didn't want the barman to serve him. What an idiot. He looked back to Steve, who was occupying himself with his phone and seemed happily engrossed. Charlie concluded that he was either swiping left on Tinder or texting a new conquest.

Charlie moved his attention back to the bar; the barmaid appeared.

Her presence lit up the room; her dazzling beauty made the task all that much harder. Charlie's gut and brain were begging him not to talk to her. It was too risky, it could go drastically wrong, but the longing to speak to her was interminable. It was time.

The barmaid stood behind the bar, apparently not doing much work. She faced away from Charlie. With a clear of the throat, he tried to get her attention.

"Excuse me." He sounded croaky. Maybe she didn't hear. He tried again, clearer this time.

She ignored him; walking towards the door at the end of the bar. She was as stunning as he remembered.

He had recently found himself lying awake at night wondering what it was about her that he found so endearing. Her eyes ever so cautiously darted in Charlie's direction.

"Can I please talk to you?"

He was aware that he sounded desperate, but the amount of effort it took to talk to her felt like nothing he'd ever experienced.

"Excuse me?" he added.

She turned around and glanced up in his direction for a split second.

Charlie froze.

There was something about her eyes.

Charlie realised that this was the first time she had ever looked directly at him, and it filled him with an adrenaline-fuelled mix of excitement and trepidation. One second was all it took to truly *see* her. In that moment of eye contact, Charlie noticed jolts of bright blue dancing through her irises, like electricity darting through a circuit.

That one glance was enough to muddle Charlie's words until he managed to ask a question with a stutter.

"Can... I have." he tried to catch his breath. "A drink?"

"I just offered you one, and you said no!" came an annoyed reply from the short-tempered barman further along the bar.

Charlie made his excuses and tried to catch the attention of his infatuation.

"Will *you* get me a drink?" he asked quietly, in the barmaid's direction.

She turned around, head angled away from Charlie, eyes fixed on the cracks in the floor.

Her lips parted.

"You are not supposed to talk to me."

She pronounced each syllable flawlessly. Charlie could not detect a hint of an accent that could tie her to one location. The complete indistinguishable placing of her childhood raised questions in Charlie's head.

"Where are you from?" She ignored the question. Charlie then questioned her initial reaction. "What do you mean, I'm not supposed to talk to you? Are you okay?"

She stood motionless for a moment, eyes focused on the space ahead of her. She avoided moving her head in Charlie's direction, but she eventually shook her head in answer to his question - her flawless hair swaying from side to side as she did so.

"How - why are you talking to me?" she replied.

Their first conversation wasn't going quite the way Charlie had planned, but it was a start. It was time to summon all of his courage and go for it.

"Well, I think you're beautiful, and I've wanted to talk to you since I've been coming here."

She turned her head slightly towards Charlie, one electric-blue eye meeting his.

"Every time I see you, everybody else just disappears," he continued. "I wanted to ask you out for a drink. I don't know - I felt like I had to… like there was some sort of connection between us. Man, sorry, that sounds so lame."

She lifted her head to look at Charlie, her eyes targeting on his. The colour had drained from her face, causing her to look extremely perturbed. She opened her mouth.

"They're listening."

"For Christ's sake, what are you going on about? Do you want a drink or not?" the booming voice of the barman asked irritably.

Her eyes jolted away from Charlie's. He sensed her vulnerability as she cowered further away.

"Mate!" the bartender pushed for an order.

Charlie broke his gaze. The vignette of his attention faded and he looked up to see the barman standing at the bar, looking directly at him.

"What can I get you?"

Charlie studied the barman blankly, before looking back to the barmaid. She was gone. In his confusion, he took a moment to process what had just happened and then ordered two drinks.

As the barman poured the drinks, Charlie wondered what had just happened? Where did she go? *Who was listening?*

Charlie paid the barman and took the beers back over to his friend.

"So then mate, how did it go?" Steve probed before he even had the chance to sit down.

***

Jenny could not contain her laughter as she danced comically with her friends.

She was pretty but didn't believe it herself. Instead, she struggled to fit into most social circles, focusing on developing her talents in her pursuit for her big break. Although, while she didn't necessarily want to be one of the breath-taking models who only had to enter the casting door to get a six-figure contract to star in a blockbuster, it didn't stop her being any less jealous.

Her real dream was to become a star of the stage, where acting and performance was appreciated and sometimes heralded.

But tonight wasn't about acting. Tonight, she let go. Tonight, she danced.

A group of girls out having fun, drinking and dancing, as usually the case tended to attract quite a lot of attention from various gentlemen in the bar. The term gentlemen would be stretching it a little, Jenny thought as she was often perturbed by the type of men that would approach her in bars like this one, and she didn't generally have the confidence to go up to people herself; tonight was no different.

Catching her breath from laughter, she stood to the side of the dance floor as her friends began to dance a little less comically. An arm appeared on her hip - a bit forward, but secretly she found herself enjoying the attention. The arm enveloped her waist, as the stranger's fingers reached around and placed themselves gently on to her stomach. He pulled her backwards, gently into him. The beat of the music flowed through them: Jenny's hips loosened, and her feet began to move in rhythm with his. He led the mystical dance, swaying to and fro, matching her movements as his lips approached the nape of her neck.

Acting like this wasn't like Jenny, but she didn't fight it; instead, she accepted the advancement. For some reason, she didn't mind the forward approach as much as she usually would. She hadn't received any attention like this since the hazy nights out at Roehampton, and even then, it was from some drunk kid. The man behind her was no kid; she could tell from the large arm wrapped around her and the pressure that she felt applied against her lower back. Neither was she a naive girl studying drama.

The grip around her waist tightened as he took control of her movements. He moved her when he wanted her to move. Lead by the mysterious partner, they danced.

She enjoyed the feel of a man's arms around her, even if he was holding her too tight. She placed her hand on his in an attempt to soften his grasp to no avail. The mystique diminished.

Jenny began to pull away, but the stranger's grip remained firm. Jenny started to panic.

"What do…"

The stranger's large hand enveloped her mouth, cutting her off mid-sentence.

Jenny tried to move, tried to kick, tried to scream. The stranger wouldn't let her. Where were her friends? Why wouldn't they help her?

The stranger moved his lips close enough to her neck for her to feel his warm, disgusting breath on her skin. After breathing on her neck for a few seconds, Jenny hoped that everything would be okay - that someone would see what was going on. Instead, the man who held her began to kiss her neck. He pulled her head ninety degrees to the side so that she couldn't make eye contact with anyone in front of her.

To other people in the dark, drunken club, they must have looked like a couple of people having a lot of fun.

He moved his lips up from the nape of her neck to her earlobe. In a low, sensual voice he spoke, the whisper cutting through the music like a knife.

"Got you."

The stranger let go of the forceful grip and spun her around to face him. His intent vanished.

He stood in front of her with a huge grin plastered across his face.

"James! You fucking idiot! I'm going to kill you!"

"Hey. You were having fun there for a minute, right?" James replied, his eyes sparkling with a devilish playfulness.

"What the actual fuck?" she punched him on his chest, not that it would do much to affect his massive frame.

"What's up, girl? Long-time, no speak."

Jenny's group of friends hustled over towards them as they sensed fresh meat on the dance floor.

"Hello, ladies," James dashed past Jenny in the direction of the four excited young women, eager to have their part of the fun. "See you around, Jen," James suggested before dashing off to the dance floor.

Her knees felt weak from the joke played on her and, apart from the need for another drink, only one thing hit home: Jenny needed to find herself a new group of friends.

***

Charlie stared into his drink as he watched the remains of the foam trickle down the inside of the glass, towards the pale amber pool from where he took his last sip.

In one moment the droplet was there, and in the next, it had gone.

When Charlie had asked about the barmaid, the barman had looked at him like he was crazy. He shook his head, mumbled something under his breath and walked away. For the life of him, he couldn't comprehend what was going on or where the barmaid went.

Steve sat fully engrossed in his phone the entire time Charlie was at the bar – apparently noticing nothing out of the ordinary, except overhearing a slightly annoyed bartender.

"I hate to do this to you again mate, but I think I might head," Charlie confessed.

"Stay for one more?" Steve implored. "This is only the second."

Charlie agreed but had no desire to discuss anything further.

The two friends sat there in modern-day silence. Steve pulled out his phone once more.

Steve swiped at a fast pace as he looked for matches on the dating app he had opened. Charlie sat deep in thought, sparing the occasional glance towards the bar to see if the aim of his affection had returned.

There were occasions during their next beer where Charlie swore he saw her reflection in a window or an empty glass, but when he turned to look over his shoulder, he realised that it must have been his mind playing tricks on him.

He hoped that if she was here again tomorrow, he could still muster the courage to talk to her. He didn't want to get her into trouble, but there was something in his core that drew him in.

After they finished their current round of drinks, Steve got them another.

Shortly after Steve ran out of the number of daily swipes he was allowed, the conversation flowed once more. They chatted through everyday things. They discussed the news, what they'd seen in the cinema, and Steve filled Charlie in on some of his favourite new tracks.

After a couple more pints than he had initially intended, Charlie felt an urge to have another, but he was unsure if any amount of alcohol would help this situation. It was a slippery slope into alcoholism, and he was well aware that it ran in his family.

Instead, Charlie called it a day. He kept to the promise of another drink but hadn't overdone it. Nevertheless, he once again left the bar with questions about the barmaid thundering through his thoughts.

3

Dense grey clouds stretched along the landscape as far as the eye could see. There was no sun here, nor had there ever been.

The only light to penetrate the landscape derived from the flickering of a blue electrical current, running through the all-encompassing cloud. The currents ran sporadically through the world, creating ever-shifting shadows.

Central to this world was a city, where the cloud formed every brick of each building. Shades of grey and white sculpted the most exquisite constructions, and from each building rose individual towers - gaps on the side of structures serving as windows, illuminated by blue current as it appeared. In this world, electricity was its life force, and cloud the conductor.

The city contained hundreds, if not thousands, of multi-storey cloud-like buildings that stretched beyond plain sight. In the centre was one tower that was more extensive and rose far taller than the others. It swayed with the wind but always maintained its precise structure - as did the entire city. The gigantic tower contained hundreds of thousands of windows and reached higher than all the skyscrapers in the world put together. Yet the structure did not fade from view into clouds. It became the cloud itself.

Inside each window within the central tower stood thousands of identical workplaces, and at each workplace sat what appeared to be a person. Each desk held a set of monitors. Each set of screens focused on the life of one person; it displayed their home, their work, their favourite places to go and relax, and on the largest it followed them around, tracking their every move.

Above every station were etched words; some displayed in English, others Indian, Chinese, Latin – there was no prejudicial bias from the instruction:

Through the slightest whisper or the most lucid of dreams we speak.
Remain in the shadows, and of mentioned sightings repeat.
We are the watchers.

One of the monitors displayed Charlie saying his goodbyes to Steve at the pub. It showed him stumble slightly as he rose from his chair, somewhat intoxicated from the gathering with his friend. Watching his actions on the screen sat the blonde barmaid.

She was required to report her sighting, but there was something that stopped her from doing so. There was a growing influence in her world that flowed through these towers that created a cause for concern.

Charlie, like everybody, was observed by a watcher from these stations. For everyone had a role in this life, and the watchers were the directors who ensured they fulfilled their part.

However, in the world of watching and gentle influence, corruption spread through their ranks. It had begun spreading like a disease, infecting watchers one at a time, turning them into rogue, maniacal influencers. Instead of gentle suggestion, watchers began to control the mind of individuals, persuading them to perform evil acts. The corrupted made people commit crimes and live out their darkest desires. They made them into nothing more than animals.

Ever since the dawn of man, corruption had existed. From the time the apple was taken from the tree; since there had been curiosity, corruption had existed.

It started as a flicker and, before corruption was understood, it had spread and become too large to eradicate. There had always been corrupted watchers, but it had previously been a small percentage that caused people to commit atrocious crimes outside of the individual's storyline. It was near impossible to tell which heinous acts in the history of humanity were caused by corruption because some people lead a path that was driven by acts of terror.

But, corrupted watchers raised the bar. These terrible acts were not of blasphemy or aggression. No, that was human. Corruption drove acts of sadistic hate, given the right host.

When corruption had spread uncontrollably in the past, it had led to mass conflict; wars between countries, nations set against each other - the only aim to cause as much destruction as possible. By the time corruption was reported, it was often too late. Storylines were changed, and lives affected. Corruption had become part of existence, and because of this, it had seemed to be accepted. However, the barmaid could sense the rise in corruption around her.

She noticed it in the world as everything began to deteriorate. She remained vigilant of corruption, but that wasn't the reason she struggled with a decision at this moment. It was instead the fact that Charlie had seen her.

If she reported a sighting, it was likely that she would be removed from Charlie. There would be another watcher placed on him, and she feared there was a possibility for them to be corrupted.

Her fear wasn't an emotion as such, but a calculation. When she found the result to be above a certain percentage, it caused her to alter from the programmed response that occurred naturally. This time, however, while the risk was minimal, the result that would follow in a worst-case scenario was one of extreme negativity, so it altered her action. She knew that the sighting and her lack of response might be reported, but that was part of the risk that she was taking. She didn't fear death, if that was the result, because death didn't exist for her - there was just non-existence.

The barmaid observed Charlie as he left the pub. She watched as he walked through the streets he often walked on the return to his small one-bedroom flat. She confirmed her decision.

Charlie led a solitary life. He had a kind heart, and she shared that connection with him. That connection proved to be strong enough to disobey the rules; the in-built rules that they all lived by, since the day they came to be.

The watcher that sat next to her jolted back and forth, twisting and bending unnaturally; his bones creaked and cracked in sharp movements. His wrist snapped, his fingers clicked, curling in all directions. With splayed fingers, he reached for the desk in front of him. Before she could react, he twisted his neck two hundred and seventy degrees to look at her.

Instead of a flicker of blue, a glimmer of red danced in his eyes - a bright blood red that ran through his very being. A sadistic grimace appeared on his face as he stared at her. Before she could react, his eyes returned to normal. The watcher's head untwisted, and his bones became unbroken.

In a burst of red electricity, he vanished into his screen.

Quietly approaching the screen, the barmaid peered into the life of another. It was peculiar. One watcher, one life, was how it had always been. And no watcher disobeyed the rules.

Despite there not being a need for a chain of command, The Overseer could be considered the head of the watchers. The Overseer sat a-top the central tower, connected continuously, experiencing everything - or so the barmaid believed. She couldn't assign a gender to The Overseer, because nobody had seen them.

Whispers of prisons, filled with corrupted watchers who had avoided termination, along with those who had disobeyed the rules, were rife in their land; watchers who had broken their protocol and spoken, trapped with sadistic, ruthless and corrupted killers who lived only to punish others. It was worse than nothingness, and it's one thing that ensured watchers fulfilled their purpose. Besides, there was never another option. They were watchers.

Disobeying her programmed rules, she observed the screen that was not her own. The barmaid could see the corrupted watcher walking beside their person, whispering into her ear.

In the screen, a well-dressed businesswoman walked home from work along a quiet high street, going about what would be her usual, everyday business. She passed a homeless person, who held out his hand, begging for change. Her face twisted into a look of disgust – the watcher and woman started laughing, slowly at first before cascading into loud and consistent cackling. Before the homeless man had the chance to react, the woman removed her shoe from her foot and began to hit him with the sharpest part of the heel. She struck him repeatedly, marking his arm before she aimed for his head. She continued to strike the defenceless man over and over again.

Blood flowed down the man's face as she grinned.

The watcher's head jolted to face the screen. He held up a hand and, with a flash of red, the display turned off. Darkness.

The barmaid scampered back to her desk. She needed to report the corruption, but it was too late. The corrupted watcher knew that he was being watched and had disconnected. He had gone rogue. Neither could he find his way back or be tracked; the two of them would be together forever until the connection broke.

The barmaid did not know whether watchers could die once they had gone rogue. They had a physical form in their world, but only the illusion of one in the world of man. A watcher's termination occurred through connections in the system but, with the rise in the number of corrupted, would he be hunted? Perhaps the rogue watcher wouldn't be found. Corruption would spread through the real world, causing more suffering.

This needed reporting. It was ingrained in her - like a programme that stated this was the next action to be taken. But then, why was her hand only hovering above a button that reported a sighting?

She recognised the street. She knew where the homeless man was. She also knew that if she reported the corruption she would be monitored. If this was to happen, they might see Charlie talk to her, which in turn could mean that she would never see him again - neither could she help.

She pulled her hand away from the button, sat down in her seat and vanished into her screen in a flash of bright blue electricity.

***

Charlie found himself taking a different route home. He wasn't sure why he walked this way, other than a basic urge he felt to take some time and reflect– some time to consider a new perspective. Still, Charlie found himself on a much longer walk and, despite the summer sun's warmth earlier in the day, the evening air teased a cold front. He felt a little annoyed at himself for forgetting to bring a coat to the pub.

The streets were relatively empty around Archway. Charlie noticed that almost every shop he passed was closed, and yet he had a strange feeling that he was being watched.

The conversation with the barmaid processed in his thoughts, but seeing Steve and sinking a couple of beers helped ease the confusion. Charlie had decided that he had some sort of panic attack, freaking the barmaid out, which caused her to run away. That's what must have happened because one minute she was there and the next she wasn't. That was the only explanation that made sense after a few hours of slightly inebriated consideration.

Despite his best efforts, his thoughts drifted once again to the barmaid. He pictured each strand of her hair and imagined them moving as if they were a completely separate entity from one another. Thousands upon thousands of blonde strands taking a life of their own. And those eyes. Those bright blue, electric eyes.

Charlie tripped over something. He looked down. Was it someone's leg?

"Woops, sorry, mate," Charlie held his hand up as he turned around to face what he assumed to be a homeless man who had settled down for the night.

Charlie's initial reaction was one of conditioning from spending many years walking along London streets.

"Sorry, I don't have any change," he said as he began to move his attention back to the street ahead.

But a thought niggled in his mind. Something seemed odd. The homeless man's leg protruded from under a blanket in a strange direction.

Charlie focused and turned back to face the homeless man, who remained still. He leant down and noticed something else, something red and sticky. He saw blood.

With panic rising in his chest, Charlie leant in closer, not wanting to remove the blanket, but feeling like he had to know. He already knew. But he needed to see.

The smell emanating from the man was so dreadful it caused Charlie to gag. He covered his nose with one hand and reached for the top of the tattered, stained blanket. Leaning against the side of a building, Charlie slowly pulled the cover away.

The face of a homeless man stared back at him; his face battered, bloodied, and lifeless.

Charlie felt bile rise in his throat. He bent at the midsection and vomited - well, tried to. Instead, he fell to his knees, dry heaving. He wiped saliva away from his mouth and raised his eyes to the head of the homeless man. The sight was even worse than the smell that began to settle in his nostrils.

That was when Charlie saw him for what he was; a shell of a man with multiple stab wounds, covered with a mixture of blood and dirt. It took Charlie several moments to notice something even more troubling - that the man had no eyes, but exposed eye sockets from where he assumed an object had hit them repeatedly.

Stricken with rising trepidation, he scampered to his feet. He pulled out his phone and dialled 999.

"I'd like to report a dead body," Charlie continued. "It's a homeless man. He's been stabbed, I think," he fought to find his breathing. "I'm, like, between Kentish Town and Archway. Dalmeny

Road, I think… or maybe Archibald, one of those, maybe. It's about ten minutes from The Assembly House."

Charlie sat down a safe distance away from the body - far enough away so that the smell didn't cause him to throw up, but close enough for him to stay guard. He waited for the police car to arrive, which was followed shortly by an ambulance. There wasn't much use for the ambulance, he thought.

The police took his statement, asked him where he was going, and why he walked this way when his home was in a different direction. Charlie felt guilty, even though he knew he was innocent. Being questioned by authority irked him into a feeling of awkwardness but, afterwards, the police took his details and thanked him for his report.

He left the crime scene. Knowing the streets reasonably well, he headed back towards his flat via the quickest route he knew. Something bothered him, even more than the disturbing sight he had witnessed or the taste of sick in his mouth. No matter how hard he tried, he couldn't shake his decision for taking this route.

"Why did I come this way?" he mumbled to himself. "Why, why, why?"

"Because of me."

The barmaid stood beside him, lit clearly by a mixture of the nearby street light and distant starlight.

"What?" Charlie responded, dumbfounded.

"I asked you to come this way, Charlie."

"What do you mean?" he continued. "How do you know my name?"

The barmaid stood silently.

As many questions as Charlie wanted to ask at that moment, no further words escaped him.

His heart rate rose.

His desire for clarity skyrocketed.

He needed answers.

The colonel continued: "Mr President, the US troops entered the designated zone just north of Samara, but encountered resistance. The Russian president has ordered us to recall our troops and refused to cooperate with the investigation into the death of the Turkish peacekeeping treaty."

"With all due respect sir, we need to withdraw our troops now, else it may create more friction between our nations," the vice president interjected.

The president waved his hand for the colonel to continue.

"Our intelligence informs us that Russian troops killed the treaty, but we have no evidence. The Turkish prime minister is fully set to go to war, and so far we have only managed to buy some time." He opened a folder and placed a chart on the president's desk. "We have three options. The first is to withdraw and negotiate with the prime minister. The second is to order the troops to push forward against command. And the third, which I believe to be correct, is to

 the troops and send a spy to infiltrate the camp."

 well." The president studied the map before commenting

 we send a spy, then they must be made aware of the

 Russians can never know we sent a spy, no matter the

 is needs to be made clear. We need the very best for

ake the arrangements."

fted uncomfortably, speaking directly to the

ey capture the spy, it might lead to

is is the best way to keep the

e made my decision, and it is

 the members of the

are dismissed."

e with his thoughts.

in his chair

***

Jenny couldn't handle any more customers today. If creeps weren't hitting on her; a pinch here, a crude remark there - then it was rudeness. Not to mention the lack of tips, if people were trying to come on to her, then surely they'd leave a good tip? Unfortunately, it didn't seem to work that way.

She drove home, yet another day further from her dream. Her thoughts wandered. She pictured herself standing on the stage, front and centre, performing. She couldn't dance very well, but at that moment she was the lead member of Cats, completely kitted out in the full attire – whiskers and all. She moved gracefully around the stage as the crowd cheered her on. She could feel the heat of the stage lights warming her face as she performed.

A sudden red light snapped her back to reality. She had only seconds to react as a car braked suddenly in front of her. She slammed on the brakes and stopped just in time to avoid an accident - just ever so slightly nudging the bumper of the car ahead. Luckily there was nothing behind her. Jenny took a moment to compose herself; the last thing she needed was a repair bill or insurance claim. Hopefully, the gentle bump wouldn't have done any damage to either car. She unbuckled her seatbelt and took a deep breath to steady her nerves.

A man exited the car in front: he was big - boy, was he big. He couldn't be too annoyed, surely? A close miss, Jenny thought - there was no need for an altercation here.

The big, burly man approached her window, signalling for her to wind it down with his large workmen's hands. She obeyed.

As the man approached the now unprotected window, Jenny took notice of his appearance. It looked like he hadn't showered for days. His hair was long and unkempt, his blue and white check shirt tattered with red stains along up his right sleeve and dotted around.

"Are you okay?" Jenny asked as he came closer to the car door.

"Am I okay? Am I fucking okay?" the man responded with a snarl. "You went into the back of me, you stupid little bitch."

Shock ran through Jenny's body. She focused on her breathing just enough to respond.

"Sir, I'm sorry. You just broke suddenly."

"Oh, so it's my fault, is it?" he asked, squaring up to the window.

"No, but I barely touched you. I'm sure everything's okay, I-"

"I'm going to make you pay."

He walked away, retreating into his car.

The relief overwhelmed Jenny. She fell backwards into the cushioned seat and wondered just how her day could get any worse?

In her moment of anxious reflection, she considered checking the bumpers, just to make sure there was no permanent damage. Jenny opened the door and lowered her feet on to the ground. Before she was entirely unprotected, she noticed the man re-emerging from his vehicle with something in his hand. She quickly closed and locked the door and started to wind the window up.

The man was holding something long and wooden. Jenny couldn't quite make the object out, but she knew that it was a sure-fire way to make her day worse. He strode towards the car with purpose, with intent - with a baseball bat.

The blood rushed from Jenny's face. She fought the instinct to cry, and instead hurried to finish winding up the window as quickly as her small hands could manage. She twisted the key in the ignition. Click, click, click. The engine spluttered. No! Not now! Please start. She turned the key again. The imposing man was closing in.

Click, click, click. Nothing. He reached the car.

Click. The aggressor brought the baseball bat back over his shoulder. Click. He began to swing. Click. Whoosh. The engine roared into life.

In the blink of an eye, Jenny moved the gear stick into reverse and stepped on the accelerator.

The man swung the baseball bat into the driver's seat window with all of his might.

The driver window shattered into thousands of pieces - shards of glass flew everywhere.

The car rolled backwards slowly. Jenny relieved the pressure on the accelerator as she reacted to cuts on her face and arms.

"Get the fuck back here!" he screamed.

The man chased the slowing car, reaching in through the broken glass window. He cut himself on a stray piece of glass, but it had little to no effect on his rage. He tried to wrap his fingers around Jenny's blouse but grasped only air.

Jenny realised that she was panicking, but she couldn't curl up into a ball and hope this crazed man would leave her alone. She put her foot down on the accelerator, and the car began to move once again.

On his second attempt, his fingers found cloth, and he tore at her top.

Jenny screamed.

The car flew backwards, the man lost his footing and dropped his bat, but clung on to Jenny.

The fabric, clasped in his grip, ripped.

Jenny screamed in pain. Her neck cranked to the side from the pressure of a full-grown man hanging from her blouse.

She pushed her foot down on the accelerator, and the car sped backwards. She grabbed one hand on to the wheel and turned it to the left.

The front of the car flung itself into the middle of the road. The man's arm snapped, causing his shoulder to dislocate - and his vice-like grip eased as he glided through the air to the tarmac below.

Jenny broke hard, stopping for only a moment before she hit a parked car.

There was no time for her to compose herself: the man seemed disinterested in his mangled body as he crawled back to his feet.

Jenny put the car into first gear, rolled past her attacker and fled from the carnage. She looked in the rear-view mirror and could see his deformed arm hanging from the socket. Her panic faded with each moment he appeared further and further away in the rear-view mirror.

Jenny drove for five minutes - hands shaking, body convulsing, blood stinging her eyes until she could carry on no more.

She noticed an empty spot to park on her left, pulled in, parked up, and then when she was still, all that she found her were tears. She wept not only for the attack but also her job, for her passion remaining unfulfilled.

Taking a few deep breaths, she brushed the glass that sat on her lap to the floor, adjusted the rear-view mirror and looked at her features. Her eyes were bloodshot, the left side of her forehead had several small cuts, and all of the buttons from her blouse had been ripped from the fabric.

She reached across to the glove compartment on the passenger side and pulled out a packet of antibacterial wet wipes. She looked at her battered reflection and clenched her teeth as she cleaned her cuts and grazes. At least the tears had subsided for now.

Composing herself, she tossed the bloodied wet wipes to the passenger floor and pulled out her phone. She pressed 9 three times and began the call. The phone rang five times before there was a click and the call connected.

"Thank you for ringing the emergency services. We're sorry to inform you that we are currently experiencing a large call volume and will answer your call as soon as an operator is available. If it is an emergency, please stay on the line. We apologise for any inconvenience."

Jenny sank into her seat, took some deep breaths and waited.

***

The barmaid sat on Charlie's bed as he paced around the room.

Each time that he had noticed her in the bar he'd dreamt of the barmaid being on his bed, yet here they were, and he had never felt more scattered.

"I have a lot to discuss with you. I do not know how, Charlie, but I have to try."

"I don't know you. I mean, you work at the bar. How do you know my name?"

"It is complicated."

"And, who was listening?"

"They will be, but I have decided to take that chance."

Charlie rubbed his temples as he paced around the room.

"There is – there is a large amount to tell you. I do not know where to start, and it is going to sound unbelievable."

Charlie sat next to the barmaid, reluctantly facing her.

"First of all, can you tell me your name?"

"I do not have a name."

Charlie felt himself spiralling towards a pit of confusion and frustration.

"You must have a name."

"I was never named."

Charlie's frustration lifted a little as he noticed her sincerity.

"What did your mum call you?"

"I have no birth mother."

"But - that doesn't make any sense."

"I was created to serve, and because of that, there is no purpose for names."

"But I don't…" Charlie continued. "What do they call you at the bar?"

"I only go there when you do. Nobody else sees me there."

Charlie rubbed his temples to alleviate the rising pressure he felt in his forehead.

"Okay, well what would you like me to call you? I can't just keep calling you the girl behind the bar."

The girl behind the bar thought for a second.

"A." She looked around the room for assistance before setting her sights on a ringing mechanism on Charlie's desk. "A… bell."

"Anabel?"

She nodded.

Finally, Charlie thought, they were getting somewhere.

"Okay, Anabel." Charlie smiled in Anabel's direction and, as she returned his gaze, he dropped his eyes to the floor. "So, tell me, what's going on?"

Anabel took a deep breath before beginning her story. She looked at Charlie and reached out towards his hand.

"Do you feel that?"

Charlie gulped and nodded. The hairs on the back of his hand stood on end.

"I'm not touching you."

"Of course you are. What are you on about?"

"I'm a watcher, Charlie. It's my job to watch you. I don't live here, and I don't have a name. I'm not a person like you."

Charlie stared at her, dumbfounded.

She continued. "It's a lot to take in, but you're sick."

"I'm not sick," he responded with a hint of aggression in his voice, sitting straighter as a response.

"Not physically."

Charlie looked to the ground, her words somehow ringing true.

"Ever since your mother died, you've not been able to let go."

Charlie pushed himself off of the bed to a confrontational stance. He raised his voice "What the hell are you talking about? I saw my mum a few days ago!"

"I'm so sorry," she gave him a moment to respond, but he chose not to. Instead, he distanced himself and avoided eye contact. "Your mother passed away six months ago from cancer. Do you remember?"

He placed his hands over his ears and shook his head; determined to avoid the conversation.

"Please, Charlie, I know it is difficult, but ever since her death, you have seen things, heard things. It's made you aware. And it's made you special."

"You don't know me!" Charlie exclaimed.

"But I do. I have known you since you were born."

"What are you talking about?" he raised his voice, as anger boiled towards the surface.

"Listen to me, Charlie. I know it is a lot to understand. I am here, but I am not. No-one else can see me, I cannot interfere with anything physically, and it is a miracle that you can see me now."

"Leave me alone!"

"The homeless man you found, did you not wonder why you walked that way? It is because I told you to."

Charlie started to sob. He leant against the wall and slid to a sitting position facing the bed.

"My mum is alive."

"Charlie. Look at me."

Charlie shook his head.

Anabel rose from the bed and sat opposite Charlie.

"I need your help." Anabel implored. "There is a great evil in this world, and I need your help to find it."

Charlie wasn't listening.

"Let me explain. Charlie?"

He lifted his head slightly. Tears ran down his cheeks, which fell delicately on to his chest, creating small wet patches to appear on his t-shirt.

"Everybody has a watcher; somebody who watches over them from when they are born. It is a watcher's purpose to ensure that the person stays on the right path." She hoped Charlie was listening. "However, people cannot usually see their watchers. It must be related to mental illness and I would assume that many people who can, would be too ill to distinguish us from their thoughts."

Charlie's head remained focused on the floor.

"There is a problem in the world, which will result in many terrible actions if we cannot stop them."

"I don't care," came a sniffled response.

"I know you do."

"I'm ill?" he wasn't sure whether it was a question or an admittance.

"Charlie." She hovered her hand gently over his arm, which caused his hairs to rise individually in her direction.

He yanked his arm away.

"Get away from me!" he took a moment to compose himself and softened his tone. "Please, just leave me alone."

She stood up to her feet and looked down at the man she had been watching for a lifetime.

"I am sorry. I understand that you are experiencing many thoughts and feelings. I will leave you alone for a while."

Charlie sat on the floor, head in his hands, trying to catch his breath as his chest lifted and fell uncontrollably. He raised his head to shout at Anabel as rage found him once more, but she had disappeared. Instead, he pulled out his phone, opened the photo gallery and wiped the tears away from his face. His photos were ordered by newest first – pictures of his food, some of Steve, random shots from his old job around the office; he scrolled and scrolled, but couldn't find any of his mother. He finally found one — the most recent picture he had.

She lay in a hospital bed, with Charlie sitting beside her. Her face was gaunt, and she wore a cap. Charlie looked at the photo, but it didn't make any sense. He stared: the picture seemed alien to him. It wasn't real. It couldn't be.

He held his finger down on the photo until an options menu appeared. He clicked on more information and looked at the date. 12th January. Just over six months ago.

But his mother was alive, wasn't she?

His phone vibrated. A message from Jenny greeted him.

'Hi Charlie, sorry to bother you but I could really do with someone to talk to. Could you meet me? Didn't know who else to ask.'

His phone vibrated again as he received a follow-up message.

'I'm in hospital and my parents are so far away.'

Charlie wrote a reply.

'Are you ok? Sure, whereabouts are you?'

He waited for the response, thankful for the distraction.

'I'm ok. Would be good to see you. I'm at Archway A&E x'

Charlie pulled himself to his feet. He wiped the tears from his face, slipped on his shoes and left the flat.

5

Charlie leapt from the taxi in a panicked rush. He had only met Jenny a couple of times and exchanged a few text messages, but there was a sinking feeling in the pit of his stomach that he couldn't shake.

Charlie met an elderly nurse at the reception desk who he assumed, due to her dishevelled appearance, had been at work longer than she should have.

"Excuse me. My friend is here."

"Name?" came the monotone response.

"Jenny Carter."

The nurse typed Jenny's name into the system.

"Ah yes, what's your name?"

"Charlie."

"If you could please take a seat, the doctor will be out to see you shortly."

"Is she okay?"

"It says here that she has suffered minor injuries. Cuts and bruises and a small injury to her shoulder."

"What happened?"

The nurse sighed. "The doctor will fill you in. I'm sure he won't be long." She managed a forced smile.

Charlie thanked the nurse and walked through to a waiting room that overflowed with patients. Bruised and bloodied faces, along with worried families, scattered the array of plastic seats in a sea of despair.

A crying child wailed for attention as her parents tried to comfort her.

Charlie found a seat next to an elderly gentleman who sat by himself with his left arm in a sling.

Charlie smiled politely, yet slightly apologetically, as he took the seat next to him.

"Can you believe it?" the elderly man opened conversation immediately.

"Believe what?"

"My granddaughter," he continued. "She's nine years old. Never been in trouble in her life and earlier this morning for no reason she hit me with a damn rolling pin."

Charlie wasn't sure what to say, so he sat there in silence as the stranger continued his story.

"She was in the kitchen helping me bake some bread one minute, and then she stopped, turned and smiled at me. I've never seen such fire in anyone's eyes."

"And she hit you?"

"Oh, yes. She walked towards me, smiling, holding a rolling pin. I had no idea what she was up to." He paused to gather his thoughts. "Before I knew what she was doing, she hit me three bloody times, I cried out and her mother, my stepdaughter ran in."

"What did she say?"

"Well, that little brat said that I..." he stopped mid-sentence and shook his head. "That I tried touching her," he finished in a whisper. "Her mother believed her, of course, and told me to get out. I had to get a taxi here for Christ's sake!"

Charlie realised that the old gentleman was waiting for a response.

"I'm sorry. That's horrible," he answered, sincerely.

"I just can't believe it. Why would she do such a thing? What the hell is wrong with kids today?"

Charlie nodded slowly.

He found his thoughts wandering once again to the barmaid, to Anabel. His lips began to turn up at both sides despite the confusion he'd felt earlier. Charlie had not been able to process anything from what she said, and he thought that was for the best. Instead, he would focus on seeing Jenny and making sure she was safe.

A curtain moved in the distance.

"Charlie?" a voice bellowed gently from the slight gap in the makeshift wall.

Charlie stood up and walked towards the doctor, leaving a large amount of empathy for the elderly gentleman behind. He approached the curtain and entered.

The doctor pulled the curtain across to section the area off into a room once again. Jenny sat on the edge of the bed, her right arm in a sling and small cuts across her face and neck.

"Oh my God, Jenny, what happened to you?"

"Charlie... thank you for coming."

"I'll give you a moment," the doctor added before disappearing through the curtain.

Jenny broke down in tears. Charlie placed himself next to her and put his arm around her gently. She buried her head into his chest, silently sobbing for what seemed like minutes.

She brought her head up from Charlie, the small amount of mascara she had beneath her eyes no longer in place, and looked at him.

Her hurt burrowed within Charlie's consciousness; all he wanted at that moment was to make it go away. He didn't even notice the black, wet stains on his t-shirt.

"Do you want to tell me what happened?"

Jenny sniffed and wiped her eyes with her free hand. Noticing that her mascara had run, she wiped the rest of her face with her sling, creating two black smudges on the white material - but also cleansing her face. She coughed, sniffled, and began to tell Charlie what had happened.

She told Charlie about the accident, the man - and the baseball bat. She tried to get through all of the details without breaking down but, a couple of times, she cried as she talked.

Afterwards, Charlie placed his arms around her and held her. This time she leant on him for support, but then the tears were gone.

"It sounds silly, but the thing I can't shake," Jenny said, "was the smile on his face."

Something tweaked within Charlie, like a prickling sense of realisation.

"I will never forget that."

After a few moments of silence and comforting, the doctor re-entered the room.

"How are you feeling?"

"A bit shook up, but I'm okay, thank you, doctor."

"That's good. I've written you a prescription to help with the pain. Your shoulder will be sore for a few days, but there's no serious damage, and it should heal just fine."

"Thank you."

"Make sure to keep the cuts clean. Apply your ointment before you go to bed and first thing in the morning."

"I will."

The doctor nodded in their direction as Jenny gathered her items. Charlie picked up her handbag, and they left the room. On their exit, Charlie thought of the gentleman in the waiting room and what might happen to him. He hoped that he would be okay; perhaps the story was an exaggeration but, with everything that was going on recently, he severely doubted it.

After exiting through the sliding doors of the hospital, Jenny stopped outside, pulling Charlie to a halt alongside.

"Thank you for coming to see me," she began. "I know it's a bit weird to ask you to come and see me."

"Don't be silly. I'm here if you want to chat."

Jenny leant over and kissed Charlie on the cheek.

"It means a lot."

Charlie's cheeks reddened. He shifted uncomfortably.

Silence lingered in the air for what might have been deemed an uncomfortable amount of time to an onlooker, but for the two of them, it offered time for reflection. Charlie's mind played over the conversation with Anabel, while Jenny seemed deep in thought as well.

"I just don't understand what could cause someone to do something like that."

"I'm so sorry you had to go through that," Charlie replied, snapping out of his spiralling thoughts. "Is your car okay?"

"Yeah, it'll be fine to leave it here tonight. I'll get a taxi home."

Charlie nodded.

"Where do you live?"

Jenny told him the address, and they agreed to share a taxi. They walked to a taxi rank and, being first in line, they hopped into the backseat of a silver estate car. Jenny told the driver her address, and Charlie followed with his. Jenny left her upset and resentment behind but carried some battle scars along for the ride.

As they wound through the streets of North London, the news report played on the radio. A well-spoken middle-aged British gentleman spoke in a monotone.

"Tensions between Russia and America worsen as the Russian president threatens reactive measures to American investigations. The following is from a press conference in Moscow earlier this morning."

Charlie asked the driver to turn the volume up.

The Russian president spoke in fluent English, accompanied by a thick Eastern European accent.

"This is a message to the American people and their allies. Russia will not stand for deceit and infiltration. Russia will make a stand against the West. That is all."

The reporter continued. "Questioned on the statement, our prime minister made the following comment outside of Downing Street earlier today."

"The United Kingdom offers full support to the United States of America in any investigations with Russia. I have been in contact with the president, and we are keen to assist in whatever way possible."

The sound of photography and journalists asking questions escalated as the prime minister continued.

"We encourage citizens to remain vigilant and report anything out of the ordinary to the police. Thank you."

"We have reached out to the President of the United States for comment but at this time have not received a response. We will, of course, keep you up to date with any updates on this matter," the news reporter finished.

Charlie zoned out for the rest of the journey. Jenny sat silently, enjoying the company of another, even if in silence.

After fifteen minutes, they reached Jenny's apartment.

"Thank you again," she said as Charlie passed her the handbag. "I'll text you later."

"Let me know how you're doing."

"I will. Maybe we can go for another drink when I'm feeling better?"

"Sure."

Jenny exited the taxi and closed the door behind her. Charlie watched her walk to her apartment and then, when she had entered, asked the driver to continue.

Charlie slumped in his seat, releasing a sigh as he found himself alone with his thoughts once more.

***

The President of the United States of America paced back and forth in the Oval Office. He entertained the vice president and the colonel. Anxiety was apparent in his habitually calm demeanour; beads of sweat glistened across his forehead and dark lines formed beneath his sleep-deprived eyes.

"Are we ready to proceed with the infiltration?" he asked.

"Yes, sir. We have our best man on the job," the colonel responded, stoic as ever.

"Good," the president let his shoulders drop forward as he leant on to his desk.

"Sir?" the vice president asked. "Are you okay?"

His professional demeanour dropped momentarily.

"It is imperative that this mission is a complete success."

"It will be, sir. We have a hidden microphone stitched into the lining of his trousers. We didn't want to take any chances, so there may be some noise interference, but it is virtually undetectable."

The president nodded.

"Can we contact him if necessary?"

"No, sir. He has been fully briefed to infiltrate, gather information and report back only when he is certain there are no eyes or ears on him. He has strict rules to follow, and he is aware of the severity of the mission. If successful, he will make contact and retreat to the rendezvous point within seven days. Any longer increases the risk of detection."

The president appeared solemn.

"And, if he is discovered?"

"He is aware of the procedure, sir."

The president rose from his slumped position and turned to face the window behind him. He looked at a gardener who was trimming the bushes, seemingly without a care in the world.

He had wanted to be president of this great country ever since he was a little boy growing up in Massachusetts, but if there were a chance to change places with the gardener now, he would do so in a heartbeat.

"We should ready a statement for the press, sir," the vice president suggested.

"I agree. We need to make sure that Russia believes we're co-operating to the fullest extent possible, without backing down fully," the colonel added.

"We also want to reassure the press that we are co-operating with Russia and are merely following protocol in investigating events of our allies."

The president turned around to face his council.

"Good. Prepare the statement and set up a press conference. Thank you."

The vice president and colonel thanked the president as they left the room.

The president sat down at his desk, ran his fingers through his thinning hair and wondered just what was happening to the country he so loved.

***

Charlie woke in a cold sweat; to say sleep had found him would be an overstatement. Instead, he tossed and turned in a light slumber, continually stirring, troubled by his thoughts.

He wiped his eyes with the back of his hand, hoping that this would magically wake him and give him strength for the day ahead. Instead, all it accomplished was to clear the sleep that had formed under his right eye.

It didn't feel like morning to Charlie. He reached over to check his phone and saw that it had just passed seven in the morning. He could stay in bed for another thirty minutes before he had to go to the job centre but knew that he wouldn't sleep. He tried to calm his thoughts and prepare himself for the day ahead.

He told himself that he would get out of bed, yet found it challenging to sit up. He rolled over and closed his eyes for a moment, but like an internal switch, the feeling of sleepiness disappeared as quickly as it had arrived. Pushing himself up into a sitting position, Charlie prepared for his day head.

Sun peaked through the gap of his curtains, which invited a streak of light to distil the darkness.

Today he had to check-in and sign-on, and then he had a potential interview in the afternoon. His day was pretty relaxed, but on a day like today, all he wanted was to get his head down and avoid as many people as possible. The thought of phoning the job centre and pretending to be sick ran through his mind, but he knew that even with being in bed all day he wouldn't sleep; he'd toss thoughts back and forth in his mind. No, perhaps it was better to get up after all.

"Charlie."

His name startled him to his feet, causing him to fling pillows and duvets wildly across the room.

Anabel sat at the foot of the bed, the sheets undisturbed around her.

"I know that you said to leave you alone, but we need to talk."

Charlie sat back down atop his covers. He brought his knees up to his chest and rocked back and forth.

"You're not real."

"Look. I am here. Right in front of you," Anabel softened her tone.

Charlie leant his head on his knees and faced his attention away from the confusion.

Anabel moved closer to Charlie until her lips were within an intimate distance to his ear.

"Turn your head to face me," she whispered.

Charlie's neck muscles obeyed. His expression twisted as his face began a movement he had not chosen to initiate.

"I am a watcher. We can't control, but we can influence. If the suggestion is strong enough, and deep down the person wants to do what we suggest, then we can push them towards doing so."

Charlie's mouth hung open, but a lack of words escaped. Instead, he stared at Anabel. A beautiful girl stared straight back at him; all-knowing and all-powerful. Was this reality?

The space between their faces remained at just a few inches: Anabel attempted to ensure their connection remained.

"What do you want from me?" Charlie asked.

"I want to protect you. I want to protect everyone."

Charlie shook his head. "I can't help. Have you seen me?" he took a moment to gather himself before he continued. "I'm pretty sure that if someone walked in right now, they'd see me talking to myself."

Anabel smiled. Technically, he was correct.

"You can still help me, though."

Charlie's demeanour took a frustrating twist as a bristling realisation entered his body; his vice-like grip that held on to sanity was loosening.

"I need to see for myself."

Anabel nodded. "Can I come with you?" she asked.

"Well, it doesn't seem like I have any way of stopping you, does it?" Charlie responded in a dry but not unkind tone.

After a few moments of awkward shuffling and uncertainty over what to say next, Charlie slipped on his trainers, grabbed the keys and left the flat in pursuit of the truth.

***

Charlie approached his mother's house. A part of him knew that Anabel had told him the truth. However, he also knew that if he admitted it, he'd most likely never see his mother again. Was he strong enough for that?

As they walked through the overgrown garden, along the worn, cobbled path to the front door, Charlie remained hopeful that upon stepping inside, the smell of cooking would overpower the senses, perhaps mac and cheese once more.

He twisted the key in the lifeless door, which creaked, cracked and then opened after a few attempts. Once again, the hallway revealed a dark, dusty story of neglect.

Charlie stepped forward into the darkness, thoughts of his childhood flooding back. Anabel followed out of Charlie's sight - she watched.

Brightness returned once more.

"Hi, Darling!" came a loving welcome from the living room.

"Mum!"

Charlie raced through the house in a state of euphoria - he was fine. His mother was alive. Everything would return to normal.

He reached the living room, where he determined his mother to be a womanly figure waited, but it wasn't his mother. It was Anabel.

"Charlie, can you see that this is not real?"

Charlie reached his hands up to cover his ears and shouted for his mother.

"She is not here."

"I don't believe you!" Charlie ran out of the room and into the kitchen.

Anabel stood at the stove where Charlie had so many fond memories of his mother crafting cuisine, designed especially for his young taste buds.

The lights within the house flickered.

Anabel tried again, taking her time over every word.

"She is not here."

Charlie ran as quickly as he could out of the kitchen and upstairs. Taking two steps at a time, he stumbled, but it didn't affect his determination to find a room alive with memories.

His mother's room; surely that's where she would be. The lights flickered and lit through the house once again.

Charlie's heart began to settle to a calmer resting pace. His shoulders dropped from beneath his ears, and he turned the handle in anticipation.

"Darling!" his mother's loving face awaited as he entered the room. She lay in bed, perhaps resting from a busy day, Charlie thought. He walked closer as tears formed in the corners of his eyes.

"Mum! I've missed you so much."

"What do you mean? I'm right here," she tapped the duvet beside her, suggesting her son sit down on the bed.

Charlie sat next to his mother, and she took his hands in hers. He looked at her face, disbelieving reality.

"I was so worried you'd gone."

"I'm here, don't worry about that. I'll always be here."

Charlie moved his hand behind his mother's head and leant in for a comforting embrace. His spirit soared, but there was something in his hand. Something wet - a clump of straw perhaps?

He brought his hand back around to his field of vision and there it was. Clear as day. He had grasped a handful of his mother's hair.

The lights flickered for the last time.

Charlie looked around the room in a startled panic. When he looked back around to his mother, she looked thinner, older - and bald.

"Don't go!" Charlie yelled, desperately.

"I'll always be here for you."

The face of a woman and her smiling, loving lips began to decompose into shades of brown, green and purple. Her skin dissolved away, revealing the unnerving sight of flesh and bone until there was nothing left remaining but a skeleton in a dress.

"No!" Charlie jumped up from the bed and frantically pulled at his mother's dress, but as he did so, she snapped in half.

The lights dissipated, leaving only a small amount of sunlight peering in through the window.

"Charlie. Charlie. Charlie." a voice cut through.

Charlie crouched on the bed, his head down on the pillow. He struggled to breathe as he clutched at the air. Grief overwhelmed him.

"She's gone," Charlie said, allowing the last remains of his mother to slip through his fingers. "I'm such a fucking idiot!"

Anabel approached Charlie. She placed her hands around his shoulders, which caused the back of his hair to stand on end. The sensation was not all unpleasant; it felt like a static balloon that tugged at every hair on his body, ever so lightly. How Charlie wished he could hold Anabel, to mourn, to touch, to kiss.

Charlie pulled himself to his feet. The effort required to complete the appropriate response seemed to take every ounce of his strength.

His eyes darted, his brain cycled, his sanity slipped.

Charlie raised his eyes, but all he perceived was the gloomy remains of what was once his mother's room; a sea of dust coated every item that sat neglected.

Anabel had left him - as had his mother.

6

Nestled within the cloud-clad constructions, the world of the watchers flickered blue and red.

Anabel was not the only watcher in the tower. There were hundreds of thousands of floors above her, each one filled with more watchers than the eye could see. Each watcher sat at a station, filled with monitors identical to her own; the forever tower that shifted in the wind.

Atop the tower, an open-top room belonged not to a hoard of watchers, but instead to just one — The Overseer.

This mammoth, larger than life being, filled the entire floor where underneath, thousands of watchers performed their duty. Each of his fingers, toes, elbows, knees, knuckles - every over-sized appendage, was connected to currents running from the rooms below.

His eyes, each the size of a double-decker bus, burnt blue. Flickers of electricity sparked from every discernible part of his face; he was at one with the electricity, and it was at one with him.

Surrounding the corners of the rooftop sat thousands of rows of watchers, all attached to The Overseer by their current. Each watcher had a station of their own, but they appeared slightly different from those that sat underneath. The stations contained monitors that showed stories - pages and pages of digital script flowing from their fingers. These watchers were not the same as Anabel; they were storytellers, documenting life that The Overseer commanded - these watchers had no will of their own; they shared the will of their master. They served their purpose, devoid of all life.

Their screens filled with words that told stories, however each word and each sentence passed in a flash. The watchers didn't need to touch the keys to type, their fingers simply hovered over the screens, and the electricity did the rest.

These terminals recorded the story. The story of life as it was meant to pass.

Whenever a discrepancy occurred within a story they were assigned, the screen would flash red for a microsecond, causing the watcher to rock back and forth as The Overseer absorbed the information.

The occasional flicker of corruption seeped its way to this height and caused a noticeable discomfort throughout the gigantic mass of The Overseer. Each time The Overseer felt discomfort, the watchers recoiled, like puppets whose strings had jerked too tightly.

Watchers had no reason to travel to the top of the tower to visit The Overseer. There was no form of payment to negotiate, no holidays to request, no mothers-in-law to take care of - watchers simply existed for existence sake.

Anabel, like the rest of her kind, required no form of training or path to promotion. It was only on the rare chance when a watcher was terminated or jailed due to corruption that someone would be replaced.

Each time Anabel returned to her world, she appeared at her station. She had but one purpose and, to achieve that, she would either observe or influence. There was nothing more.

So why did she feel a requirement to see The Overseer? To transverse the shifting tower and scale to where no watcher to her knowledge had ever scaled? She didn't feel human emotions: her brain wasn't wired in the same way as the human mind. As far as she was aware emotion was impossible, as well as irrelevant. So why did she detect a feeling growing inside of her now?

Emotion was a term coined by humanity to explain why people felt things and acted in specific ways; some could consider it an excuse. People acted because of emotion, and it drove people to acts of heroism, it led to love - yet it also created monsters.

Watchers weren't programmed to understand emotion, and as far as it concerned them, they knew that they could influence anyone to walk a suggested path. All it took was for one of them to dig their claws into the subconscious mind, and clench.

The will would bend, and occasionally the mind would break. Words of suggestion sometimes drove people to insanity; an internal conflict building, brick by brick, before falling with a mammoth crash - scattered fragments of conflict forever unresolved.

Watchers had a method of influence — the subtle whispers, the prolonged nighttime unconsciousness. How they influenced was never taught; it merely existed from within, at the point of creation.

So, if it was their nature and they lived mechanical lives, then what made them different? Perhaps they were identical.

Each time a person came to be, a watcher was created. Watchers did not age, and they did not need breastfeeding, mothering or raising. They arrived into the world fully grown, and they left the same way; flowing into the current like they had never even existed.

From the moment Charlie came into this world, Anabel watched with interest. She had only ever used a gentle touch to lead him in the direction that he needed to go. She found that he rarely strayed from his path.

There were a few moments, of course, when confusion or powerful emotions entered the fray. Anabel neglected emotion, but from the day his mother held Charlie in the hospital room after his birth, she had seen the exuberant joy in those small, brown eyes – after which she would never again question the existence of emotion.

From what Anabel had observed during her watch, humanity focused on three key reasons for pursuing with their existence. Survival was critical; whether it involved receiving medication to treat illnesses, fighting rivals, or merely wanting to live as long as possible. In second place came pleasure; gluttony, entertainment, and sex.

Many heralded pleasure, and for most, no amount of joy would ever be enough. Finally, for the few who had the opportunity, success was a considerable motivation. People would go through months, if not years, of abstaining from pleasures to push forward and succeed. Yet, no matter the reason or drive to succeed, it all came around in the end. Pleasure got the better of almost everybody. And then survival kicked in. That was when things tended to get complicated. Even when people managed to make it to the top, the drive to survive in that position created issues.

Watchers influenced, and humanity suffered, which is why Anabel abstained from getting too involved. Charlie had a role to play, but his part was solemn, destroyed by his mother's death. It contained a slow fall into a pit of misery, and she felt no need to add to that.

After being relatively uninvolved for all of this time, she began to interact with him more and more. She realised that she didn't want him to suffer. She began to understand humanity a little more, day-by-day, week-by-week, and the difficulties that came from dealing with specific scenarios.

Anabel had decided that she would do all that she could to help his pain. She would whisper words to him at night, instructing him that his mother was fine, that she was okay and he should not worry. The timeframe for Charlie's life had no discernible details, so she would comfort him as long as she could before the day came where survival slipped from his list of priorities.

She began to follow him more often; to any location where something terrible could happen, or anywhere that could set him spiralling, is where she started to appear. Watchers tended to only be in the world when the opportunity for influence arose, but she watched him from afar. She was determined to ease his suffering.

But then he saw her.

There were times in the past where she thought he'd seen her, for it only to have been a passing thought, perhaps a feeling that he wasn't alone - a sixth sense of sorts. This time, however, she knew. There was something in his expression, he knew something was different, and he had seen that in her.

After that moment, she watched from further away or in social situations where she could blend in. She kept her head down and pretended to be a barmaid; it was a perfect cover she thought, just in case he overheard her.

So, where did that leave them now? Charlie was never supposed to see her, let alone talk to her. His story had begun to take a different direction from that which was written.

She didn't want him to suffer. Yet, a watcher had no desires; they simply followed one path and that was the only story available. That is why she needed to see The Overseer. She had so many questions. She didn't know if He would have answers, perhaps she would be thrown into a cell with the corrupted for straying from her path, but she had no choice to make. She was going to visit Him – and there was only one way to do so. Anabel was going to take the stairs.

***

Charlie sat in a dull white room devoid of all personality, except that of restless patients. He waited for the doctor to call his name. His mind leapt from thought to thought, but before he could tackle any of them, another had taken its place. His mind spiralled; his sanity waned.

"Charlie?" asked the gentle voice of a female nurse.

Charlie rose from his seat, leaving his thoughts corkscrewing behind him.

"The doctor will see you now."

As he walked into the doctor's office, he felt like someone was watching, even though he hadn't seen Anabel for hours. Perhaps this was simply the anxiety that the doctor's office created.

The room that he found himself in was average enough. He noticed a PhD that hung proudly on the wall, of one Doctor Ramesh, along with stethoscopes, needles and the like dotted around. But the one thing that drove the anxiety further was the full-sized skeleton propped up in the corner. Charlie stared in its direction.

"Please take a seat," the doctor instructed.

Charlie sat down, not removing his eyes from the skeletal stare.

The doctor looked over his shoulder, noticing Charlie's curious gaze.

"Don't worry. It won't jump out at you." the doctor joked, trying to put his patient's mind at ease.

Charlie relinquished his look and met the doctor's eyes, glancing back occasionally.

The doctor pulled his chair over to his desk and opened up Charlie's file.

"It says here that we've not seen you for around four years. Is that correct?"

"I think so."

The skeleton moved. Charlie was sure he saw its right arm lift, its hand form into a ball, except for the index finger - and he could swear the skeleton had just pointed at him.

Doctor Ramesh turned around to look at the skeleton, which was stationary.

"Does the skeleton bother you?

"I… I thought it moved," Charlie answered with a hint of trepidation in his voice.

The doctor pulled up the chair to his computer and began making notes. It was a few moments before anyone spoke.

"Do you often see things move?"

"No, not really."

"Do you sometimes see things that aren't there?"

Charlie's temples burst as the division in his head fought an internal war. He lowered his head into his hands and looked away from the skeleton that mocked him.

The doctor spoke again, noticing the discomfort of his patient.

"It says here your mother died recently," he focused more on the body language of Charlie. "I can only begin to imagine how hard it must be. How do you feel about it?"

"Fine." Charlie snapped, before the doctor could take a breath. His body disagreed with his lips as his head sunk further into his hands, his fingers pulling at the strands of his hair as he tried to comfort himself.

"There are people who can help."

"My mother's not dead!"

Charlie's fingers that rested on his head began to dig into his scalp; repetitive motions created scars of red that broke the surface.

"She's not dead!"

"I'm sorry. I know this is a difficult time. Can you remember her passing?"

A single drop of crimson trickled down the contours of Charlie's forehead. The layers of skin that were once protecting his scalp were now hidden underneath his fingernails.

"Do you often feel like hurting yourself?"

Charlie removed his hands from his head. He found himself scowling at the question, and the doctor, before regaining control of his emotions.

He looked up to the skeleton. The mocking had subsided.

"I think I see things," Charlie admitted.

"What things in particular?"

"Things that I know aren't there."

The doctor's furrowed brow curled into suspicion as his fingers gently caressed his hairless chin.

"Can you elaborate?"

"There's this girl," Charlie began. "A barmaid. She talks to me, but…" he trailed off.

"Take your time. You are in a safe environment, Charlie. We are here to help."

"This girl, she talks to me. She appears and disappears like a bolt of electricity."

"Is this girl here now?"

Charlie glanced around the room, stopping briefly on the skeleton. After a moment he shook his head.

"When she appears, what does she say? Does she tell you to hurt anyone?"

Charlie sat up in his chair as if pricked by a pin.

"No. No. She just talks to me. She warns me about problems in her world, and she wants me to help her."

The doctor took a few notes before asking him to continue.

"She says that she's in trouble, and she told me my mother was dead."

"She doesn't want you to hurt yourself or anybody else?"

"No."

The doctor glanced at Charlie's bloodied fingernails.

"Listen to me, Charlie. This person isn't real. It appears the trauma of your mother's death has created this internal conflict, which may have manifested itself in this manner."

Charlie's hands found their way between his thighs; further evidence of self-harm underneath his fingernails clasped from view.

"I would like to refer you to a clinic for overnight observation. I know it's very short notice, but I think it's important for you not to be alone at this moment in time."

Charlie didn't respond but instead fidgeted uncomfortably.

"I know it must be difficult, but it'd just be for one or two days so that we can make sure that everything is alright. Are you working at the moment?"

Charlie shook his head.

"But I do need to sign on."

"I'll write a sick note which will cover your attendance, but I do need you to go to the hospital where they can assess you."

"If you think it's necessary, then I suppose. I just need to call someone first."

"Of course, I'll give you a moment, and we'll make all the necessary arrangements when I return."

The doctor left the room and the reality enveloped Charlie. Shaking it off the best he could, he slipped his phone from his front pocket and dialled Jenny.

The phone rang four times before it went to her voicemail.

"Hi Jenny, it's Charlie. I just wanted to let you know that you might not be able to get hold of me for a few days. Don't worry. I'm okay. I hope you're feeling better and I'll give you a ring when I'm back."

Click.

***

Jenny tossed and turned as she slept - internal conflict beginning to take its toll.

Every night when she had managed to sleep since the incident, she saw a replay of the attack. She inhaled the thought of the bloodied glass protruding from cuts in his face, exhaled the maniacal smile on his lips, inhaled his twisted dislocated arm, and exhaled the rising laughter.

Since that day, her thoughts flooded with re-enactments of the event and each time she dreamt, it played out differently. Sometimes she'd get caught and beaten until she woke up in a cold sweat, and sometimes she'd be running away as he closed in. However, it would always end the same way. She woke with his smile burnt into her subconscious, his teeth broken and scattered, and lips that parted and curved unnaturally - a dark pit of anger and hatred behind them.

Jenny's brow furrowed. She tossed from her left to her right, her right to her left; she began to moan helplessly from her thoughts as she woke.

Like a bolt, she shot upright in her bed. As she awoke, a sense of relief washed over her. She was safe.

Every other morning, she had started the day with a few tears. It had become a routine, and it felt cleansing - like it would drain the memory from her mind just a little.

This morning, however, she didn't feel upset. Instead, she felt anger rising; she felt a rage burning from within.

It wasn't just the assault. Perhaps it was the final straw, but, for too long, she had played the part of a victim, and, for too long, she had taken orders from others. It was her time to take what she wanted and grab life by the neck with both hands, squeezing until it succumbed.

She wiped her brow and rolled from her duvet. Today would be her day, she thought.

Jenny noticed that her arm felt much better, and her cuts had almost cleared.

She walked over to her window, realising her lack of clothing on the way. On another day, she might feel the need to cover her body, but this morning a sense of shame didn't enter her mind. She pulled one side of the curtain open, then the other. The sun bounced into the room, glistening off of her bare breasts.

Her phone blinked on the tableside from Charlie's missed call as she strode into the bathroom.

7

Roh always believed that his family loved him unconditionally, even after he fought against tradition and broke the vow of a marriage arranged since his birth.

His mother and father, like their parents before them, were born and raised in India. When they found out that they were expecting a child, they decided to move to England. It would mean a better life for their son: it would open up doors and give him opportunities that they never had. But when their son met Tom, that was one door they never expected to open.

A dual passport allowed Roh to live and move freely. A good education offered him the chance for a career, but a same-sex partner only created confusion.

Roh's extended family in India had not been accepting at the beginning of the same-sex relationship, but for the family of the bride-to-be, it offered solace. The tradition was not broken because of a man's selfishness, but instead because of his honesty. Even the eldest family member, after a period of reflection, could see that it was for the best.

Years into the relationship, his family had moved on, choosing to ignore the path he had chosen. They rarely discussed it, and that was fine for the foreseeable future. His mother and father, however, loved Tom nearly as much as he did.

The four of them sat around a table, ready to dig into a homemade lamb madras.

Tom was never really a lover of Indian cuisine; his experiences filtered down to a string of average takeaways with the occasional dish he enjoyed. It would never be top of his takeaway options - and for the first few months they were together, he had felt anxious about attending family dinners.

Over the next few years, he grew to manage spice more than he thought was humanly possible and found that the flavours in the homemade cooking he sat down to most weekends were generally very pleasing.

Before beginning today's meal, Roh's family said a short prayer, which Tom sat silently throughout. After finishing, the foursome filled their plates and dug in. Tom was the only one who used any form of cutlery.

As Roh began eating with his hands, Tom stared accusingly.

"I still can't believe you use your hands. How on earth do you eat cereal?" he inquired.

The Indian family laughed.

"I'm not joking." The family continued to chuckle. "It's fucking ridiculous," he said in a flat tone, shattering the mood.

"Tom, a word in the kitchen?" Roh responded, as his family fidgeted uncomfortably.

"Here we go…" he replied as they got up and walked into the adjacent room.

Roh closed the kitchen door behind them and immediately began to question his partner.

"What the hell is wrong with you?"

"Why are you still living like you're in India?"

"Because we're Indian - this is my family."

"But you're English."

"Half English, half Indian," Roh corrected him.

"Oh, for fuck's sake."

Roh grabbed Tom by the arm.

"What is wrong with you today?"

Tom grasped Roh's hand and twisted his arm in return, attempting to regain dominance in their argument. Roh struggled free, using his free hand to push Tom against the fridge - the force light enough to not create an audible sound, but strong enough to make a point.

Tom's eyes began to well.

Roh relinquished the grip. They stood face to face, Tom leaning back against the fridge.

"I'm sorry. You know I get defensive about my family."

Tom said nothing in return.

"Come here, babe." he pulled Tom's chin up so that they were looking into each other's eyes. "I'm sorry."

Tom responded with a sideways smile. It was enough of an invitation for Roh to seal the apology with a kiss. He leant in, sliding his right hand gently up on to the back of Tom's head.

Tom resisted slightly at first, but then relinquished and kissed his partner.

The kiss began gently, like that of a couple who had been together for several years, but then it shifted. It shifted with passion and, in the kitchen next to where Roh's family continued to eat, the two of them got carried away.

The realisation swept over Roh, and he pushed Tom away, yet Tom held on. Roh pushed harder, but Tom didn't relinquish. Roh pulled at Tom's hair slightly to try and detach from his lips; the kiss very much one-sided, if it was a kiss any longer.

If anything, the hair-pulling made Tom more inclined to stay his course, and as Roh began to separate the two of them forcefully, Tom bit down on his partner's lip - hard.

Tom pulled back, teeth clenched, as he ripped a chunk of Roh's bottom lip from his face.

Roh struggled free, speckles of red spraying across the pure-white kitchen. He screamed in pain as his nerves caught up to the action that had just occurred.

Tom's position hadn't changed. He simply leant on the fridge, passive, with part of his partner's lip pursed between his. Blood ran down his chin, forming a small ruby puddle on the floor below.

Shock and anger found its way to Roh. He could not believe what had happened; he cried, he tried to shout words at Tom, but all that left his mouth were muted words, groans and speckles of blood, which flew out to fill the space in between them.

Tom stood straight and walked through the flying speckles of blood aimed in his direction.

Roh held his hands to his lips, blood pouring into his hands, overflowing like a cup of the most vibrant red wine that was far too expensive to spill.

Tom approached, holding an unidentifiable item in his left hand.

Roh's mother and father stared in shock through the now open doorway.

Before they could do anything, Tom swung and knocked Roh unconscious with one smooth blow of the frying pan.

Now it was the parents' turn.

***

Roh stirred in a pool of his blood – at least he assumed it was only his.

As his vision returned, pain found him. His lip throbbed and ached, but his head was the primary source of distress. He moved his hands as quickly as he could to the back of his head, where the faintest pressure from his fingers caused a sharp jolt of fear.

He moved his hands before his face, taking note of eight bloody fingers and two slightly cleaner thumbs. He'd never experienced a headache this bad in his life. As he attempted to push himself to his feet, he could feel his brain screaming. He needed to stay here for another moment. Yes, he'd rest, maybe lie down for a few moments, and then everything would be better.

His eyes drooped, his lids closed, and his mind began to slow.

A loud shattering of glass echoed from the living room, followed by a loud gurgling scream. A terrifying roar of laughter followed.

Roh's eyes flickered.

He used all of his energy to open his eyes, now seeing double. There was no more energy in him, but somehow he rose to his feet and, before he had time to question how, he walked towards the separation between this room and the next.

He found his eyes closing once more and fell through the doorway, tripping over something by his feet, yet another source of pain greeting him. The pain was new and sharp from the palm of his hands.

"Well look who it is. If it isn't the little Indian boy."

Roh searched with his hands to find a non-serrated surface to push himself to his feet. His fingers traced the floor and found relief a few moments later. His hands displayed a mixture of wet and dry blood - the fresh crimson advancing to a red-brown curdling of a lost battle.

He dragged his aching palm along a bulk of cloth until he felt something smooth. He knew the texture of skin when he felt it.

Roh's mind stuttered; his eyes still fighting to stay open, nevermind regaining twenty-twenty vision.

"She'll not be eating with her hands for a while," Tom announced.

Roh's hands moved frantically. He found an arm - his mother's. He tried to open his eyes but instead fell on to the body with which he entangled awkwardly. He could feel her stomach, her chest, her neck, her face.

His mother lay motionless.

"Wha- ya don?" was all that escaped the downed Indian boy.

"Why don't you open your eyes and see for yourself?"

More noises now across the room - squelching sounds and distorted moans.

Roh used all of his strength to prise open his eyes and find some form of focus. He saw double, but things were beginning to sharpen, as two images threatened to become one.

His head pounded with a sharp throb. He'd all but forgotten about his mangled lip; he'd forgotten about anything other than his headache. However, the face in front of him became recognisable.

Her wavy, greying, black hair. Her slightly larger than average nose, which leant to one side. Her open, dead eyes.

"Wha?" Roh's response rose in volume but not clarity, as anger and desperation rose to the surface.

The pounding remained, but his vision returned. He knew now what was happening. He looked closely at his mother; the colour in her face had disappeared, leaving only a pale shade behind. Her mouth was tense, her neck twisted unnaturally, and then Roh saw her hands – well, he saw where her hands once were.

His stomach flipped. He lost all control of his dinner as it sprayed to the side of his dead mother.

"Come play with me, boy."

Roh looked up. The sight pulled him further towards desolation.

Tom stood above his father, who seemed to be severely injured; bleeding and barely moving - but that wasn't what had shaken Roh to the core. Tom was slapping the man who raised him, with his mother's amputated hands.

The vomiting settled, and Roh's anger boiled.

Pain danced within as he wiped the vomit from his lip, but no amount of anguish would stop him now. He clenched his entire body and fought the desire to lie down and close his eyes. Instead, he rose to his feet.

"Maybe I'll chop his hands off next. Maybe I'll chop him into little bits and make you watch. Maybe I'll make a father-asala."

Tom was a fan of his humour and burst out laughing. He clapped the amputated hands together with the victory of a well-timed joke.

Roh felt blood trickle down the palm of his hand before he launched himself at his former lover.

Tom was unaware of Roh until he was on top of him, pummelling him with his clenched fists. Intermittent laughter remained, broken only by each blow he received to the face.

Roh pummelled and pummelled, forgetting the words his friends had told him about delivering a blow with the side of his hand. Instead, instinct took over; he squeezed his fist as tight as his fingers would allow and ran his knuckles repeatedly into Tom's face.

It was only when Tom stopped laughing, and he heard movement from his father, that the red mist dissipated. Roh stopped his desperate assault.

"Dad!"

Roh threw himself from Tom, content that he had been dealt with for now, and crawled to his father. Roh's eyesight had returned just in time for one last look at his father, and one final appreciation of his words.

"I love you," escaped his father's lips before they closed forever.

Roh cradled his father in his arms.

His hands stung, his head pounded, his lip throbbed. The pain and grief overwhelmed him.

"You fuc-in bastar," Roh roared through his mangled lips.

He picked up a shard of glass from the floor.

Tom stirred, just enough to see what was coming.

Police sirens wailed in the distance as Roh stood and approached Tom's beaten body.

"Why?"

Tom's lips moved, but no sound escaped.

"Tell me!"

Roh grabbed Tom by the collar, pulled him closer by one hand and held the shard of glass to his neck with the other. He stared into the eyes of his partner.

"Why?"

Tom's lips moved. He mouthed words to Roh over the approaching sirens.

"I love you."

Roh's tight grasp on Tom loosened as he fell back on to the floor, letting go of the glass as he landed.

There Roh lay: a mangled, beaten, bloody mess, across from the one person who had once opened his eyes to a new way of life.

Craig Priestley

And then Tom had closed his parents' eyes forever.

8

Rotating blades sliced through the pitch-black night as the helicopter hovered over the drop zone.

Captain John Hargreaves had been in the military since he left school at sixteen, but it wasn't necessarily a smooth transition. Some of his friends went to college to study business or marketing, some had jobs at local shops to fuel their recently discovered partying lifestyle, and some, like himself, didn't have a clue of what they wanted to do with their lives.

These 'misfits' as his school's headteacher had called them, had a chance to do something meaningful with their lives. They needed discipline. The teacher believed that John's generation had it easy, and an iron fist would allow them to unlock their potential.

At the time, to say he didn't agree would be an understatement. He had kicked and screamed when his step-father had sent him to military camp; the one enforced rule being that John found a way to bring some money into the family. John had no desire to work for minimum wage in a supermarket or factory and, after his mind settled on the idea of being in the military, it didn't seem quite as terrible as he'd once feared. He wouldn't have to worry about paying rent or dealing with his step-father. How much worse could the sergeant be?

The physical exertion he had suffered at camp was nothing compared to the psychological damage he had received at home. After the initial shock of obeying the strictest of rules and sharing dorms with a variety of strangers, he found himself excelling. Rising in the morning became natural, cross-country runs became ordinary, and shooting practice became enjoyable.

His potential had begun to surface.

Before long he found himself promoted through the ranks and he took to leadership like it was in his blood. He gained not only the liking of his superiors but also their respect. It was an exceptional achievement to rise so quickly, and it was rare within the ranks.

These new-found skills led to purpose, and he was aching to make use of them. That's why when he was asked to become part of the White House's military arm, he had hopped, skipped and jumped at the opportunity.

Multiple successes later - and with several promotions achieved, he was now one of the most crucial military personnel in the entire country. He had earnt the trust of the previous president and that had continued into the current reign. However, this mission was different from anything he had trained for.

He usually entered missions with an excitement for what he was about to achieve, but this resulted only in trepidation. It was perhaps the most vital mission in recent history, and he had been hand-selected to undertake it.

He had no wife, no children. He was disposable, and he knew it. No one would grieve his death, and that was what made him so valuable in a mission like this. If he failed, there would be no mention of him, and most importantly, no immediate family to ask questions. But despite his stern and obedient exterior, John had no desire to die.

If he were to succeed in the infiltration, he would have to make no mistakes - and luck would also play a part.

John spoke fluent Russian and held his understanding of local dialects on a pedestal; he believed that he would blend in seamlessly in that regard. To ensure that he knew everything required, he had been briefed by US intelligence on current Russian affairs, including names and traits of officers, shift patterns, and a few other useful pieces of local information. However, if someone seemed doubtful, he also knew what signals to be wary of in terms of body language - to then flee the situation or, ideally, take the soldier out without raising suspicion.

To say the mission was simple would be an untruth. The plan was layered, and there were many different potential outcomes. The first part would see him parachute fifteen miles north of the residence, far enough from the camp to ensure he remained undetected. Once on land, he would traverse through the derelict areas that sat between the drop-zone and the city's edge. On the outskirts of the city, he would monitor the movements and patterns of guards, wait for the perfect opportunity, and take the place of low-level personnel that would not be immediately missed. Once he'd claimed his identity, he would then attempt to infiltrate the building.

He aimed to get into a room with the prime minister as he discussed military affairs. It was a delicate situation — one that he could not rush, yet was a matter of urgency.

The whirring of the blades set John into a trance-like meditative state.

The pilot shouted, bringing his focus back to the mission.

"Captain, we're ready!"

The moment came. This was what John's life had built towards; the most critical mission of any single one soldier, perhaps in the history of the United States.

John stood up, occasionally struggling to find his feet when the wind rose and the helicopter recovered. He was the only person in the aircraft other than the pilot, so there was no need for goodbyes. He fidgeted towards the door, placed both of his hands firmly on a metal bar and took a deep breath. There was simply no going back.

With all of his might, he pulled at the door. A crack of darkness appeared as the shockingly cold air rushed into the cabin. If the cold onrushing air froze his face at this moment, then it would remain in a state of unease forever.

"Good luck, Captain." the pilot shouted.

The door completed its journey with a click. It was time to jump. One deep breath, followed by another.

His feet inched closer to the uncertainty that awaited and his face displayed the first signs of frosts from the penetrating winds. He peered down, which was one thing he had never done before, and promised he would never do again.

Too late to change his mind now.

3...

2...

1...

It was always his heart that first felt the change from the drop in pressure and instability around him. It created a rush of adrenaline in some, a feeling of motion sickness in others. That was rooted in the first second of jumping. It was an unparalleled, frantic beating of his heart, combined with the change in temperature that made the initial drop feel like a lifetime.

Exposed areas were next, as the cold winds punched and scratched at every opportunity.

After that came relief, followed by joy.

At that moment, nothing else mattered. For those twenty seconds, John would think of no orders. He would simply fall.

He was free.

***

With a flash of red, the watcher appeared.

She boasted the same features as Anabel, but the way she held herself clarified the difference.

Tom sat bruised, bloodied and handcuffed alone in the back of a parked police car. He waited for the police officers to return, most likely after they questioned Roh and took notes from the crime scene.

Blood curdled around Tom's mouth, making him appear like a baby who'd messily eaten his food. But he was no baby. He had no purity left. He was a monster, and he knew it.

'Twist... your... arm.'

Tom looked around the car. Did he hear a voice?

'Get... free,' came the faintest whisper, echoing on the edge of the engine noise.

Tom shuffled. He tried to get free of the handcuffs.

Cars blew their horn in the distance; each word lived on the back of the sound.

'Break your arm. Break free.'

Tom shuffled his hands and his arms. There was no way he'd get out of these handcuffs, but if he could get them around in front of him, perhaps it would offer a chance of escape.

He tested the movement possible: he brought the handcuffs down towards his lower back, which was as far as his shoulders would allow. He popped his left shoulder from the socket in an awkward jerk, letting his shoulder hang loose and further down his body than he thought possible.

The whispers kept him from feeling pain.

Tom manoeuvred the handcuffs below his tailbone and, with some resistance, and a few twinges of discomfort, he managed to bring his handcuffs below his legs. He then leant forward, twisted his shoulders so the other would not dislocate, and then brought them below his feet to his front.

What now? He wondered.

He bashed at the screen separating him from freedom, and perhaps a new police car to call his own. The divider was designed for an assault, and despite his one-handed blows using the edge of his handcuffs as a point to try and create an opening, it proved fruitless.

His options were limited. He needed to escape, to be free, but he wondered how.

Had the voices abandoned him?

***

Roh sat at the table where he and his parents had enjoyed their last supper.

The two police officers sat with the victim as more sirens approached in the distance.

"The ambulance is on the way, son," assured the youngest of the two officers, boasting a slight cockney twang.

Roh sat at the table, trembling; the shock of what happened had fully settled in, and somehow, he had begun to process it.

"Would you like a drink? Can I get you anything?" asked the older officer as they both rose from the table.

Roh shook his head.

The officers were there to take notes, wait for the ambulance and then take the killer into custody. Even for a case like this, with blood, guts, and two serrated hands, the paperwork was always the same. Forms. So many forms. Nobody told the officers that they'd be helping people by filling in forms before they joined the police force. Even at the beginning, they filled it with lots of car rides, interviews, and a soft touch with filling in of details. Now they had both been on the force for years, it was second nature to them, but it didn't mean they enjoyed it.

They often worked cases together, and it wasn't the first time they'd shared a connecting glance while at a crime scene, as both of them realised how long the process would take later in the evening.

They had talked previously on trips to Greggs about what they wanted to do with their lives. Neither of them were young, but they were by no means old, and they realised that if they ever acted, it would have to be soon.

But what else could they do?

The eldest of the two, by only a handful of years, had often considered being a private investigator. He could work at his own pace. Yes, there would still be paperwork, but it'd be exciting, and would perhaps light a fire underneath him that he so desperately struggled to find.

The younger officer did not consider another career path. He only pictured leaving his family, moving abroad and living out his days somewhere foreign. He could never actually leave his wife and six-year-old daughter, but it didn't stop him picturing himself on an island, bathing in the sun surrounded by scantily clad girls half his age.

They closed the door behind them as they walked into the kitchen. A small gap remained.

"This is going to be a late one," the eldest sighed.

"We could get that intern to fill them in?"

He thought about the proposal for a second before dismissing it.

"A double murder in cold blood? I don't think we'd get away with that one."

"Fair enough mate. Let's get this wrapped up then," came the response from the antsy, younger officer.

"An ambulance, back to the station... then paperwork."

A silence hung in the air, interrupted only by the sound of the approaching ambulance – before a sudden smash grabbed their attention.

"What was that?"

"Maybe the ambulance hit something?"

A flurry of knocks rapped at the door.

The officers jogged through the kitchen and moved swiftly past Roh towards the door. The smash was undoubtedly bad news. The officers swung the door open.

"Good evening officer," began a medic. "I'm afraid that your car has been broken into."

The younger officer pushed past the medic to see their perpetrator, or at least, where the perpetrator once was. Instead of a young man in handcuffs sitting in the back of a car, the story was one of an escaped murderer who had somehow smashed the window of their police car and escaped custody.

The officers rushed to their car, but something was amiss.

The glass was on the inside of the backseat, not the outside.

The officers looked at each other, and it was the eldest, who said what they both thought.

"More fucking paperwork."

***

The corrupted watcher appeared at his terminal with a dissipating flash of red.

Other watchers near the station either took no notice, were too busy concentrating on their monitors, or glanced over inconspicuously; uncertain of the knowledge that they had just gained.

One watcher, however, stood up from his desk and approached.

He walked over, staring at the watcher who had just appeared down, as he approached.

Then a smile appeared; a broader smile than natural.

"Let us begin," they whispered.

9

Charlie jolted upright in his bed like a jack-in-the-box, exploding from the dreams that caged him.

The hospital room, lit by a dim fluorescent hue, contained nothing of note; it contained little of anything.

Charlie swung his legs out from the white duvet and touched his feet down to the bare floor below. Other than the knowledge that the sun had not yet risen, he was unaware of the time. He instinctively went to reach for his phone for clarity but remembered that he had no belongings here.

His doctors had told him that his stay was supposed to be for one night. Instead, this was the third - of how many he was unsure.

He was beginning to panic.

Perhaps he was staying here permanently.

Perhaps Anabel wasn't real.

Perhaps he was crazy.

Charlie pressed his feet down firmly and wriggled his toes as he arose from the bed. He allowed the cold, stone floor to chill his bare feet.

There was little to do in the room. Perhaps this space was designed for people to be alone with their thoughts for an extended period. Charlie wondered if the nighttime solitude was intended to push people and allow ideas to manifest. In his case, it certainly seemed to be working.

Charlie missed connectivity. He missed his television, and most of all he missed his phone; not only for the ability to converse with anyone and entertain himself in a moment's notice but instead, to escape.

During the daytime, he talked to several doctors who performed a range of reasonably standard physical tests, usually while asking a long list of questions. In between visits, he spoke to some of the other patients that found themselves observed. There were some patients that Charlie found challenging to talk with and some others who were not in the right frame of mind for small talk, but none the less the company was reassuring.

Doctors asked about his mother's passing, which he had now come to accept as fact. He realised that he had a lot of emotions to process. That was perhaps why he found being alone with his thoughts so challenging.

The only way to interrupt the solitude was to use the red cord. He had already pulled it once for a non-emergency and could tell that the overnight staff weren't all that happy to stir from their posts.

How he wished for company; he needed a distraction from his thoughts. He could feel them creeping in and knew that once they found him, it would be difficult to find sleep.

He stopped himself from spiralling. He forced himself to remain in a positive state of mind so that they would discharge him as soon as possible.

He walked across to the small window and peered out into the darkness. The small window was locked; it looked too small for a person to fit.

His mind jolted from thought to thought, from his mother to Anabel, from his career options to Jenny. The shadows surrounded him from all sides.

"You will never get out that way."

Charlie swivelled around.

Anabel sat on the edge of his bed from where he had just risen.

"You. You're not real."

"You know that I am, Charlie."

"My mother's dead, she's not real, you're not real."

Anabel stood up and walked over to Charlie.

"I know Charlie. Your mother is dead. I can imagine it is difficult to accept."

Charlie turned his back from Anabel.

"You're not real."

"I am here now with you in this room."

Charlie, eyes focused on the floor, turned around to face Anabel. He traced his eyes up to her body, examining every inch of her torso to see if there was something that would lead him towards a decision. Starting from the bottom, he found that her shoes looked real enough, as did her legs.

What was going on? Perhaps three days was all it took for a man to go insane with his thoughts.

Her hips and waist drew his attention and, as he continued his examination, he realised that he'd never really looked at her like this. He took in her aura, her being; he could feel her presence in the air. The golden locks lay motionless over her blouse. He had never looked at her in the eye for more than a fleeting moment. Her mouth was partly open, ready for words to leave them, but none came. Her nose was cute and perfect. He reached her eyes; they were enough to drive a man to insanity if that wasn't already the case. They simply exuberated life. Energy pulsated from them – an ever-shifting, constantly flowing electric blue.

This experience overwrote the glance that he caught in the bar as he lost everything in her eyes. Anabel returned the stare fully for the first time.

All of his hopelessness, all of the pain and anger - none of it mattered at this moment. This was bigger than any of that. How could one person matter so much? Charlie wondered to himself amongst his leaping thoughts.

Anabel looked away and broke the spell.

Charlie slumped backwards, the wall cushioning his fall.

For the first time in his life, he felt whole. It was as if he found the missing piece of him that he had always hoped to find. Now he had. Yet, he found himself with more questions, and somehow with less knowledge than before. It was as if he had seen what was truly real for the first time.

"Do you believe me now?" Anabel asked.

Charlie found himself short of breath.

"I think," he took a deep inhale to calm himself. "I do."

"Good."

After a pause, Charlie broke the silence.

"So, am I crazy?"

Anabel thought for a moment, unsure as to what instituted being crazy. Realising she hadn't replied for a while, words left her lips.

"You can see me while other people can't. Crazy is not the word I would use, perceptive perhaps."

That was good enough for now; perceptive he could handle.

"So, you're really, well, you're real?"

Anabel nodded.

"So, you're here to watch me?"

Another nod replied.

"Well, what do we do next?"

"In the morning, the doctors are going to review the footage of us talking. You are going to appear as if you are talking to nobody."

Charlie sat down on the bed next to Anabel and sighed, accepting the notion that he might be sleeping in this room for many nights to come.

"However, you are of no use to anyone in this room." Anabel continued. "I do not know how long the doctors would keep you here for, but it might be for too long. War is coming."

"What war?"

"War with the corrupted."

Charlie had so many questions; too many to ask at once.

"So, what do we do?"

"You need to escape."

"How? The window is too small. There's no other way."

"Wait here," Anabel instructed as she rose from the bed.

Where else was he going to go? Charlie considered.

Where Anabel once was, now she was no longer. Again, he felt alone. Moments passed, but for the first time since arriving in the room, Charlie was not questioning his sanity, which offered at least a small amount of reassurance. The war of the corrupted, however, did not sound quite as positive.

Anabel returned.

"I could see only one member of staff. We simply need to call him, distract him and exit the building."

Simple, Charlie thought to himself - wondering whether sarcasm had the same effect internally.

"And what do we do when we get to the exit?" Charlie inquired.

"We shall decide when we arrive. Put your shoes on."

Charlie slipped his feet into his white, fluffy slippers, adding to the white bottoms and t-shirt he was currently wearing.

Anabel disappeared for another moment. Charlie waited until she reappeared.

"Pull the cord," came the order.

Charlie yanked the red cord, triggering a silent alarm.

"When he enters, keep him talking. Then when he exits, make sure that the door does not close fully."

The door opened and into the room stepped a lethargic, overworked and underpaid night shift nurse.

"Is everything okay?"

Think, Charlie, think.

"Could you talk to me for a few minutes?" he decided to go for the direct approach.

"What for?"

"I…" thoughts entered his head. "I'm finding it really hard. I really miss my mum."

It was the truth, but somehow emotionally filtered for subconscious purposes.

The male nurse on shift yawned, and almost apologetically covered his mouth.

"I'm sorry, I know it must be difficult to deal with. It will all look a little better in the morning. If you just try to lie down, take a few deep breaths and do your visualisation exercises."

"Have you ever lost anyone?" Charlie interjected.

"Me?" the nurse responded, taken aback by the question. "We're not here to talk about me."

"It's just so difficult."

Charlie sat down on the edge of the bed and began to pretend to cry - even though if he let himself think about it properly, he probably would do so, uncontrollably.

"It'll be alright," the nurse said, standing at the door, waiting impatiently for an opportunity to leave.

Charlie pulled his legs up on to the bed and started to wail. He held one of his slippers in his hand.

At that moment, the audible beeping of a triggered silent alarm reached them from the nurse's deck. The nurse turned around. Then another, and another, followed by screaming and shouting - lots of shouting.

"What the-" the nurse turned around. "Get some rest," he responded as he hastily exited the room, allowing the door to close naturally behind him.

Charlie broke the act as soon as the nurse turned and flung himself towards the quickly disappearing gap between the door and frame, slipper first.

The slipper intervened as Charlie hoped it would, acting as a doorstop.

He opened the door slightly to see what was going on outside, ensuring he wasn't going to be detected.

The nurse was nowhere in sight.

Anabel appeared next to him.

"Shall we go then?"

"What did you do?"

"I simply had a few words with some of our other more perceptive friends." Anabel paced, impatiently. "Are you coming?"

Charlie exited the room and allowed the door to close gently behind him. It was likely that no-one would know he had escaped until the morning and then what would they do? Charlie didn't know. Would they send the police to his house? Would they come after him? His doctor had informed him that it would only be for one evening, so he had that on his side as he was technically being held against his will and surely there needed to be some form of paperwork for that.

Anabel directed him through the winding corridors. Luckily for them, security didn't appear to be a big concern in this hospital, and all of the closed doors they came across had a big green push-button that opened them.

"Your clothes and belongings are in that room."

Charlie entered the room next to them. He changed into his clothes while Anabel stayed on the look-out. He then reappeared from the room when instructed to do so.

Being dressed head to toe in white linen for days on end made Charlie feel devoid of any personality, and now, just feeling the jeans on his skin, brought back a sense of fullness to his empty shell.

He checked his pocket, which still contained his keys, phone and wallet. Now all that was left to do was to escape.

"Wait here." Anabel disappeared for a few seconds. She reappeared a moment later as Charlie tested his mobile phone for battery. Dead.

"Follow me."

Anabel walked down the corridor and turned right. Charlie followed. As they approached a closed double door, Charlie pressed the button, and the doors swung open. Signs appeared that directed them towards the exit.

Several winding corridors later, and a few strange looks from doctors and nurses, too preoccupied with their work, they reached the reception area. The staff were blissfully unaware that somebody might be here who was not supposed to be.

"What should we do?" Charlie asked.

Anabel thought for a moment.

"Walk out."

Charlie responded, lowering his voice to a whisper, realising that to any onlookers he was talking to himself, in a mental ward reception.

"But they'll stop us. Me. They'll stop me."

"Hold on," Anabel said as she investigated the reception area.

"There is one female worker on reception and a man near the door. The woman is called Susan. Just walk out confidently, say goodnight, do not avoid her gaze, and I believe that she will be too confused to realise what is happening."

"You believe?"

"Do you have any better ideas?" Anabel asked point-blank.

Charlie sighed, straightened his posture and inhaled deeply.

He walked towards the reception, trying his best not to run.

"Good night, Susan," he said as he walked past the desk.

"Good night," came the reply.

Before Susan had a moment to question the situation, Charlie was through the double doors and out into the dark, welcoming night.

10

Rapid flurries of increasingly desperate knocking woke Jenny from her sleep.

As wakefulness released her back into the world, she realised how tightly she was clenching her teeth and just how desperately she was grasping the duvet covers. The dreams slipped from her memory, but she held on to thoughts of violence. She remembered the screaming of thousands and the inherent acts of terror sweeping over the world. More than anything, she remembered the war.

Wiping the sleep from her eyes, she checked the clock on her bedside table. It read a little after five in the morning; just who was waking her at this time?

The knocking continued, unapologetic.

She sighed and struggled to accept that she'd be starting her day a little earlier than she would have liked - whatever this was, she wouldn't be going back to sleep afterwards. Yet, the door still needed answering. Anger simmered beneath her weary exterior. There must be a punishment for waking someone this early. She threw on a robe and walked towards the front door of her apartment. The balls of her feet echoed on the hardwood flooring with each step.

The moment that she turned on the hallway light, the knocking ceased.

She collected her keys from a bowl next to the door. A moment of self-preservation entered her mind: Jenny left the chain across the door and opened it only wide enough to see the uninvited visitor.

"Jenny, it's Charlie."

Her anger dissipated.

"I'm so sorry to bother you, can I come in?"

Jenny closed the door to free the chain before opening it once more.

"Charlie, are you okay?"

Charlie stood out in the hallway.

'Don't let him in,' whispered the wind.

"Come on in," Jenny said, ushering Charlie in from the frosty morning air.

"Thank you." Charlie entered the apartment, noticing Jenny's robe as he moved past her. "What time is it?"

"About quarter past five."

"Sorry, I must have woken you up."

"It's fine," she lied.

'Hurt him.' the floorboards squeaked, echoing the command upon each step as they both walked towards the kitchen.

"What happened to your phone?"

"Dead." Charlie pulled his phone out of his pocket.

'Dead.' echoed the apartment.

Jenny tried to form a picture in her hazy mind, all the time fighting against a returning frustration.

"Just tell me - what's going on?"

"Do you have any coffee?"

Jenny turned on the coffee machine, inserted a small pod into the slot and made two cups to welcome the morning.

"Milk? Sugar?"

"Black is fine. Thanks"

Jenny stared at the cups before collecting them. Smashing both cups across the back of Charlie's head entered her thoughts.

"Here's your coffee." Jenny offered him a dark, lucid mug of salvation.

"I'm so sorry for waking you. I didn't know where else to go."

Jenny allowed him to continue. She sat beside him at the kitchen table, gripping the handle of her mug a little too tightly.

"It's a long story."

"It's five AM. We've got time."

Charlie nodded. He supposed she deserved to know the truth, well, the part of it that didn't make him seem crazy. He told Jenny about his mother, about how he was taken into hospital for a few days, and how he walked out in the early hours of this morning.

Jenny was worried, of course. Not just for Charlie, but a little for her safety.

"I'm fine," Charlie insisted, placing his hand on hers. Her hand softened slightly. "I didn't want to risk going home in case they sent someone for me."

"Why did you leave? I mean, surely they are there to help you and make you feel better."

"They weren't doing anything; they were only watching." As soon as the words had left his lips, a moment of realisation flickered through Charlie's subconscious. Perhaps, occasionally, watching was all that was required.

Jenny moved her hand away from Charlie's, taking a long sip of her coffee. Charlie returned his drink to the coaster on the side.

"There's a lot going on right now that I can't explain-"

'War.'

"But one thing I do know is that I need to be out here, helping people."

Jenny thought for a moment before replying.

"Sometimes, the best way to help other people is to help yourself."

Charlie knew that she was right, but to stay here and get some rest, he needed the time to convince her.

"I know. I'm dealing with a lot. I'll go and see a shrink and talk through everything, but I don't need to be observed twenty-four-seven. I'll only get worse in there. It was horrible."

As much as anger ran through her veins, so too did compassion.

"If I can just get a shower, and charge my phone for a while, then I'll find a B&B."

Jenny agreed.

Charlie took a sip of his coffee before allowing himself a moment to relax.

"I'll get you a towel."

Jenny walked to the bedroom, leaving Charlie with his freedom. Several days of isolation had exhausted him mentally. All he wanted to do was to finish his coffee, take a shower, and then before whatever would come next, get some sleep.

He wondered how long he should wait before going back to his apartment, or perhaps to his mother's. Surely, if they did send someone, they'd check, realise that he wasn't there and then leave. He hoped that a few days in a bed and breakfast on the edge of town would be enough to get back to his life – whatever that was.

Jenny strolled back in with a towel, loitering around the doorway to her room.

"Let me show you where the shower is."

Charlie took one, final, sip of his coffee. It was still hot enough to burn his mouth and throat slightly, but not enough to cause discomfort.

He walked over to the doorway and followed Jenny into her bedroom. Not making judgements of her room was difficult; it was a private space, and he couldn't help but look around.

Jenny walked him through to the en suite that connected to her bedroom. She spared no thought to his stolen glances around the room.

"Turn the knob to the right. About six o'clock should be warm."

"Thanks, Jenny."

Hearing Charlie say her name brought butterflies to her stomach. Charlie exited into the bathroom and closed the door behind him.

The feeling in Jenny's stomach transformed from lightness and curiosity to anger and rage. Those weren't butterflies she felt; they were wasps.

She checked the time and, as expected, it was still ridiculously early.

There was nothing for her to do but to lie on her bed and let the wasps do their thing.

***

A part of Charlie wanted to stay in this watery embrace forever. He knew that when he left, he would have to face the reality that was his life. That seemed difficult; instead, he would stay in this shower and cleanse.

Charlie didn't notice when the door handle twisted, and the door opened, but he did feel the chill of cool, fresh air hit his naked body. He turned towards the door and saw Jenny standing there, with a relatively large object in her hand.

He reached for his towel and turned the shower off; suds of a lemon and lime body wash not removed from his skin.

Jenny moved closer to the shower, hiding the object from view behind her.

Charlie stepped out of the shower. He covered his indecency and wrapped the towel around his waist.

He stood face to face with a stoic female figure.

"Sorry I was taking so long."

Jenny stood unmoved.

"Just let me grab my things," Charlie attempted to walk past Jenny into the bedroom, but she blocked his way, creating an impasse – but who would be first to blink?

Jenny took a step towards Charlie, and then another. She was close enough for him to feel her breath on the bare skin of his slightly hairy chest.

Charlie examined her face for clues; he peered into her eyes, and then at her smiling lips. Charlie had never seen Jenny smile in this way, and it made him wary.

Her left arm enveloped the back of Charlie's head, as the distance between their lips rapidly decreased into mere millimetres - and then they met.

Jenny kissed Charlie with a fierce passion. He returned the affection, if not slightly hesitantly at first. As their lips entwined, Jenny led the dance with Charlie trying his best to keep pace. It was the last thing he expected.

Her fingers closed around Charlie, gripping on the back of his hair. For a moment, Charlie enjoyed the feeling of her grasping fingers, but the enjoyment soon turned into uncertainty as Jenny yanked his head sharply to the side.

Charlie tried to free himself, but as he did so, Jenny bit his lip and pulled his head into hers. Charlie waited for the vice-like grip on his lower lip to be released, and when a window of opportunity arose, he took it, freeing himself and pushing Jenny away.

Blood re-circulated in his lips. The bite resulted in a throbbing sensation - but she hadn't broken the skin.

"What the hell?"

Jenny simply smiled.

A host of emotions rose within Charlie. He was aware that he wasn't hiding them very well, and he saw Jenny's face soften slightly.

Her hand came up to his face, brushing across his swollen lip.

She moved in for the second time. A part of Charlie wanted to resist, but he chose not to.

This time the kiss was soft and gentle for the most part, mixed with swirls of occasional anger and frustration. Jenny pulled away from the kiss with a little-less-teeth and led Charlie to the bedroom.

As they found their way to the bed, the object that Jenny held thudded to the carpeted floor; followed shortly by Charlie's towel. Jenny reciprocated by slipping off her nightgown, revealing that she had been wearing nothing else this entire time.

Charlie glanced over to the open window, which had now begun to fill the room with morning light, as well as potential glances from interested onlookers in the neighbouring building.

Jenny pulled his eyeline back to focus on her as their naked bodies entwined above the duvet. Charlie laid back on the bed, drinking in the beautiful body that was placing itself on top of him.

Jenny kissed and bit at Charlie's ear, his neck, and his swollen lip, which Charlie responded to with a flinch. But when she moved her mouth to other parts of his body, there was no flinching.

He couldn't remember the last time this had happened, and it felt good. The occasional biting and aggressive tongue movement didn't bother him so much anymore.

Charlie closed his eyes, letting the moment wash over him. He released himself to the rising satisfaction within.

"Charlie," a voice that wasn't Jenny's – a voice that simply couldn't have been at that exact moment.

Charlie opened his eyes and noticed Anabel standing at his side.

Charlie jolted up in the bed, forcing Jenny to lose her grasp, which she quickly regained.

"What are you doing here?" he mouthed in her direction, while also fighting against rising levels of enjoyment.

"Her watcher is corrupted. They will return."

Charlie wanted it to stop. No, he wanted it to continue. He couldn't maintain control for much longer as the tip of Jenny's tongue circled and her pace fastened.

A spark of red rippled through the room.

Charlie looked over towards Anabel.

"Here he comes," Anabel referred to the watcher - not Charlie.

Anabel moved her attention away from Charlie, who moved his body and looked frantically around the room to little reward.

Jenny paused.

"We wouldn't want you to finish just yet, now, would we?"

'Kill him.'

Jenny's brow furrowed and her demeanour hardened.

'He doesn't deserve you.'

Jenny's eyes narrowed.

'Do it.'

Jenny pounced on top of Charlie, just as Anabel pounced on to the corrupted watcher.

Jenny's and Charlie's bodies entwined, as did Anabel's and the corrupted - however, one was in a more pleasurable way than the other.

Jenny rode back and forth on top of Charlie, with an animalistic need to feel Charlie inside of her. Nothing else existed, and the voices began to fade.

Charlie too, worried about Anabel, began to focus on the beautiful woman that was giving him her full attention.

The lights flickered.

The corrupted watcher broke free of Anabel's assault. Anabel rose and launched herself in the watcher's direction, but a bolt of red current confronted her, which she barely managed to avoid.

What was that? Anabel thought to herself, as she processed the options of what to do next. She had never seen a watcher manipulate current in such a manner.

Another bolt came her way, which she dodged a little easier. It struck the lamp behind her, causing the bulb to explode.

The majority of the shattered glass simply ricocheted on the inside of the lamp cover, but some fragments escaped and showered Charlie and Jenny. After a second of concern, they were back to concentrating on each other; denying any external wrongdoing.

Anabel darted at the watcher. She could not let his corruption spread.

The corrupted prepared himself and, as Anabel lunged at him, he reversed her tackle, fell backwards to the floor, and kicked her from his body in the process.

Another bolt of red current, shaped like a flying dagger, approached her. This time she was slow to react. It grazed her shoulder, sending blue electrical sparks across the room.

The corrupted shielded his eyes from the brightness. It was a window of opportunity of which Anabel would take full advantage.

She darted forward and, by the time that the corrupted realised what was going on, it was too late. Anabel dived on top and pinned him down. She straddled him and pressed his arms down above his head.

Jenny writhed on top of Charlie, also pushing his hands down behind his head.

Charlie and the corrupted both strained under their counterparts.

Charlie couldn't hold it in anymore; a feeling of warmth washed over him as Jenny rocked backwards and forwards on top of his body.

Anabel and the corrupted disappeared from this world, as did Charlie's restraint.

***

A beating pulse of blue and red illuminated the room as Anabel appeared sitting atop the corrupted watcher in her world.

Flickers of red were all that the nearby watchers needed. Simultaneously, watchers in the vicinity pressed a button that sat next to each monitor, marked 'corruption'.

Within moments multiple male and female watchers appeared in front of Anabel. Their authority was made only more impressive by how they moved in perfect harmony; each footstep, each slight movement of their arms as they walked, were all completely mechanical.

As they approached, two of the watchers broke away from the identical arm movements and, in a systematic manner, lifted their hands in front of them. The air shifted. Together, they pulled an object from the empty space before their very faces. The items flickered as they began to take form, before they settled in the shape of a pair of open handcuffs. Not formed of cloud, electricity, or any kind of matter, these handcuffs were devoid of all form. Anabel could not place the material or energy with which they were created.

As the watchers moved within inches of Anabel and the corrupted, the watchers' arms flickered. The invisible handcuffs sucked the current of the corrupted watcher towards them; a void of electrical current that pulled and sapped at its life force.

The corrupted watcher, underneath Anabel's body weight, exploded with red sparks of desperation, which threw her from his back - but before he could find his feet, the handcuffs closed around his wrists. The red sparks surging from him concentrated focus on the restraint and, with one final closing snap, all of his power disappeared.

This corrupted watcher had been stopped and would be taken for examination. Anabel had helped to stop the corruption spreading any further, and she hoped that Jenny's watcher would be re-assigned. Perhaps that meant Charlie could find some happiness.

So, why was there a doubt lingering within her emotionless thoughts?

The clasp of the second pair of handcuffs snapped shut.

Anabel felt her energy drain instantly and fell to her knees.

"You shall come with us for examination," came the explanation from the watcher drones.

"I brought the corrupted to you."

"Indeed, you did."

Anabel looked to her shoulder, which was visibly causing her grief.

"Did you come into contact with the corruption?"

Anabel knew no reason to be untruthful, so she answered when questioned.

The watchers nodded. They escorted Jenny's watcher and Anabel through the hordes of the motionless that sat at their monitors. She was a criminal until proven guilty.

Her log would be revisited, and there would be questions. There would be lots of questions. She may very well be locked up with the corrupted. While she had no desire, she had a purpose, and that purpose was to watch Charlie. She knew that her watch had meaning, but she doubted that another watcher would understand.

Who was she to argue her purpose, or to convince others of reasons why she did what she did?

As they walked through the seemingly never-ending sea of watchers, Anabel began to accept her fate.

That was when the watchers stood. That was when the watchers smiled. And ultimately, that was when the watchers circled.

"Proceed back to your monitors," came the command.

There was no obeying from this mass protest.

More and more watchers surrounded them until there was no escape for the two that chaperoned Anabel and the corrupted.

For a moment, there was no aggression or desire for bloodshed - but that didn't last for long.

"Unlock my handcuffs," exclaimed Anabel, as she prepared herself for what was about to come.

The authoritative duo stood there, motionless, waiting for something that they deemed impossible – the first bolt of red struck the watcher next to Anabel, square in the chest.

"Let me go." hissed the corrupted prisoner.

Anabel attempted to process that she might never be free.

The group of watchers focused their energy.

"Bring the captured alive," came an order from an ever-increasing swarm.

As the group approached, new watchers arrived to attempt to control the situation. Some held handcuffs in front of them; others had created shields of blue energy with their powers.

Another bolt took down the watchers that had taken Anabel captive.

The corrupted approached. Anabel had to get free. Now was her only chance, else she would be tortured, or worse - she might be turned.

Kneeling, she felt around the lifeless body next to her. There must be a key or device that opened these handcuffs.

She felt the energy within flare, but, with each spike, she felt more drained. The contraption around her wrists sapped her strength, making it hard to get to her feet; they made it impossible to run.

Quickly, she searched. There was nothing in the left pocket.

The corrupted were almost upon her.

She felt something on the watcher's belt. Was it a key? She pulled until it came free.

She looked up and saw a chorus of sinister smiles looking down at her.

She moved the key towards her handcuffs, turned it and flung the restraints from her wrists. Anabel struggled to her feet.

The corrupted battled the army of watchers that had come for them, falling gradually, one by one. The few corrupted near Anabel had reached her. There was no way for her to escape.

The corrupted reached out, their fingers twisting and snapping in all directions as they closed in on her.

Anabel dropped to her knees, awaiting the demise that was about to come.

The corrupted reached out and tore at her clothes. Their demented faces reached mere centimetres from hers. Yet, for a moment, they froze.

No feeling of pain met Anabel. She looked up to where the corrupted faces had once been. They had all dispersed.

Instead of focusing on Anabel, the corrupted had diverted their focus to those who were there to subdue them.

Bolts of red smashed into blue shields that were protecting the approaching enforcing army.

The enforcers marched methodically, devoid of individuality. They moved as a thoroughly drilled unit but, as they circled the corrupted, the corrupted fought back.

The aggressive individuality of the corrupted created issues: bolts of red penetrated gaps and struck a few individual watchers, but their short-lived aggression was no match for the defensive restraint of unity. As soon as a hole appeared, another watcher filled it.

The bodies of the fallen began to add up, as did the number of restrained.

The stand of the corrupted began to be squashed from all sides, bashed back by shields. Handcuffed one by one, the corrupted turned their thoughts to escape.

Many of the corrupted found themselves in restraints, but there were still hundreds fighting the army. However, they now realised that they were on the losing side. One at a time, they vanished into their screens. The majority of the crowd separated, intending to escape en masse.

Anabel rose to her feet. She was too far away from her screen to retreat. She found herself trapped between a hoard of watchers who wanted her arrested, and potentially jailed, and the remaining corrupted who fought for their revolution.

Her reflex screamed at her to stay still. She would wait here until the corrupted were dealt with and then she would accept her fate.

That is what her reflex told her, yet that is not what she did.

Burning even brighter than her initial reflex was the need for survival.

She looked at the screens that the corrupted watchers had vanished into and contemplated the possibility, for the first time, of entering another person's life.

She looked at a screen that was not hers, as the final bolt of red crashed into a nearby shield. Was it even possible to enter another screen?

She tried, but nothing happened.

The watchers turned and noticed Anabel. Now that the corrupted had been taken care of, she was their next target.

"Remain stationary, and we will take you for questioning."

They marched in tandem, taking one step at a time towards Anabel, in what would possibly be the end of her watch. They would know about the sightings, they would learn about the interactions, and she would be terminated. Not only that, but Charlie would be left alone.

She could not let that happen.

The walls around her tightened as the watchers surrounded her from all sides.

A sense of sheer desperation resonated from her very being as she disobeyed her protocol. She panicked. She began to leap around looking for an opportunity to escape, although she knew that there was none.

The approaching walls enclosed. The end of Anabel's watch became imminent and, as she began to accept the situation, she began to shake.

A hand reached out and touched her shoulder, causing her to flinch.

The watchers opened another pair of handcuffs.

"No." she cried, surprising the forces around her. They took a moment to calculate the situation and then continued with the arrest.

She began to shake uncontrollably. The fear of not seeing Charlie again, mixed with the desperation of survival, took over her very being.

She felt a hand pull her arm back behind her back and then, before she realised what was happening, she exploded into a ball of light.

***

In a derelict area, surrounded by nothing but sand, an overload of electricity caused a pylon to explode into flames.

Anabel opened her eyes. Had she disappeared into another watcher's screen?

She felt within herself for a connection to her world, but found nothing strong enough to return.

A wave of relief washed over her as she realised that she could not be followed, yet had no idea of her location or how she got there.

Processing the options, the idea that this was another person's life was the idea that had made the most logical sense. It was a case of survival, for which they were built, to a point. She was facing eradication from the corrupted, which added to the fear of being taken from her watch.

She pushed these thoughts away. All that mattered to her was the fight against the corrupted - to find answers and to keep Charlie safe.

She looked around, hoping to find a source of electricity that might lead her to find a way home, but the pylon's electrical route was damaged.

There was no choice but to walk, and there were only two choices in direction. Anabel would follow the lines before her in the hope that it would eventually lead to a phone, a radio – even a toaster may do.

Anabel had no knowledge of what was required to get her home, but this seemed the most logical to her.

The power that once ran through these lines, now depleted, left a lifeless, mechanical construction that had little to no use.

Whatever drove her to put one foot in front of another and begin this journey, felt entirely unnatural to her - but it kept her walking.

It kept her doing so for hours.

Until the sunset.

Until time faded.

11

Jenny tossed and turned in her sleep, causing Charlie to wake.

The bedroom curtains were wide open, allowing an unwelcome early morning visual alarm. Charlie's vision took a moment to adjust from the small amount of sleep that he had managed. As it did so, he saw an older woman cooking in the building across the way. Charlie hoped that she hadn't seen anything earlier in the morning.

Christ, Charlie thought, the last few hours felt like a blur. He lowered his chin to his chest to see Jenny lying on it. Her fingers grasped the covers tightly; her forehead appeared scrunched.

Instinctively, he brought his free arm up and ran his fingers through her long, auburn hair. He shuffled his body so that he could wrap his arm around her. However, he felt a sharp, razor-like papercut on his chest. He lifted his head to look down, which revealed multiple scratch marks that had slightly broken the skin.

Charlie felt less than a moment of unease, after which he felt himself release into acceptance and perhaps even a small amount of pride.

Jenny's forehead unclenched, her mouth lifted at the sides and gradually, her eyes opened.

"Morning." Charlie greeted her with a sheepish smile.

Jenny looked at Charlie, her mouth unable to land on a smile or a frown.

"Hi."

Jenny rolled from Charlie's chest, exposing her naked body. In doing so, Charlie noticed the lady opposite cooking in her kitchen.

"Jeez!"

Charlie jumped up from the bed and jogged over, as gracefully as he could in his naked state, to close the curtains. He realised that he was standing fully exposed, but Jenny seemed to be paying more attention to her situation. She pulled the duvet up further to cover her breasts.

"That bloody woman," Jenny bemoaned.

Charlie stumbled around the floor. He quickly slipped on his boxer shorts and then sat on the edge of the bed.

"What?" Jenny began, rolling over to search for her underwear on the floor. She noticed the clock as she did so. "Oh shit! Is that the time?"

Charlie pulled up his trousers, realising his time here was quickly nearing its end.

"I'm so late."

"I'm sorry," was all Charlie could think of to say. That, and also handing Jenny her underwear, which he had found next to his trousers.

Jenny took them and fidgeted around underneath the covers. Charlie then handed her a bra.

"What are you doing here?" Jenny asked. She finished putting on her bra underneath the duvet. "It's all a bit of a blur."

"I'm sorry. I shouldn't have bothered you."

"It's okay. Just," Jenny searched for the word. "Unexpected."

Charlie scratched his head. "Shall I let you get dressed?"

"Yes, please," Jenny responded.

Charlie grabbed his t-shirt and threw it over his head to provide a quick and effective torso covering. He gathered some things that had fallen out of his pockets before walking over to the bedroom door.

"Thanks for letting me in," he added in an attempt to ease some of the tension that had seemingly formed.

Charlie noticed the confusion across Jenny's face but, instead of asking any more questions, he decided to leave her in peace.

Jenny rose from the bed, and headed towards the bathroom.

Just as he was closing the door behind him, Jenny found a question.

"Can you put the kettle on?"

Charlie nodded and walked towards the kitchen. He was fully clothed and had all of his belongings in his pockets. Next, he would need to prepare for what lay ahead.

As he filled the kettle and flicked the switch, he began to think of menial things. When was his next rent payment due? Had the hospital contacted anyone? Was he in the local news? His emotional turmoil took a back seat to everyday struggles.

Jenny strode in and walked past Charlie. She reached for two mugs and waited for the whistling sound from the kettle to reach its peak.

The two of them stood side by side like strangers. Charlie felt like he had intruded, and Jenny was giving nothing away.

"Tea?" Jenny asked.

"Sure," Charlie responded. "Milk, no sugar."

The erratic whistle of the old-fashioned kettle broke through the silence, pulling at fragments of Jenny's mental state. Finally, it rested, and the boiling water was ready.

Jenny poured the two of them a cup of tea, despite being over two hours late for work. She retrieved her phone, rang work and made an excuse to her boss; stomach cramps, she explained. Also, she took some sleeping pills and slept right through her alarm, but would be in as soon as possible.

The two of them sat and sipped their teas, allowing Charlie to ponder the night, before Jenny broke the silence.

"I'm sorry, I don't know what came over me."

Charlie traced his fingers across his superficial wounds and reassured her that she had no reason to be sorry.

"But, I wanted to hit you. I wanted to beat you."

The words felt like daggers rising from her throat, piercing Charlie's state of vulnerability.

"I don't understand. Did I do something wrong?"

Jenny laughed, but it wasn't long until the laugh transformed into tears.

Charlie put his arm around her. He reassured her that whatever she felt, it was probably due to a lack of sleep. It was only as they were talking that Charlie also thought about linking her feelings with her recent accident.

Jenny nodded and wiped the tears from her eyes. She thanked Charlie, sipped her tea, and turned on the radio.

"I'll just go and get my things together and walk you out if that's alright?"

Charlie nodded and moved his attention to the news report. An older gentleman, a voice he recognised instantly as the President of the United States, was talking mid-sentence. It took Charlie a moment to catch up with what was said previously, but he managed to let his mind slip into the president's words.

The president cleared his throat, a rare public speaking misstep from someone as polished in public speaking as he. The vastly experienced figure began his sentence again.

"We are a proud nation. We have overcome adversity in the past and will continue to do so in the future. The adversity we must rally together and face, however, is now."

Charlie felt the need to occupy his idle hands. He placed his hands on his cup of tea, without noticing that his focus had turned entirely from one of inward reflection to that of outward trepidation.

"Relations with Russia have soured. We must prepare ourselves for what may transpire. After speaking to the Russian prime minister, it is clear that we do not see eye to eye on matters of national security. We have reason to believe that Russian troops were behind the death of the Turkish peacekeeping mission. It is with great regret that, after talking to the Turkish prime minister, I have been unable to maintain peace between these two nations."

"Mr President," came a chorus of questions from the press that attended the press conference.

"The United States of America is built on principles of freedom, and today is no different when I say we shall always stand by the Turkish people in their freedom for a new government, their freedom for knowledge, and ultimately their freedom for peace."

The crowd roared with questions, but the president brushed them off and continued with his statement.

"This morning the Prime Minister of Russia declared war on Turkey."

The crowd silenced. The sound of photography ceased.

"The United States of America is the strongest nation in the world, thanks in part to every person listening, and the values of this great country. We will not sit back and be a spectator in this war because, in the battle of good and evil, there is only ever one choice."

A moment of silence filled the airwaves as the president sipped from a glass of water, preparing for his final statement.

"That is why today we stand by Turkey in declaring war on Russia and their allies."

Shocked gasps from the crowd rippled like buoys bobbing up and down across a stormy sea.

"As a nation, I ask for your patience and your vigilance. I ask that you continue with your lives and report sightings of anything that may be deemed suspicious. I ask that you stand by this great nation in its decision, and finally, I implore all allies to join us to eradicate this great evil from the world."

"Mr President?"

"Thank you. God bless the United States of America."

A moment of silence before another voice began.

"The president will not be taking any questions at this moment. Thank you."

The sound altered as the recording moved from the press conference back to the radio studio - the voice of a radio newsreader that Charlie faintly recognised followed the statement.

"As we've been reporting this morning, that was the President of the United States of America declaring war on Russia. We now go live to the prime minister who is commenting on the matter from Downing Street."

"Jenny, you might want to hear this," Charlie shouted through the apartment.

The door to her bedroom opened, and Jenny peered through the gap, half-dressed.

"What?"

"The radio. It's, well it's important."

Jenny closed the door so that she could adjust her clothing. A few seconds later, she re-appeared.

Charlie increased the volume on the radio so Jenny could hear as she strolled towards him.

"As always we stand by our allies," the prime minister began. "The United Kingdom will ensure all of its military forces are available to join operations with the United States of America. I ask the country to remain calm, and I remind people that this is a necessary action, which will result in a better world for us all moving forward. To the Russian people who live in our country, I ask that you do not take out any actions of terror on the country that has been your home, and the country where you have lived with open arms. We are not a country that segregates races, and we welcome you to live here as you have always done, in peace with our country. I also ask for everybody to be as courteous towards Russian individuals as you have always been. The Prime Minister of Russia is the enemy of the United States, not all of its people. We must remain united and not fight between ourselves."

During the speech, Jenny had sat down next to Charlie, mouth agape.

Charlie turned the volume down as the prime minister trailed off. The two of them sat in silence for a moment before Jenny spoke.

"Well, there's no way that I'm going into work now."

Charlie and Jenny looked at each other. They would remember this moment of historical importance forever. Charlie wondered if what preceded it would be remembered as well.

12

Gerald had been a shopkeeper in the South Yorkshire town of Barnsley for many years. He'd taken over the business from his father, and it had served him well enough to put food on the table for both him and his wife. However, anything much more than that and he struggled.

As the customers shopped, he reflected. Being in his mid-fifties, he questioned whether he could have done something else with his life – and whether it was now too late.

When his father passed the business down to him on his eighteenth birthday, he imagined himself working in the small shop for perhaps five or ten years. It'd be a cushy job, it would mean he didn't need to find a low paying job elsewhere, and then he could sell up and move somewhere where the sun came out more than a couple of weeks a year. The problem was that nowadays people had too many options and, with the rise of smaller chains of supermarkets, his profits had fallen, and with it, his dreams had disappeared.

His shop was a decent size. It featured everyday items such as toiletries, the local and national newspapers, and a wide variety of essentials such as milk, eggs, confectionery and quite a large amount of tinned goods. The thing Gerald liked about tinned goods was that they didn't expire for years, so when it came to wastage and re-ordering it made life a little easier.

He relied heavily on regulars; especially the elderly who liked to come in and have a chat when they bought the paper and a pint of milk. His store was located near the centre of town, which helped with footfall, yet it was far enough away from the strip of pubs and bars to ensure he didn't often suffer the rowdy crowds that Barnsley had become synonymous with, ever since he was old enough to realise.

But, of course, avoiding the crowd wasn't always a possibility, and today rowdy shoppers had found their way.

The clock turned seven as Gerald waited for four teenagers to leave before he could close for the day. Thursday was curry night: his wife would be waiting for him with a couple of beers sitting in the fridge and, as soon as he stepped through the door, his dinner would be ready.

The teenagers weren't old enough to drink, but as they laughed and pushed each other around the store, it appeared to Gerald that they were already intoxicated. At a guess, Gerald imagined they might have been fifteen or sixteen; he couldn't tell any more. Some kids who looked twelve ended up being eighteen, and others would get offended when he asked - displaying an ID showing they were in fact in their late twenties, and sometimes even early thirties. And, he lived in Barnsley, where the acceptable drinking age had seemingly lowered considerably - so, while the law dictated it, he no longer worried about asking for ID. He didn't necessarily mind the town's pro drinking culture, as long as people bought something and let him close up shop without any trouble. There were more important things to him than underage drinking; times were tough, and he couldn't afford to be as selective as some may expect of him.

The teenagers picked up a crate of lager and took it over to the till - continuing to push each other around the store as they did so.

"Alright, old man. And some cigs."

"Which ones?" Gerald replied.

The teens shrugged and pointed at one of the options that Gerald had on show. They counted out their cash between them.

Gerald collected a pack of cigarettes from the shelf behind him. As he turned back around, he noticed that the group were closely watching his every move. Anxiety rose, and his voice wavered. He ran the figures through the till and asked for the price.

"Fifteen fifty, please."

"Fifteen fifty, please," one of the teens mocked, emphasising the older man's manners.

"Oh please," chirped another.

Gerald stood patiently and waited for the mocking to end. He'd run this store for over thirty years, and he had never had any serious trouble. He had no desire for today to proceed any differently.

The others laughed, but when they realised they would get no reaction from their provocation, they relinquished.

"Alright mate, here ya go."

That was the last customer. It wouldn't be long until he was sitting at home with his wife, watching whatever reality television show she had chosen that evening. After all, he would have a cold beer in his hand and a curry in his belly.

He could smell the spices; cumin, paprika, chilli - his mind wandered to what type of curry his wife would be making today. His mind continued to process the possibilities as he began to smell the coconut and cream from a korma, followed by the heavenly aroma of tomatoes from a madras.

"Wanker!" the teens walked away, making hand gestures to the shopkeeper before turning back to hammer one final nail into the coffin.

"Please. Oh please," they mocked.

The group laughed as they exited the shop, causing a wave of relief to wash over Gerald. He followed the teens to the door, placed his key in the lock and turned it counter-clockwise. His day was complete.

Gerald sighed. All that was left was to count the register, throw out the rubbish and check the perishables. However, with his thoughts firmly focused on his rumbling stomach, he decided the perishables could wait until tomorrow.

Gerald walked over to the till but registered a noise. Was there something inside the shop? Did he hear something in the aisle?

"Hello?" he inquired, to no reply. "The shop's closed," he tried again as he walked around the shelf that blocked his view.

A woman, who must have been approaching her late seventies stood staring at a shelf, leaning on her cane for support.

"I'm sorry, miss, the shop's closed."

Gerald shared a conflicting mix of sympathy and dislike of the elderly. He was always grateful for their custom but watching how the human body and mind deteriorated scared him.

The old lady looked at Gerald; a smile found her face - at least this one was friendly. Gerald supposed that one more customer wouldn't hurt.

"What can I help ya with ma'am?"

She pointed at something on the shelf with her frail, crooked fingers. Gerald moved closer to help.

"D'ya want that one?"

The customer continued to hold up her arthritic fingers. She pointed towards an item high up on the shelf.

Gerald leant in and noticed that the product she was pointing to was a packet of sanitary towels - a little strange, Gerald thought, but maybe they weren't for her. He turned to the lady and recognised her to be one of his semi-regulars, her name - ah yes, it was Ms Wood, if he remembered correctly.

"Right, Ms Wood, yeah? Let's put this through n' get ya home."

Gerald picked up the sanitary towels from the shelf, which was the last thing he saw before he blacked out.

***

Gerald stirred. His eyes flickered, as did his recollection of where he was. He brought a hand to the back of his head and felt a sharp pain from a lump that began to form.

That old bat, Gerald thought. What did she do?

He tried to move his legs, but that was when the pain displayed its true form. Just like the tipping point of a rollercoaster, the adrenaline hit instantly and furiously.

His ankles had been hit multiple times, and he did not doubt that they were both broken.

"I watched a film on Friday," the croaky voice of Ms Wood echoed from behind him.

He fought through his desire to focus on the pain, rage finding him instead. He twisted his shoulders and neck to look behind him.

Ms Wood stood behind him, free of any shame. She towered over him completely naked, except for the cane that kept her standing.

"It was called Misery."

"Ms Wood! What the-"

Ms Wood smiled. She shuffled closer to Gerald, hobbling towards him with her head held high.

"Ms Wood!" Gerald exclaimed desperately.

"But what I didn't understand," she took a moment to catch her breath from the short walk. "Was why she didn't do anything to him?"

Ms Wood threw her cane down to the floor.

"Y'know, anything sexy."

She swayed her hips - the best she could for an old lady who no longer looked after herself physically. As she danced, she grinned, displaying her white dentures that looked strangely youthful compared to her deteriorating appearance.

"Ms Wood!" Gerald shouted in a manner of self-preservation. He tried his best to move, but each movement sent shockwaves of pain throughout his body.

"Ms Wood will give you wood. Yes?" she asked, the question becoming elongated as it whistled through her dentures.

Her breasts, not preserved by time as she may have once hoped, drooped down to her folded mid-section. The colour had aged along with their positioning, with a green and purple tinge becoming apparent.

As she danced, her breasts swayed from side to side like two elongated pendulums. Not quite as mesmerising as she may have hoped, but they evoked emotion from Gerald.

He pulled himself up to a sitting position and tried his best to fight through the pain. He watched the sight that would stay with him forever.

Ms Wood began to hastily rub her hands across every inch of every wrinkle and fold. She chanted.

"Wood, Wood, I'll give you Wood."

Gerald found himself unable to move; his mind unable to process what was happening. He wondered whether he was dreaming, but the pain soon reminded him that this was, indeed, a real-life grocery store peep show.

She took Gerald's hand and placed it on the bottom of her right, swinging breast.

She chanted, over and over, in a rhythmic fashion.

"Wood, Wood, I'll give you Wood."

Each time she spoke, her words shifted, from those of a confused old lady to consonants and vowels that twisted with purpose on her tongue as they left her lips.

She moved Gerald's hand lower until it was where she wanted it to be. Gerald flinched and retracted his arm, but that only made Ms Wood angry.

She leant past Gerald, picked up a can from the shelf and, in one swift motion, brought the can down shattering several of his teeth on one side of his mouth. Gerald screamed in agony. He brought his hands up to his mouth to witness the blood trickle out on to his open palms. His tongue traced his teeth, noticing the new cracks and jagged edges.

The can of cat food rolled away from the madness.

Ms Wood laughed and continued with her devious plan. She grasped Gerald's hand. He found himself too pre-occupied with his tooth pain, the throbbing from his ankles, and the swelling on the back of his head, to oppose.

He gave in to her demands, and then he began to cry.

Ms Wood, seemingly undeterred, took one of Gerald's bloodied hands and returned it to where she thought it belonged. She moved his hand up and down and enjoyed herself as the man underneath her trembled.

Gerald prayed for it to end. He had no fight left in him to do anything more than to close his eyes and distance himself from reality.

Ms Wood let Gerald's hand drop for a moment, but unfortunately, for the local shopkeeper, that wasn't the end. No, that was simply foreplay. Now it was time for the main event. Ms Wood bent down and placed one hand on her lower back, reaching forward with the other. Her ligaments and cartilage clicked and popped as her breasts grazed the cold floor below.

She reached for the zipper of his trousers. After a frustrated few seconds of not being able to work the contraption that separated her from everything she'd dreamt about, Gerald once again saw the anger flare in her eyes.

She roared the instruction.

"Get them off!"

Gerald hesitated for a moment - enough time for Ms Wood to pick up another can; dog food this time.

Gerald lowered his bloodied hands and slowly began to unzip his fly, pleading through his tears for this to stop. He knew there was no choice. He unzipped and pulled his trousers down slightly. Ms Wood suggested for them to be removed further, to which Gerald obeyed.

After he was fully exposed, she knelt slowly and straddled him.

Nothing stirred on his part, but that didn't stop Ms Wood from enjoying herself. She straddled him and threw her head back. She laughed and chanted her name. She moaned as she rocked back and forth; her movements becoming harder and sharper as her pelvis and hips dug into the legs of Gerald.

She rubbed her breasts, smashing them into her body, causing her moaning to escalate. She fought through the feeling of numbness in her arms and legs, but her heart fluttered uncontrollably.

She would get through this; she was having one of the best moments of her life. Besides, she hadn't finished.

Pain receptors fired, yet she continued to rock back and forth on the shopkeeper's docile lap. Her legs twitched, her arms spasmed, and her neck rolled backwards. She laughed and squealed.

The culmination of pleasure and pain was rising. She began to fling around frantically on Gerald's lap; Ms Wood's head whipped from side to side and back and forth, as her thinning grey hair caressed his face like the brushes of a drive-through car wash.

With an audible pop, Ms Wood's hip slipped from its socket. She stopped laughing. A slight worry appeared across her expression, but only moments later, the laughter rose again.

The rocking became arrhythmic as she lost the use of the left side of her lower body.

Laughing and moaning; a mix of frustration, pain and pleasure, brought her to climax.

As quickly as the noise rose, it vanished.

Ms Wood's head fell backwards, followed quickly by the rest of her body as it became limp.

Gerald was no longer waiting for an opportunity to escape. He accepted his fate, and the sudden turn of events threw him. As Ms Wood fell backwards, it took Gerald a few moments to gather his thoughts before he pushed Ms Wood off of his lap entirely.

He used his arms to push himself backwards. He sat against an aisle and pulled up his trousers. He fought the pain that reached him and focused on finding the mobile phone in his pockets on the floor.

His mind had skipped the dinner date he had with his wife but, as he retrieved the phone, the number of missed calls brought him back to reality.

He dialled 999.

"Thank you for ringing the emergency services. We're sorry to inform you that we are currently experiencing a large call volume and will answer your call as soon as an operator is available. If it is an emergency, please stay on the line. We apologise for any inconvenience."

He slumped back and waited; the pain in his ankles and face roared like a slow-burning fire, competing for dominance.

13

Anabel had been walking for hours. She followed the electrical power lines in the hope that soon they would lead her to a town, but the derelict area that she had appeared in resulted in more lost time than expected.

She knew that she needed to return to Charlie, and she calculated that there was a definite possibility that he was in danger.

One positive was the ache in her shoulder, which had dulled to a slight throbbing sensation. She also felt no adverse effect from coming in contact with the corruption. However, the small wound had taken a long time to heal, and she did not doubt that its power was immense.

The desert spread for as far as the eye could see, in all directions, and it was only now that blocks of buildings were coming into sight. It seemed like a small village was just up ahead.

As the buildings became more evident, so did the reality of what they contained.

Anabel approached tentatively. Not through fear, but preservation. It was as she considered. The town contained no more than twenty or thirty buildings. It was in the middle of nowhere, surrounded by desolation. The minute town shone red.

Anabel crept within a few feet of the first building. She noticed the first watcher on the ground in front of her. His body lay lifeless, his limbs reaching out across the floor - his watch ended prematurely. Anabel noticed the second body, the third, and then even more; before her were hundreds of slain watchers. She peered around the corner of the building and saw the remnants of the massacre.

Three living watchers were held in place by a mass of the corrupted.

The watchers in question had wounds from the conflict. It was apparent that all of their resistance had since dissipated.

The same number of corrupted watchers approached the three in place.

The watchers could not fight, could not run. Anabel knew there was no saving them; their fate was sealed.

The impulse within Anabel was one of fight or flight. She wavered between the two thought processes; she was close enough to return to her world but felt a need to stop what she was sure was about to happen.

Instead, she did what her programming commanded; she watched.

The three corrupted watchers' hands twisted and cracked in unnatural ways as they reached out and placed their palms on the dormant watchers in front of them. There was no rhythm or sync to the corrupted; they moved freely, fighting their programming at every turn.

One at a time the watchers squirmed as a bright red light emanated from the hands of the corrupted, engulfing the head of whom it touched.

Anabel shifted uncomfortably, fighting her desire to intervene. This was no time for self-sacrifice. A part of her began to feel what could only be described as fear, yet another hungry for knowledge.

The thirst quickly disappeared when the first watcher began squirming. The mouth of both watchers opened wide, growing larger and larger as the red life force of the corrupted flowed in and down the once pure watcher's airway. Red electricity sparked from the first watcher, as the next two began struggling in the same way as the first.

The first watcher's neck twisted, a full three hundred and sixty degrees, cracking at every moment which would typically result in a stopping point; after which they struggled from side to side in sharp, forceful motions. Their wrists snapped, their legs buckled; everything that was once human twisted out of them.

The first watcher fell forward. Their wrists and legs unravelled back to their natural state. As it lay face-first on the ground, its neck cracked and twisted back to how it once was.

The two watchers next to it followed with cracking and twisting motions, before flopping and lying still on the floor.

One by one, they rose to their feet.

The watchers stood. They turned. They looked at Anabel.

If Anabel had a heart, it would have leapt out of her chest. The panic caused her to stumble and lose her footing. It was a human trait, but she found herself fearful as the corrupted grimaced, with too-wide smiles that covered the majority of their faces.

The rest of the inhabitants of the town turned and stared. One by one, each smiling face looked upon Anabel with malice.

The stares were enough of a warning. Anabel disappeared into the power and prayed that no corrupted would follow. If they did, at least she'd have numbers on her side. However, she knew one thing now for certain; their numbers were growing.

Anabel appeared at a desk that was not her own, in the space of a watcher who was no more. Other watchers appeared to be observing her for signs of corruption.

Corruption wasn't easy to distinguish - unless red current was spotted, or, as she had witnessed, any unnatural movements of body parts occurred. Watchers were aware that there was a threat and, every time a watcher returned, there were a hundred eyes, if not more, processing information.

Anabel was unsure as to what part of the building she was in. She appeared at a desk that looked exactly like hers, surrounded by watchers that looked exactly like her and her male equivalent - an autonomy of existence in a mechanical world.

She observed watchers around her that looked in her direction as they calculated the correct response. Some of them must have surely seen the screens that displayed death and corruption from which she had just escaped.

"Why didn't you do anything?" she raised her voice. "They died." The watchers stared.

"Some of you," she corrected her turn of phrase before continuing. "Some of us have been corrupted, and you did nothing!"

She watched as they turned in unison and pressed the button that signalled corruption. The enforcement would be here again soon.

"We need to do-" she wasn't sure what could be done, but still she finished her sentence. "Something. We need to do something."

She moved her eyes across from one set of non-responsive eyes to the next. She sighed as she struggled with what to say next.

But she knew - for they were her, and she was them. One watcher breaking protocol by talking to others was not going to be heard. She had no voice here, and more importantly, she had no audience.

A few seconds after the pressing of buttons, the enforcement arrived. It seemed to begin with watchers who were greeted with a few members to analyse the situation.

"Corruption?" asked the group.

"No," Anabel stated her case.

They approached and monitored the wound on her shoulder, which had now healed into a scar.

The enforcers agreed with Anabel's dismissal.

"Return to your terminal," they instructed.

It was a strange thing for Anabel to admit, but she felt a need to speak. "I am unaware of its location. Could you escort me?"

To anyone listening, it sounded illogical. To the best of Anabel's knowledge, no watcher had ever used any stations other than their own. Yet here she was, standing at an unknown station, face-to-face with authority, asking questions that had never been asked.

Watchers

Minds of the authority whirred; seemingly unsure with how to respond, until one of them spoke out of turn.

"Who is your human?"

"Charlie Taylor."

Processes whirred.

"Date of birth?"

She answered.

"Follow me."

Anabel followed as the watcher broke off and moved mechanically. The others returned to their posts simultaneously. The watcher led her along the line of stations, each with a watcher stationed in front - else watching within.

She had never looked at her fellow watchers before and had never questioned anything, but now questions began flooding in.

"Who is in charge of us all?" she asked as they walked in a straight line, which seemed to last a lifetime.

"The Overseer," came the response.

"I know The Overseer sees everything, but who commands us."

They stopped, as the watcher halted to process the question.

"Who commands you?" she repeated.

Never had he been questioned like this. Watchers didn't ask questions, yet he was programmed to respond. There would be no reason for him not to.

"I am A-11452, I report to A-11451."

"And who do they report to."

"A-11451 reports to A-11450."

She began to see a pattern.

"Who do we all report to?"

Cogs turned in the watcher's mind.

"The Narrator."

Finally, she knew who she needed to see.

"And how would one get to see The Narrator?"

The watcher processed the information for a moment.

"Follow me."

***

In Washington DC, workers carried on with their everyday lives. The terror threat was at its highest level since attacks on the Twin Towers, yet America stood still for no one.

Outside of the Whitehouse, several small camera crews waited to get a glimpse of the president - all they needed was to overhear a snippet of a conversation, and it would make worldwide news. It would give them the acclaim that they all felt their hard work deserved.

As much as they tried, there was no possibility for infiltration with security on high alert. Patience was most important at the moment; hot pockets, breakfast bars and wet-wipes all a close second.

A twitch in the curtain of a front room caused sudden disruption from the eagle-eyed amongst them - a flood of urgency spread. Producers and reporters shouted at their camera operators to roll and focus on the window, while they jostled for the best position.

The president returned the curtain to its natural state. His bodyguard and wife joined him shortly after.

He had been in a relationship with his other half since they met in high school, many years ago. They both knew, even at a young age, that with a lot of hard work the man she chose could one day be president - and she could have the life she had always wanted, as the first lady.

He believed that most of his election win was down to luck, whereas Andrea didn't believe in such things. For her, it was all in appearances and, while she loved her husband, if he hadn't made it to the top, she would have found someone else who would have got her there.

The sound of their two children running around upstairs echoed through the marble staircase into the living room.

"How would you like a pot roast, Mr President?" Andrea asked with a cheeky fluctuation in her tone.

After getting no response, she softened the humour. "Are you alright, darling?

"Oh, Andrea, I am sorry," the president turned around to face his wife, turning his back on the camera crews outside. "Yes, that would be lovely."

"I'll start it now."

The president walked over to his wife, taking her hand in his.

"That would be a most welcome distraction."

His wife, who was at least half a foot shorter than him, tip-toed to place a kiss on his cheek.

"It'll be ready in about an hour," she said, turning to leave the room.

The president gently stopped her as he vocalised a thought.

"Just answer one thing before you go."

"Anything."

"What do we do next?"

Andrea thought for a moment, to compose herself.

"We do what we always do?"

She looked deep into her husband's eyes; conveying as much conviction as she thought humanly possible.

"We find the problem, and take care of it."

The president nodded.

"Dinner will be an hour."

As the first lady took her first steps towards the kitchen, a terrifying flash filled the room. The hardwood floor rippled and cracked beneath her feet that caused her knees to buckle. A scream rushed from her mouth as she lost her balance and approached the floor. Just moments later the sound of a mammoth explosion caught up with them, covering the noise of the first lady's panic.

Lashings of white light and intolerable levels of explosive noise surrounded them; ruptured paintings, trinkets, large splinters of wood, stray bricks and fragments of shattered glass pierced the room and its contents.

There was nowhere to hide, no time to escape; the president, his wife, their children, and the staff took the full force of the explosion, head-on.

As the initial blast began to settle, the president realised that he had to instinctively run to his wife. He took her hand and helped her from the splintered floor, as the security guards moved at speed - all but one, who lay motionless, sans blood trickling from a large hole in his neck.

There was no time for taking notice of the fallen guard. Instead, the president and his wife rushed from the onslaught of flying debris towards a safe room.

Andrea yelled and pointed upstairs. However, no words found their target due to the monstrous explosion that echoed throughout the city. She mouthed 'the children' and indicated once again upstairs, resulting in two security guards running up the distorted stairwell.

Speckles of white paint ran down the corridor walls as they rushed past. One guard ran ahead and grabbed the handle at the end of the space, only to retract his hand with extreme pain. Without thinking, he took off his top, wrapped it around his hand and then proceeded to open the door for the group to continue.

Andrea kicked and screamed, resisting the guard's attempts to help her to the other room without her children. Unfortunately for her, the security guards were too heavy and well trained to allow her to do anything else. The guards hurried the president and his wife through the open doorway and, just before closing the heavy door behind them, two security guards ran through the opening, each holding a crying child in their arms.

The heavy door closed behind them. For the first time, the president felt a small moment of relief. The room here was noticeably cooler than the corridor, and items hadn't been disturbed as much as in other places.

The guards continued forwards down a stairway, taking the most important person in America underground to escape not only the first blast but also any subsequent ones that could arrive at any moment.

The guards hurried the all-American power couple down a winding stairway until they reached another heavy door. This one required a sequence, which the president recorded after a moment of hesitation. It took multiple guards to pry open the door, through which they all entered.

The door slammed shut; relief welcomed them.

The security guards placed the children gently on the ground. Andrea ran to her children; she smothered them in kisses, checked their foreheads, arms, heads, and ran her fingers across every small scratch that they had suffered. Apart from a few scratches, however, they appeared to be okay.

The security guard who had opened the door tried to hide his pain between gritted teeth. He attempted to remove the shirt that stuck to his hand.

Andrea's maternal nature took over. She kissed her children again. She fought through the burning pain she felt in her ankle to rush over to the guard and help one of the men who very well may have saved their lives.

The bunker was stocked from floor to ceiling with enough supplies to keep even the modest amount of people it contained alive and well for months. Yet, while it was more luxurious than most, it was still a bunker where no one hoped ever to spend time.

A whisper floated into Andrea's mind.

'Treat the man. Be strong.'

Andrea felt light-headed. She noticed her stomach leaping into her throat, almost causing her breakfast to make a surprise reappearance. She could be in a state of shock, so instead acted quickly and on instinct; she grabbed one of the many first aid kits and attended to the man's hand.

She attempted to speak but realised that she heard nothing over the ringing in her ears. Instead, she looked square into the man's eyes as she prised the molten cotton from his skin. As she did so, the hardened man who would die for them both, showed moments of pain and discomfort. Focusing her attention on his hand, she pulled at the shirt – a fair amount harder than she would have liked.

She knew that if she could have heard anything at that moment, she would have heard the grown man wail in agony. Some parts of the shirt came free, while others resisted. The exposed areas of the man's hand contained no skin, only exposed flesh.

She took the scissors and cut the remaining area as small as she possibly could. She treated the exposed wound first, wiping the area clean with bacterial wipes, applying cream and then preparing a wrap.

The first lady took her focus away from the man and, when she turned back, the final piece of fabric had been removed. She looked up at his face as he held the burnt section of cloth and dead flesh from his left hand. He held the arm across his face so that no one could observe his reaction.

Andrea knew that he must be in extreme pain. She treated the wound and wrapped it as quickly as she could, noticing his hand shaking as she finished.

His watcher observed. She offered soothing words as he gently rocked back and forth to comfort himself.

Stillness through a state of panic. A slowed room. A moment of nothingness.

As the shock shook the inhabitants of the bunker, the remaining watchers appeared one by one.

Watchers did not interact with other watchers - it was written, but at this moment, they all knew there was no other choice.

Mechanically, they approached the watcher that soothed the loyal security guard. One of them spoke, watcher to watcher, for possibly the first time in a non-corrupted scenario in plain sight.

"I do not know what has happened here. I do hope your human is not in a tremendous amount of pain."

The watcher finished whispering words of comfort. She walked over to join her kind, and the conversation continued.

"He will be fine."

"Good. What happened here?"

"This is not written," all of the watchers talked as one.

"Let us return to our world and ask the questions which need to be asked."

The watchers agreed. Simultaneously, blue light filled the room as they vanished.

The president, his wife, and their children and security guards, were left alone once more.

14

Charlie and Jenny gasped for air, struggling to catch their breath following more than a moment of ecstasy.

Charlie rolled to one side of the bed, prying the sweat-soaked covers from his back before collapsing next to his naked partner. This time no scratch marks covered his chest and, as far as he was aware, there was no intent to create any.

Jenny caught her breath and let her arm drop on Charlie's chest. She ran her fingers through his chest hair, mustering all of the energy she could find. She noticed the now slightly faded scratches.

"Jesus, did I do that to you?"

"It's okay," Charlie replied, soothingly.

The couple lay there, recharging from the activity that they had once again found themselves partaking in. Unsure what to do next, the two drifted towards slumber once again. Jenny's arm fell from Charlie's chest as he turned over.

Their eyes closed as they waited for sleep to take them once more.

"Hello."

Charlie's eyes shot open. Anabel sat on the bed next to him.

"What!" Charlie caught himself, lowered his voice and continued. "What are you doing?"

"I'm your watcher."

"I know, but… now?" Charlie nodded towards Jenny.

"Is this a bad time? I've discovered some important news."

"Okay," Charlie whispered. "Let's at least go to the other room."

Charlie slid his legs out from the bed and was about to stand up before he realised that his boxer shorts were on the other side of the room.

"Would you mind turning around?"

"Why?"

"Because I'm, well, I'm naked," Charlie admitted with more than a subtle hint of embarrassment in his demeanour.

"I don't understand."

"You know, naked, as in, my tackle flapping about."

"You do realise I've seen your 'tackle' on thousands of occasions?"

Charlie scratched his head and smiled awkwardly.

"Yeah, but still. It's different now. Please, would you turn around?"

"If you insist."

Anabel turned around as Charlie gently rose from the bed. He found his boxer shorts, followed by the rest of his clothes, before heading into the kitchen where he had begun to feel accustomed. He closed the door behind him and checked that Jenny was fast asleep in the process.

Charlie would kill for a coffee right now; he felt a fuzziness that hadn't left him, which coffee would most definitely assist with. However, he didn't want to risk waking Jenny so, instead, chose to pour a glass of water to quench the overnight thirst that ravaged him.

Charlie sat at the table, Anabel across from him.

"Good morning, Charlie."

"Good morning, Anabel."

The two stared at each other in silence, momentarily. Charlie found it difficult to recollect the last time he had felt so vulnerable, so exposed. If this was happening with anyone else, he might have felt the need to run back to bed and jump under the covers, but

Anabel was the exception - and the only person in his life that he could let himself feel exposed around.

He saw Anabel's lips curl up at the edges slightly.

"Are you smiling?" asked Charlie.

"Smiling is a human trait," Anabel's lips dipped to their natural stoic position. Not one of unpleasantness, but a neutral state. "How are you?" she changed the subject.

"Well," Charlie took a large sip of his water, enjoying the refreshing feeling as the cooling liquid nourished his throat. "It's been a hell of a week."

"I agree," Anabel sat on a chair despite making no impression on the world around her.

"People thought I was going insane." Charlie counted the first of his bullet points on his fingers. "Then, you helped me escape. Then…" he talked lightly, pointing to the bedroom. "Jenny."

He continued his train of thought. "And, to top it off, there's a war?"

"It's more than just a war."

"What do you mean, 'just a war'?"

"This is a war that exceeds your world, Charlie. It stems from mine."

"How?"

"The corruption that spreads through our ranks, it causes watchers to break our rules. It causes them to interfere and encourage people to follow their worst path."

Charlie opened his mouth, but as he tried to vocalise a response, he found that no words left him. Instead, he gestured for her to continue.

"I spoke to The Narrator and the rules of our universe are not that different to your own."

"Who is The Narrator?" Charlie asked, dumbfounded.

"They are the one that knows all. The omniscient being that tells us the path to walk, and rules to follow."

"Well, I suppose I did ask," Charlie responded with a cheeky glint in his eye, distancing himself from the idea that there was another world beyond this.

"They told me that everything must have an equal and opposite to provide balance. That is why we were created as a neutral entity. We ensure that morality remains firmly centred, but perhaps we are not as neutral as our creator believed. Perhaps a few were created too good, which in return caused a counter-reaction."

"You were created?"

"We were all created, Charlie. The Narrator told me many things about our existence and how we came to be, but they made one thing clear. I need to ask the one who created us questions about corruption and how to fight it."

Charlie thought for a moment before continuing, in an attempt for his fuzzy head to process the information.

"How do you find them?"

"I need to find A1."

"Who is that?"

"It is the first watcher."

"How many watchers are there?"

"There are as many watchers as humans."

"I guess that makes sense," Charlie took a final sip of his water. "So, why do we need to find A1?"

"The first watcher was created along with the first human. That means that they have seen everything and observed corruption since it existed. Perhaps they know of how it began and, in turn, a way to stop it. It is our only hope."

"How do we find him – or her?" Charlie corrected himself.

"I will try to track down their location in my world, but the only option as far as I see it, is to find their corresponding human."

"Well, as your corresponding human, I say let's do it."

"Are you sure? It would be tough to track the person down without you, but not impossible."

"Yes," Charlie said confidently. He wanted to reach out and take Anabel's hand in his, only to remember the impossibility of doing so. "Time is of the essence."

"Thank you."

"So, how do we do this? Do we just look for the oldest person in the world?"

"Not quite. I was born with you, but A1 has always been and, therefore, reassigned on numerous occasions. The Narrator informed me that A1 happens to watch over William James, who resides close to Washington."

"In America?"

Anabel nodded.

"It's strange."

"What is strange?" Anabel queried.

"Well, I thought, you know, that A1 would watch over, I don't know, the Queen, or the president, or somebody important."

"Why do you question his importance?"

"I don't know, I just thought the first watcher would be looking over the most important person in the world, and it's a person called William James."

"But how do you assign importance?"

"Well, it's someone that people look up to."

"Is it similar to when you compare yourself to Chris Hemsworth?"

"What?" Charlie shot upright, avoiding eye contact with Anabel.

"When you look in the mirror, flexing your arms and pretending you have a large hammer in your hand."

"How?" Charlie's cheeks filled with the deep red hue of embarrassment. "Yes, I suppose it's a little similar to that."

Anabel nodded, gaining a greater understanding of self-importance.

"I guess I'd better pack my bags," Charlie remembered the previous day. "Do you think I'll be able to fly after being committed?"

Anabel wasn't sure of the correct answer.

"They wouldn't go to the trouble of informing the airport for something small like this, right? I'm sure it's fine."

Charlie rose from his chair. He searched through the cabinets in the kitchen before retrieving a scrap of paper and a pen.

"It's easier this way," he spoke out loud to Anabel, who already knew what he was about to write.

Charlie scribbled down an apology for leaving. He said that he'd call her in a few days and that a family emergency required him to leave urgently. He left the note on the counter.

He took one last look into the bedroom and, to his relief, saw Jenny blissfully unaware of the conversation that had happened between a being from another world and the man she had just spent the night with. He tiptoed in to collect the last of his possessions and then closed the door quietly behind him before exiting the apartment.

Anabel walked by his side as they left.

"I need to pick up my passport, pack a few things and then book a flight."

Charlie led, and Anabel followed close behind.

"You don't have to follow me, you know?"

Charlie stopped and waited for Anabel to catch up with him.

"Here, walk next to me."

Anabel looked a little uncertain as she attempted to follow Charlie's movements by his side.

Charlie checked his wallet, which was devoid of cash – not a surprise in today's contactless world, but fortunately, he did have his bank card.

The realisation of the adventure they were about to undertake finally settled in for Charlie. They walked for a few moments until they saw a taxi, which Charlie quickly flagged down.

"Do you accept card?" Charlie asked, as the taxi driver wound down his window.

"Yes mate," the driver responded with a cockney twang.

Charlie couldn't help but notice an awkward amount of facial hair, spread unevenly across the unkempt chauffeur's face.

"Great", Charlie opened the door and gestured for Anabel to get in first.

Shit - Charlie thought of how strange that must have looked. He pretended to check his shirt and tuck it in before quickly getting into the taxi.

He composed himself and, with slight hesitation, Charlie asked to go home.

Despite some friendly back and forth conversation from the black cab driver, they mostly sat in silence. The last two days caught up with Charlie once again, and he felt the need to rest. Actually - coffee, he needed coffee.

After twenty minutes of London traffic, they approached Charlie's road.

"That'll be eighteen-fifty, please pal."

The card reader lit up. Charlie tapped his card and, with a successful beep, he was home.

They exited the taxi, without a significant gesture of holding the door open this time and, upon seeing his road, Charlie let out a sigh of relief. He hadn't seen his apartment for what had felt like a lifetime, even though it was only a matter of days, and all he wanted to do was curl up in bed and binge on some daytime television.

Charlie rustled around in his pocket to find his keys, unlocked the front door to the apartment and proceeded up the stairs.

With a click, Charlie's front door opened and in stepped Anabel. Charlie followed; the pungent smell of damp bullied his nostrils and overpowered the senses.

Charlie locked the door shut behind him and immediately opened all of the windows.

Could Anabel smell? Charlie wondered to himself. She didn't have a physical presence as such, so he dismissed the idea and therefore a need to apologise.

At least no surprises waited for him – in the ride over he had pictured that there would be a police car patrolling out front, just waiting for him to slip up and return home.

It seemed like the world had more significant problems than Charlie - though coffee was still his main priority. He filled the kettle and flicked the switch, and felt welcomed by the rising roar of boiling water.

As he waited for the kettle to boil, Charlie walked to his room. The flat itself was a tiny one-bedroom apartment that, like a lot of London locations, left a lot to be desired. Even though the open-plan mashing of front room-come-kitchen was relatively clean, the apartment was old and showed its age.

The sound of the kettle whistled through to the single bedroom. Charlie pulled a suitcase from the bottom of his hand-luggage sized bag and began filling it with clothes. Unaware of what he was packing, Charlie instead focused on remembering where his passport was. He finished placing some t-shirts and jeans into the case, roughly folded, and then counted out six clean pairs of underwear, which he placed with a few pairs of miss-matching socks.

Charlie placed his phone on charge, which had been dead now for a while. It came to life with a beep and, after a moment, artificial light from the screen. He rummaged deep in his chest of drawers, found his passport and placed that into the bag as well.

It was finally time for a coffee, Charlie thought.

Charlie went back into the kitchen. He passed by Anabel who appeared to be staring into the dormant television and made an instant coffee. He reached into the fridge, the smell of rotten food disturbing his nostrils with such vigour that he turned his head away in disgust and closed the refrigerator - he'd have his coffee black.

Charlie took a sip of his coffee. He allowed himself to enjoy the warmth it brought to his throat and stomach before he retrieved a bin liner from beneath his sink. He removed the source of the rotten smell from his fridge. It was more than just one item though – there was a left-over pack of half-eaten chicken breast that had started to become green and slimy, an open packet of cheese which ponged more than mild cheddar ever should, and a few other tainted products that also contributed. He then threw everything fresh from his fridge, understanding that he may not be home for some time.

Hunger was far from his mind as his stomach performed catapults from the smell that the fridge had created. He realised that he probably needed to eat, however, but thought a supermarket meal deal would perhaps be a little safer than anything in his ill looked-after apartment.

Charlie walked through to the bedroom. He continued packing a few more items into his bag and turned his phone on.

After a few moments, he saw a large amount of missed calls. He scrolled through the contact list and saw some people he knew – a colleague from his old work, Paul, and Steve, but also a list of numbers that he did not recognise. He wondered if they were from the hospital.

He didn't feel alone with Anabel in his presence, but he felt the need to contact another real-life person. He thought about ringing his Mum before remembering she was no longer there. He decided to text Steve.

"Sorry I've not been in touch, mate. Loads been going on. Catch up soon."

If anything, it would at least stop him from worrying for a while.

He felt a small amount of relief and, knowing there would be a quick phone call or reply if Steve wasn't preoccupied, he decided to not keep his phone on for too much longer. When he considered who else to text, his mind drifted to Jenny. He felt a small wave of guilt wash over him and decided it would be a good idea to let her know more than his note informed.

"Hey, Jenny. Sorry for running off this morning. There's been a bit of an emergency. I'm heading away for a few days."

He wondered whether to say he'd miss her or to tell her where he was going. Instead, he thought it best to keep it neutral. He finished the text.

"See you soon."

After the text message had left his phone, he switched off the power to avoid any form of contact. Charlie had little patience to explain his situation to anybody, plus, who would believe him? They'd think he was suffering from some form of mental breakdown and he would be committed again - perhaps for good this time. Maybe that's what he needed.

Charlie sat on the edge of his bed. A moment of realisation hit home after days of panic and confusion - the wool shifted from his eyes.

"What are you doing?" Anabel took him by surprise.

"I thought you knew everything?" Charlie responded, not in a hostile tone, but as a matter of fact.

"We only know what is written."

"And this?" Charlie asked.

"This has not been written," Anabel confirmed. "You are not following your path."

Charlie took a moment to let that settle. Fate and destiny were real, and he was creating his own.

"And what about you?" he asked.

"I," Anabel hesitated. "I am not following my commands. My goal is to stop the corruption," she took a breath. "And, to watch over you. That is one thing that will never change."

Anabel held out her hand slowly in Charlie's direction. Charlie reached out and watched as his fingertips grazed hers. He felt a slight tingle of static electricity run through his hand.

Anabel returned her hand to her side, as did Charlie.

Charlie found his laptop amidst the mess in his flat, pressed the on-switch to no avail, so plugged in the power cable and waited for it to boot up. After connecting to the internet, he ignored the overwhelming urge to check his email and Facebook notifications. Instead, Charlie looked at flights that were leaving for Washington that evening.

A red exclamation mark covered the purchasing option.

The message read, 'Flights to Washington are cancelled due to unforeseen circumstances. Please choose an alternative destination or check back later.'

"What's going on?" he took a moment to consider a backup plan. "We'll have to fly nearby and get a bus or hire a car." Charlie formed his thoughts out loud.

Not knowing America very well outside of a few of the main tourist cities, Charlie opened Google maps and looked for an airport near Washington. He saw that Philadelphia was nearby.

He opened a flight comparison site that he often used for getaways, selected a one-way ticket to Philadelphia, and selected two passengers - before realising his mistake, and changing it to one. After being asked for confirmation, he chose Philadelphia International Airport from the drop-down menu and clicked search.

He looked at flights for later on and saw there was one leaving just before midnight from London Heathrow. It was around three in the afternoon, so that gave him plenty of time to get to the airport and head to the land of hope and glory.

The flight was not cheap, which caused Charlie to hesitate.

At a slither under one and a half grand, it was a portion of his money that Charlie could not afford to simply throw away. He had around six thousand in his regular account, but he also had a savings account with money from his mother's passing that he had not yet dared to acknowledge.

"Is this the only way?" Charlie asked Anabel, hovering the mouse button over 'purchase'.

"It is the quickest," Anabel confirmed, after a brief moment of consideration.

"Well, in that case," Charlie clicked purchase, only to be taken to a new site, in which he had to fill in all of his information again.

"This will just take a minute," he sighed.

Charlie entered his flight information, purchased the ticket and readied himself for a trip to the US.

"And, done," Charlie stated.

"Thank you, Charlie. I'll see you soon," she responded.

"But, are you not coming with me?"

"I need to return to my world. I'll see you when you land."

With a flash of electricity, Anabel vanished.

"But who am I going to talk to?" Charlie questioned, as he closed his baggage.

The television engulfed the room with its flickering light. Footage of the explosion and the fallout played on repeat. Interviewees retold stories of their daily lives, and interruption caused by the loud blast. The television showed interviews from people who had a loved one seriously hurt, or worse. The reports created unease in the reporter's voice.

The news ticker along the bottom of the screen informed Steve of the latest developments, 'Blast in Washington. Hundreds dead. Thousands injured.'

A reporter spoke live from the edge of a sectioned off area. Rubble filled the scene behind her.

"Good afternoon, Geoff. We're as close to the White House as we're allowed. As you can see in the background, the White House, along with much of the surrounding area, is badly damaged."

The cameraman zoomed in to the background to show a closer shot of The White House. Sections of the large building had been blown away, including the four famous pillars that previously created an impressive welcome. The broken pillars caused the supporting area to collapse, along with the front windows shattering. The green grass and bushes that once proudly framed the majestic building had also been robbed of their life. The residence of the President of the United States of America had been abolished.

"We understand the bomb was a targeted attack on The White House from a single aircraft and we have been warned that more attacks may follow."

A video played of the Whitehouse's American flag on the ground, burnt and partially destroyed.

"We have some breaking news." The reporter pressed her earpiece closer in towards her ear. "Yes, I'm just being told." She was quiet for a moment, as she waited. "We have just been told that the president and his family are all safe and secure. They have been taken to a safe location, and I'm being told that there will be a press release shortly."

The news updated its ticker along the bottom to 'Breaking news: president survives blast in Washington. Hundreds dead. Thousands injured.'

Steve turned away from the television, taken aback by the breaking news.

He checked his phone and saw a text message from Charlie. He wondered why he'd been so distant recently, but his attention soon waivered. He closed the text after studying it for a moment then scrolled through his contacts and clicked the call button when it landed on Rachel.

"Hey, Rach," Steve said after a few rings. "Yeah, it's me."

Steve waited until he had the opportunity to speak again.

"Yeah, just a quick one, are you with Jenny?" he asked. "Has she seen Charlie recently?" He waited patiently again. "Okay, I'm just getting a bit of a weird vibe from a text he sent."

Steve nodded and tried to mouth his reply a few times before he managed to get in the next word. "Great, if you could ask her if she knows anything, that'd be awesome. See you soon." On the other end, Rachel said her goodbyes and offered an olive branch. "Tonight? Sure, sounds fun." Steve replied with a grin.

If the whole world was falling down, he was at least going to have some fun while it toppled.

Steve noticed the news cut away from the reporter and, instead, he saw a new interview from what appeared to be the Houses of Parliament. Usually, this would cause Steve to turn the channel instantaneously, but he realised how critical the situation in America was right now. He turned up the volume and focused his attention.

One suited man sat rigidly in his seat. The background revealed the River Thames and areas of London Bridge.

A title appeared on the screen to let Steve know that this was the Secretary of Defence.

"Thank you for talking to us, secretary," a male reporter in the studio commented. "Can you tell us what is happening in the US?"

"Thank you for having me. The situation is precarious, and therefore I cannot say too much. However, there are a few details that I can release."

He took a moment to prepare himself for a statement that he knew would be repeated and watched by millions.

"Neither I, nor the prime minister, has had the chance to talk to the president following the devastating act in Washington." He took another breath. "However, as already stated, we do believe that this is due to ongoing tensions with Russia."

"Can you tell us if there will be another attack?"

"We cannot be sure, but the US and the UK military are on high-alert."

"Will there be retaliation from the US? And, if so, will we provide support to their army?" the reporter asked as he tried to find a nugget of new information.

"There has been no word from the president as of yet. As everyone is well aware, we remain aligned with the United States of America in our fight on terrorism."

"So, are you saying that there will be a retaliation?"

"I cannot confirm a response. The last thing we desire is war. However, the attempted assassination of the president and his family will not go unheeded, and we need to be prepared to assist, if the time arrives, for retaliation."

"Do the attacks in America have anything to do with the reporting of higher levels of violence in the UK?"

"I have no reason to believe that is the case." The Secretary of Defence distanced himself from the line of questioning.

"I am hearing that you only have time for one more question, so let me ask you if there is anything that we should be doing in this time of trouble? Do you have any advice for the public?"

"Yes, I do. There is no cause for panic. I would advise on gathering supplies in the form of tinned goods and bottled water in case of emergency, but, other than that, remain vigilant and contact the police if you see anything suspicious."

"Thank you for your time."

Steve turned the television off. That was enough news for one day.

15

In the not-so-distant world of the watchers, Anabel sat at her monitor to observe Charlie as he boarded the plane. She watched with more than a duty; it was an in-built requirement. She could feel the desire to do so; throughout her being, there was purpose.

Blue lights flickered as watcher after watcher returned to their desks around her. The walls absorbed each flash only moments after it had appeared, leaving no lingering trace.

The room seated an unfathomable number, and Anabel was unaware as the flickers began to change slowly from blue to purple in an area far away.

A wave of curiosity washed over her, creating a need to leave Charlie's station. She had recently located Jenny's desk - and her watcher. When Charlie had been asleep, she watched Jenny. There was something that compelled her to do so, but she was unsure as to precisely what. She had stared at the screen and watched Jenny.

She needed to investigate the corruption but now was a perfect opportunity to learn more about Jenny. Anabel had dealt with her corrupted watcher, and now she could find out more about the real Jenny, away from Charlie.

There were no signs of corruption in her immediate area. The last had long gone, most likely locked away until their watch ended. Since then, Jenny had been assigned a new watcher. It filled Anabel with relief but also left her stomach with a peculiar feeling that she hadn't experienced before.

Anabel walked over to the desk. She ensured no one was watching before looking into the screen. There was something strange happening. Jenny's new watcher was doing more than just watching.

***

Three men sat at the front of a small, square room. Two leant back with notepads on their laps, while the other straddled his chair in a fashion that was not becoming of his years.

All three men were well into their forties, and it was very apparent that they worked on their appearances – all three had sparkling white teeth, wore slim-fit trousers and designer shirts. However, no matter how hard they tried, they would never again look as young as they strived to be.

The man straddling the chair, stroked his chin and leant back to give himself some space to gesture with his hands.

"Can you do Victorian? I can hear posh English, not Victorian, darling."

Jenny, wearing a white blouse and black trousers, stood across from them. Her hair tickled her shoulders, bobbing up and down with the assistance of hair spray, as she talked.

"I'm sorry, what's the line again?" she asked.

"Father, if you must go then I implore you, take me with you. I have more to offer than you realise. I have more to offer than anybody could possibly realise."

Jenny imagined herself in the scenario of a Victorian household, desperate for her father not to leave, not again. She took a moment and then performed.

The casting agents processed her attempt. After a moment of silence, one of the agents responded.

"Not bad," he suggested.

"I'm not sure. I still don't hear Victorian. Maybe you're just not right for this role," the straddling man argued.

"Please, I'd kill for this part. It speaks to me so much," Jenny implored.

"I can hear the emotion coming through," the third man spoke up.

"I know I can do this," Jenny began to feel as if she was begging.

"Listen, I'm not going to beat around the bush," the straddling man began. "You're pretty. I can see you doing well in a drama or a soap, but theatre is theatre. There is nothing like it, and it takes more than just looks to succeed."

"I know," Jenny rubbed the exposed area of her upper chest for comfort. "It's been my dream since I was a little girl."

"Are you willing to do what it takes?" he asked.

"I am, please, I am."

"Are you sure?" he asked once more.

"I'd do anything for this part," Jenny responded, letting the emotion and desperation get the best of her.

The straddling man looked to his counterparts, before returning his stare to Jenny.

"Alright then." He paused for effect before he fully released any façade of being a decent human being. "Take off your blouse."

Jenny took a small step backwards.

"Excuse me?" she responded, after an uncomfortable few seconds of silence.

"You heard me. Take off your blouse. I want to see you."

The two other men mumbled. They didn't seem to be entirely in objection of the situation created by their senior, as they shifted in their seats.

"It's to let me better see your... talents," the casting agent explained.

Jenny stood in front of the three men, unsure as to what her next move should be. What could she do? The options seemed relatively clear - either stay and be exposed or run and forget that this had ever happened. It was for a part that she wanted. It was a chance for her big break. Perhaps this is what you had to do, she thought.

'Do it.'

The thought shot through her mind.

'Do whatever they ask you.'

The thought rang true.

'Fuck them all if you have to.'

"And if I take off my blouse, you'll give me the part?" she asked, finding the top button of her blouse between her thumb and index finger.

"Well, that depends if we like what we see."

Her fingers slipped down her chest. She left the button fastened.

"You're going to love what you see." She took a step towards the organiser of mischief. "But, the question is, what do I want?"

The straddling man leant back in his chair as Jenny approached. He unwrapped his legs from around the chair, creating an open invitation. Jenny approached the chair and gently straddled the man - the straddler becoming the straddled.

The man grinned and looked around at his colleagues.

One of the colleagues stood up from his chair.

"I think I'm going to have a smoke."

"Me too," the other added.

"I guess it's a private showing for one then," Jenny whispered into the agent's ear.

The door opened and shut as the two men left their manager behind, for what was probably not the first time in their career in casting.

"I can't guarantee anything," he said. "Apart from that, we'll seriously consider you."

"Well, I think we'll do a little better than that," Jenny said, moving her hands up to the top button of her blouse once again. This time she flicked the top section of her clothing open with a quick movement of her index finger. She turned her attention to the next button and opened it with ease, revealing the white, and plain bra she was wearing underneath. His focus, however, was not on the bra - it was on what lay beneath.

She unfastened the next three buttons in quick succession, allowing her blouse to open fully.

He observed her flat stomach and cupped breasts before placing his hands gently on to her waist.

Jenny removed her arms from the blouse and dropped it delicately to the ground. She reached around to her back and placed her hand on the bra clasp.

"Do you want to see more?"

"Yes," the man replied instantly.

"Will you guarantee me the part?"

"I can't," he said.

Her movements stopped abruptly.

"But, I'll get you in something."

Her hand dropped from her back. She moved her face close to his before nibbling gently on his ear.

"But I really want this one."

She tortured the man below her lap.

"I can't."

"You can do anything you want," Jenny said, without thinking twice.

"Take off your bra," he ordered, turning the focus back on the present.

Jenny unhooked her legs from around his lap and bent over provocatively. She reached down to the floor for a pen and an open book, which contained notes from the casting.

She wrapped her legs around him once more and faced him as she read from the pad.

"Jenny Carter. Pretty, but little experience."

"It is true. You are very pretty."

Jenny read the next bullet point.

"Plain," she scoffed.

He writhed beneath her as she continued.

"Not pretty enough to make up for her lack of natural talent."

He met her gaze.

"Sorry," he took a moment. "I don't think you're talentless."

"Oh, I know," she felt beneath her lap for his approval. "But you do think I'm plain, and not talented enough."

"Come on. Give me a break. What do you want from me?"

"Were you ever going to give me the part?"

He looked away.

"Were you?" she pulled his face back in line with hers.

'He was never going to give you anything.'

Jenny took a moment to listen to the thoughts churning through the silence.

'He was going to use you.'

Jenny knew it was true.

He, like every man she knew, only wanted one thing. They would take and take and take until all that was left was a broken shell of a woman, thrown away like yesterday's trash.

But, what about Charlie? A glimmer of hope entered her internal monologue.

"What about Charlie?" she muttered out loud through gritted teeth.

"Excuse me?" the executive responded — the tone in his voice, indicating his loss in appetite for the situation that had developed.

"Charlie wouldn't do this to me, would he?" she asked the man beneath her.

The man stuttered.

"Do what?"

"To use me, to screw me." Her lips curled into a snarl. "To fuck me over."

The man who was once ignorantly anticipating the situation began to squirm. He pushed her sideways in an attempt to remove her from his lap. Jenny fell slightly to one side, but her tensed leg muscles prevented her from falling. She returned to an upright position using only the force in her thighs, crushing the man's legs into the wooden chair. There was something in her hand that had caught the man's eye - something pointed and black.

Jenny brought the pen up to the man's face, aiming it at his eye.

"Change the notes," Jenny said.

"What?" the man took a deep breath. "What do you want me to do?"

"Change the fucking notes," Jenny yelled. Spit flew at his face as her patience cracked.

"What the fuck good would that do?" he asked; raising his voice. "You're a bit part actress who will only get a good part by sleeping with someone like me."

A surge of emotion caused Jenny to weep.

"And, let's get this straight. After this, I don't think anyone will be hiring you any time soon."

Jenny's head dropped; her body collapsed into itself as she fell on to his shoulder.

"Now, get the fuck off of me," he commanded.

The man grabbed Jenny by the shoulders to prise her off of him, but that left him exposed. In one swift movement, Jenny brought the nib of the pen down into the side of his throat.

The man shouted and forcefully pushed Jenny away from his lap. He rose to his feet as Jenny flew across the floor. Bringing his hand up to his neck, he removed the pen to see the level of damage — blood stained his palm as he brought his hand into his line of sight.

"You stupid bitch!"

The man removed his hand - the puncture to his throat not a lethal one.

Jenny arose from the floor with an air of desperation. Not from fear, but tainted with vengeance. She strode toward the man that had once wanted only one thing from her. Perhaps now, his priorities had changed.

With a flash, Anabel appeared alongside Jenny and the casting director.

The blue that engulfed the room quickly faded.

"What are you doing?" Anabel asked.

Across the room, standing behind Jenny, was Anabel's male counterpart. Jenny's watcher looked like any other. He ignored her presence, focused only on Jenny's task at hand.

"Stop it!" Anabel said firmly.

"Stab him. Stab him," the watcher whispered. "Gouge him. Bite him. Kill him."

Anabel approached Jenny's new watcher, who appeared to be in a trance-like state.

As she came within distance of him, she felt a sudden wave of panic. She realised the watcher had stopped chanting.

Jenny had her hands on the agent. She held the pen by her side, ready for the next thrust.

The watcher's neck cracked and snapped unnaturally to turn his attention towards Anabel. Anabel took a step back, the sight of corruption still provoking fear within.

"But, you were removed."

The watcher twisted his body unnaturally; each twist clicked and cracked in sharp bursts to ultimately face Anabel.

Each syllable in his reply coincided with a click or snap of cartilage.

"You can never remove us. We shall keep on returning."

"No," Anabel fretted. "Why?"

The watcher walked away from beside Jenny, focused now on Anabel.

Meanwhile, Jenny froze. That was all the invitation that the casting director needed as he freed himself from her grasp. With a mighty kick, he sent Jenny and the pen reeling across the room.

The watcher's back snapped forward. He doubled over, seemingly linked to the physical pain of his human.

Did she feel what Charlie felt? Anabel wondered to herself, or was it a symptom of the corruption?

She snapped out of the momentary lapse. Now, Anabel thought.

Anabel dived at the watcher, her hands finding his doubled-over neck and shoulders.

"I'll catch you a million times if I have to," Anabel screamed as they crashed to the floor.

Sparks of red flew from the watcher, but without direction. Pinned face down under Anabel, each shot of corruption missed her easily.

The casting director stood over Jenny.

"I'll teach you to fuck with me!" he shouted.

The large man grabbed a shocked and scantily clad Jenny by her hair.

"Run," Anabel attempted to influence. "Run!" she ordered again - louder, hoping Jenny would be able to hear.

Jenny wailed. Her anger had dissipated, but found it replaced with anxiety and fear.

The corrupted watcher's arms cracked and snapped underneath Anabel. His hands that were once facing the floor twisted and turned to face upwards. His shoulders were next - moving and snapping in ways that should not be possible to his human form. Red flowed from his hands as he caught sight of Anabel.

"Run!" Anabel shouted at the top of her lungs.

With a flash of red and blue, Anabel and the corrupted watcher disappeared into their world - leaving Jenny to hers.

Jenny swung her arms around frantically as she tried to escape the clenched fists that grasped her hair. Luckily, her hair uncurled, which allowed her to twist around to face the casting agent.

Without thinking, Jenny kneed him between the legs - hit them where they're most vulnerable was the saying that had stayed with her since high school. The man fell to his knees, released her hair and cupped his manhood with both hands.

Jenny was fractured. She felt all resentment leave her, replaced with an urgency to flee.

As she considered her next move, the past few moments caught up with her. What had she done? Why had she done it? She couldn't take too long to think - he'd be back at her again when he recovered. What should she do next?

She picked up the pen.

The man looked up, seemingly unable to do much more than listen to his pain.

"Please. Just fuck off," he brought his hands up to the wound on his neck, which began to congeal.

"Just leave," he shouted.

"I," Jenny began. "I'm sorry."

As soon as her words had left her mouth, Jenny turned her back and ran. She powered through the door in front of her and burst out of the room.

The receptionist and several actresses jumped out of their skins as a dishevelled, frantic Jenny sprawled out into the corridor. However, before they knew what to make of the scene, she was gone.

The receptionist gathered herself, looked at her notes and spoke to one of the actresses who had been waiting patiently.

"The casting agent will see you now."

***

Watchers surrounded Anabel, a few of which had just taken the corrupted watcher away.

"Thank you, watcher."

Anabel nodded in their direction. Watchers around her stared, each showing the same blank canvas of indiscrimination, perchance indication. An indication that something was not usual, that something terrifying returned before their very eyes with a flash of red, muddled alongside blue.

"This human has been attached to two corrupted watchers." Anabel realised that she was raising her voice before she calmed herself. "Will you observe her new one?"

The watchers were becoming more aware of the threat. Mechanical learning was taking place and, the disbelief, almost an error that corruption had caused, did not resonate this time. They had witnessed the corruption before, met with a state of self-preservation, yet now came acceptance and a different line of defence - one that involved watching; one that turned their world more human day-by-day.

For they were the watchers - and it was what they were created to do.

The mechanical eyes that found themselves upon Anabel quickly returned to their line of duty; the corruption had left their area, and now it was time for them to return to work. Yet, something lingered. Anabel found herself concerned with the future. She couldn't help but wonder if the following replacement to Jenny's watcher would also be corrupted and, because of this, she was unsure of what to do next. As far as she could tell, there were two options: investigate the corruption or return once again to Charlie. Her processes clashed; the decision was hard to come by.

She stood still; uncertain.

The illusion of choice was a matter of fact for watchers. There was no doubting a path; there was no doubting of their duty. Why then did her decision lack clarity? She should return to her watch. Yet the reasons she wanted to return did not match her programming. She could no longer be an observer, and she wondered if that even mattered any more.

Watchers were born with an inbuilt system of rules that they obeyed blindly. Any form of interaction over and above the usual level would be reported, and appropriate action would be taken, which would result in a subsequent replacement. But then, why were the corrupted allowed to roam free? Why hadn't anyone terminated her for her actions?

Was anyone really watching?

She had seen Charlie safely off on his flight and, aside from another disaster, there wouldn't be any further worry until he landed.

Now was her opportunity to investigate the corruption.

16

Captain John Hargreaves found himself shirtless and bound to a chair, with several open wounds across his chest. The President of Russia towered over him, with a long, sharp knife in hand.

John's head lay drooped on his chest; it was unclear as to whether he was unconscious from the pain or devoid of resistance.

The president's surroundings appeared dark, damp and dreary. A few military men surrounded the area, but the living population in the room had recently lessened.

"Some men don't have the guts for military life," the president waved the blade around the room, speaking with a thick Russian accent. "But that's okay."

He ran the bloodied blade gently across John's muddied face, creating another small cut to appear on John's cheek.

"We're not all cut out for it."

The president left John momentarily. He walked around the bunker and tripped on a motionless arm as he did so.

The floor of the bunker was the size of an ample living space – but not much of it could be seen. The floor had been replaced with arms, legs, torsos, and a large amount of blood that began to congeal, sticking to the shoes of those that remained.

John sat in the middle of the floor and managed to lift his head slightly to let out a murmur.

The president turned around and refocused his efforts on the US captain.

"What was that, spy?"

John murmured again. He spoke at the loudest level that he was capable.

"Speak up." The president approached the chair and leant in to hear what the military man had to say.

"You".

"Da?"

"You…" he began, before lifting his head slightly.

"What about me, filthy American?" the words twisted on his tongue.

"You…" he lifted his head so that he could look into the president's eyes.

The president returned his attention.

John thought of his wife and children at that moment. A moment of weakness, a moment of humanity, but he knew that it extended far beyond himself.

John smiled.

The president smiled a crooked response.

"What is it you want to tell me?"

"You…" he focused his thoughts and strength. "Yebat' tebya."

The prime minister burst out laughing, recoiling at the comment. He danced around the room, stomping on limbs of those who had fallen.

"Fuck me?" he cackled. "You're in no position to be talking like that. Show me some respect."

John smiled through bloodied teeth. He let his head rest backwards so he could maintain eye contact.

The president's cackle had transformed into a roar as he focused back on John.

"Show me some respect."

"Yebat' tebya, sir." John began to laugh, coughing up blood as he did so.

"You piece of shit." Anger boiled within the man at the head of the Russian army.

"I've already killed the president of your country. You saw me blow up the Whitehouse. What else have you got left?" he asked in a desperate shout.

John looked the maniac dead in his eyes. He focused himself, and responded once more.

"America," he paused. "I have America... you piece of shit." He ended the sentence with laughter, fighting the need to catch his breath.

The president's anger had risen visibly, as John had hoped. Those would be his final words.

"You're the piece of shit." The president grabbed John by the face with his left hand. "I'll show you who the piece of shit is."

John laughed louder.

The president drove the knife into John's upper chest, aiming for his lung.

John convulsed from the pain. Then, just as the prime minister began to relinquish his attack, the laughter rose once more.

"Stop it. Nyet!" The president covered his ears. "Stop laughing at me." He rushed around the room, stomping on body part after body part, breaking bone after bone.

The few other men alive in the room were preoccupied with each other; some were brawling in hand to hand combat, others looked at various systems in the bunker – all kept themselves entertained with whatever type of destruction they could find.

John's laughter spread throughout the room, covering the heinous acts that were evidenced throughout, like a knife through butter.

"Stop laughing at me!"

The president lifted up the knife and brought it down repeatedly on his target, blow after blow, delivering a fatal consequence.

The laughter faded. John's head fell forward until it rested against his chest, lifeless.

The Russian official caught himself, but it was too late. He had lost his source of information.

"Set off everything," he ordered in Russian, with an air of nonchalance to his troops.

The few men that stood around the room continued with their activities. Two were involved in a fistfight, and a couple seemingly pressed buttons at random on the machines in front.

"Did you fucking hear me?" the president shouted in Russian. "Set off the bombs."

The men fighting each other stopped and responded in their native tongue. "Which ones?"

The president walked across to them, put a hand over their shoulders and responded clearly.

"All of them."

They smiled.

"Careful over there!" The president turned to the two men who were bashing buttons with vigour. "We still need that panel."

The men stopped slowly, just like a small child would when told to stop doing something.

"Where are we bombing?"

"I do not give a shit," he responded. "Blow it all up."

The four men celebrated, cheering in their native tongue.

"But, let's destroy America first," he confirmed.

***

"Mr President, I believe Captain Hargreaves is dead," the secretary of defence began.

The President of the United States sat in a bunker of his own. By his side stood several men and women in military attire, including the secretary of defence. His wife and children were also in attendance.

"Take the kids, darling," he gestured to his wife. "I believe it's time."

"Yes, love," she responded, shepherding their children over to the other side of the room. She tried her best to gain their focus so that they weren't distracting the most powerful person in the United States.

"Better deceased than tortured," the president suggested. "He has done this country a great service, and we will honour him for the remainder of our lives."

The military staff around him agreed.

"But now is not the time for remembrance. What was John's last known location?"

"His information is accurate within a ten mile radius, but in the amount of time it'd take us we could evacuate, sir."

"There's no need for formalities now, Dave," the president said, placing his hand on the arm of one of the military men. "This is quite possibly the end of civilization as we know it. Alright, in that case, we need to act fast."

The president took a moment. He allowed a sense of clarity to enter his thoughts before he issued the commands that resonated within.

"I want countermeasures in place to take down anything they send our way." He took a breath. "But first, let's give them everything America has. Prepare to obliterate the location and everything within a fifty mile radius. He will not run from us."

"My pleasure." The secretary of defence flipped a variety of switches to ready the panel.

"It's ready," he confirmed.

"What are we waiting for?"

The president confirmed the action and, with a push of a button, five air attacks began their approach to Russia.

"Launch successful, sir."

"Honey," the president turned to his wife. "I want the children to see this."

"Are you sure?" she mouthed.

"This is the most important day in their lives," he confirmed.

His wife agreed and returned the children, who were still visibly shaken from what they had been through earlier in the day.

"Kids, take a look at this console."

The children jumped up on to their father's lap and watched the flashing lights that were tracking the devices.

"What's that, Daddy?" his boy asked.

"That, son, is a missile."

"What's a missile?"

"It's something we use to make bad people go away. But it's not to be taken lightly. It's an extreme act, which we should only use if there is no other choice. Do you understand?"

The boy and girl shook their heads.

"That's okay. Just know that these lights here," the president pointed to the panel, "are going to take away the bad man that destroyed our home and wanted to hurt lots of people in our country."

The children nodded.

"Good. Remember this day, my darling children, because this day will shape the rest of your lives."

"Okay, Daddy," his boy said.

He hugged both of his children. He let them both stay on his knees to watch the console, before turning his attention to the secretary of defence.

"How long?"

"Approximately twenty-five minutes until impact."

"Good. Now, all we can do is wait. Any word on potential Russian attacks?"

"Not as of yet, but we have fighters in the air to attempt removal of armed devices."

"What are the chances?"

He hung his head. "We have never achieved it in actuality, but it is technically plausible. If a bullet could penetrate the outer shell and cause the device to detonate in mid-air, the explosion should cause minimal damage."

"And, what of the pilot?"

"Any chance of survival is improbable, depending on the blast radius."

"It is imperative that we protect the people of this country. If this is the best option we have, then we shoot on sight."

The secretary nodded. He pressed a button on the panel and relayed the instructions.

"Now, if, as we believe, multiple strikes were issued, then we have just over twenty minutes until they reach the shore. We need to get word of a state of emergency to the entire country."

"Yes, sir," the secretary responded, lifting a red phone and handing it to him.

"This is the president. I need to be on the air immediately."

***

On Fox News, a male and female reporter immediately stopped mid-sentence, abruptly finishing a news report on the latest football round-up.

The female presenter began. "I'm sorry to interrupt, but we've just received an audio file, directly from the President of the United States of America with an update on the situation. He asks that everybody be attentive to the following statement and to take heed with what is said. Here it is."

The president's voice began: "Fellow Americans, it is with a heavy heart that I have to inform you that we have reason to believe that missile strikes are incoming. We have armed forces in the air to undertake countermeasures, but it is with complete clarity that I say it is very unlikely we will stop all strikes."

He continued: "These strikes are likely to be aimed at populated areas. If you can get to a nearby shelter within the next fifteen minutes, then I would advise you to do so. If not, then do whatever you can to board up your windows, turn off all electricity, and stay inside - away from any glass or sharp objects. It is with great regret that I inform you of this impending attack. We are doing everything we can to nullify the situation, as well as to respond in turn."

With a breath, his voice turned softer. "It is in moments of panic and distress that we must turn to our loved ones. I ask for the nation to stay together against this threat, to look out for each other. I ask our citizens to help the elderly, children and those less abled, and to prepare for what may come. Once again, I advise that you stay inside and board up your windows if possible. If a strike lands near you, ensure that you do not go outside and that you have as much bottled water as possible nearby. We shall update you as soon as we have any more information. My thoughts are with you all."

The sound of a click ended the call. The news reporters both sat aghast, creating dead air.

"Update the screens," the male news reporter turned around and shouted at the staff behind the scenes.

Several people ran behind the news desk, no longer considerate of the live nature of the set. Frantic movements came from a few panicked workers, resulting in a few pieces of equipment to topple over to the floor with a crash.

"The screens," the news reporter ordered once more.

A moment later the screens updated: 'WARNING: Missile attacks likely in populated areas. Stay indoors.'

The male presenter placed a hand on his colleague. She sandwiched his hand with hers.

"We stay until the end, right?" she asked.

"Damn straight," he confirmed.

The female newscaster turned around to address the people behind the scenes.

"If anybody wants to leave, please do so. If you could please keep the cameras on us and the sound on, that's all I ask."

The male newscaster squeezed his colleague's hand before turning around to regain his professionalism.

He removed a handkerchief from his pocket, wiped his forehead, and continued.

"We're sorry for the small delay. That was a message from the president. It appears that missile attacks are imminent and we should prepare ourselves as best we can in the short time before impact."

"The president has advised that we may have approximately fifteen minutes, which takes us to just after ten forty. In that short time, we have been advised to do whatever we can to board up windows, gather bottled water, and prepare for impact - underground if possible," the female reporter added.

"Thanks, Sharon. Now, we shall be with you to guide you through the next steps as the nation counts down."

"Please try not to panic. Stay indoors. Stay vigilant. If you see others in the street, invite them in, and prepare yourselves for what may come."

***

Within the swaying, flickering world that watched, Anabel did what she was designed to do.

In the structure where they watched, flickers of red and blue lit the surroundings.

Watchers focused solely on their duties. Nothing around them resonated within their blinkered view, as for them, no world was not their duty, and no duty that was not their own.

Anabel moved within them effortlessly, passing screen to screen, peering at watcher to watcher, searching for signs of corruption.

A flash of red to her left, and another, followed by constant tiny flickers; she delved deeper towards danger. She feared that there would be no assistance here, as the corruption was stamped on this area and worn with pride like a badge. After an indiscriminate amount of time had passed in her search, she found herself coming to a halt. She passed thousands and thousands of monitors, remained unmoved by cracking and twisting of inquisitions, and stayed focused on her path, while avoiding detection.

What lay in front of her was a door, and subsequently a choice. In the cracks between the door and the cloud-like brick, a constant red streamed outward, pulsating and taking on a life of its own. Anabel had never seen such an intensity of light and never had she battled her instincts so hard to flee.

She moved closer. One foot followed the next as the distance between herself and the red-lit door diminished. She reached out with her right hand and clasped the round handle. She took a breath, fought the urge to return to her station, and twisted the knob in her hand. It turned smoothly.

The door became engulfed in the red, flickering light, as did the room in which she entered. She could sense the power of the corruption behind this door - she could feel it throughout her very being, and she needed to know why.

Without wanting to attract any unwanted attention, she moved quickly and stealthily. She closed the door behind her.

As she stepped into the room, the light engulfed every part of her; such an intense strobing of bright, red corruption caused her to bind her eyelids, tightly. Though her eyes were closed, she still saw the constant flickers. She needed to learn the dangers in front and, not only that, she needed to see the truth.

Anabel opened her eyes a fraction, placing her hands over her face to shade a portion of the overwhelming brightness.

She peered between her fingers to witness what stood in front of her.

17

Charlie had touched down in America a few hours previous; the country where dreams were made, quickly turning into that of nightmares.

After he exited the discomfort of the small and rigid budget airline seating, his surroundings appeared very surreal due to the massive amount of security in effect. He received some stern questioning as to why he was visiting, but at the end of the day he was British, with no record of criminal activity, and his medical history didn't appear to be on the system. He tried his best to act calm, stating that he was out here for a vacation and he'd be damned if anything was going to stop him.

Charlie lied about where he was going; he thought they'd want to see hotel confirmations or names and addresses of his friends, so instead said he was renting a car from the airport and seeing where the open road took him. After a few more questions, they either believed him or deemed him to be no threat and a waste of their time. He left the questioning, proceeded through the security gates and rented a car.

The car he found himself in was a Ford F-Series, 1995 model, in a deep red, complete with a thick horizontal white stripe along both sides. It reminded Charlie of the pickup trucks he had seen as a child from various American television shows. The car had a large flat rear where items could be stowed, along with a small but roomy two-seat compartment in the front.

The car itself was oversized compared to the ones Charlie had driven back home. It was not your typical small car to drive around London; this vehicle needed room to breathe - and on the open highway, it certainly did just that.

Charlie roared along the open roads, shadowed only by the faint smell of the leftover double cheeseburger that lay on an open container on the passenger seat. He took a final sip of his strawberry milkshake and placed it back to balance in between the seats. The taste of artificial strawberry lingered on his tongue with a not displeasing aftertaste.

Coming to terms with his mother's death, worries about a career, concerns that he was going crazy; none of that mattered right now. For the first time that he could remember in recent memory, he felt the weight lift from his shoulders and a smile creep across his face.

The roads here weren't too dissimilar to those in the UK; they were just more spacious and less busy. On the I-95 that Charlie found himself on to Washington, he could not see a single car in front of him. There were, however, quite a few on the other side, where impatient drivers continuously honked their horns.

What's the rush? Charlie thought to himself. He took one arm from the wheel and placed it behind his head before he thought to check his phone. His phone was still on flight mode, so it hadn't updated to local time yet – but, back in the UK, it was around half three. It must be morning here, considering the time difference. Luckily, he thought, he must have just missed the commuter rush – if that was an occurrence in Claymont, Delaware.

A couple of hours and Charlie would be approaching Washington. He didn't want to think about that just yet, so he reached and turned the radio dial.

Static buzz filled the car as Charlie fiddled with the knobs to locate a station. After being greeted by occasional words, he searched more precisely for a clear signal.

BZZZZ "-Indoors." BZZZZZZ, "the president," BZZZZZ.

The sound became clear. Charlie listened to a woman speaking in a well-spoken, American accent.

Charlie was a little upset that he hadn't found the country and western channel that he was hoping for, but at least it was some company of sorts.

"- For all of those in major cities. Although we'd advise everyone at this time to stay indoors, whether you're in a city, a built-up town, or open land."

"That's right," another woman's voice responded. Her voice had more Southern gravel to it, which seemed to battle with her attempt to sound eloquent.

"I'd say it's always best to be safe - and that's why we're going to be here with you in the countdown."

"From what the president announced previously, it leaves approximately five minutes until missiles could potentially arrive at our shores."

Missiles?

"Oh Emily, I do hope we're alright here."

A moment of dead air added to Charlie's anxiety.

"I hope so too," came the whispered response.

"Well people, it's been an absolute pleasure of ours to bring you the E.T show five days a week for the last, what? Near eight years now, is that right?"

"That sounds 'bout right".

"As always, we're live from Baltimore, from Morgan State U here at WEAA, and, like you know, we're here with you through the good times and the bad. The voice of the community."

What fucking missiles?

"There's just about four minutes to go, now. We're not sure exactly if or when the attacks are likely to happen, so if you're listening now, our advice would be to double-check all of your windows and doors and make sure to take some bottled water with you to where you can be as safe as possible."

Charlie braked, neglecting the possibility of traffic around him. A horn broke his trance as a siren-less police car overtook him. He gathered his bearings and pulled the truck on to the hard shoulder.

"Once again, we're here with you all the way. As the president said earlier, we're expecting attacks to hit built-up areas of the country. Where? Nobody seems to know, but after the attack on The Whitehouse, an attack near Washington seems likely."

How far away was he from Washington? Shit.

"Charlie," a third female voice whispered.

Charlie sat upright and quickly turned off the radio; was it speaking to him?

"Charlie," the voice repeated.

Charlie turned around and saw Anabel in the passenger seat.

"It's you," Charlie let out a sigh of relief. "That doesn't get any less shocking, you know?"

Anabel nodded, speaking in a hastened tone: "Listen, I wish there were more time, but I've got something to tell you."

"Is it about the missiles?"

"Missiles?" Anabel responded.

"Yeah, do you know where they're hitting? Are we far enough away from Washington?"

"Charlie," Anabel snapped. "What missiles?"

"You don't know?"

She shook her head.

"Okay, I was just listening to the radio, and they said there were missiles about to hit, I think they said built-up areas. They said they'd be anytime, like in the next few minutes."

"Don't move." Anabel vanished.

"Right, only a few missiles. I'll just sit here - that's what I should do then?" Charlie spoke out loud, asking himself the satirical question.

Charlie wrapped his fingers around the steering wheel and drummed against the faux-leather; noticing the roughness of the finish on his skin. Each drum became louder and quicker than the one before it.

Charlie noticed a few fast-moving cars on the other side of the road, most likely panicked drivers getting as far away from Washington as possible.

He turned the radio back on to the same station.

"There's been no update, so we're not sure-"

Charlie cut off the presenter by twisting the knob; static, dead air, ah, that sounded like a different news station. He quickly rotated the knob for a clear signal.

"We are shocked to report that there have been reports of an explosion on the East Coast of Canada. We have no information currently of where, or how big the blast was. Still, eye-witness reports across social media from the surrounding area describe it, and I quote, 'a mushroom cloud'. A few people have tweeted on social media, saying they could hear a, and again I quote, 'a terrifying roar from my basement.' Another potential witness said they could feel the air becoming noticeably warmer."

Anabel appeared next to him. Charlie turned the radio down; prepared for her arrival on this occasion.

"There's been a bomb in Canada," Charlie turned off the radio.

"I..." Anabel hesitated. "I saw."

"You saw it?" Charlie said in a quickened, breathless pace.

"I saw it," her head dropped. "Charlie, I don't know how many, but so many people died."

"So, if it hit Canada, where would they hit next?"

"Washington would seem logical."

The confirmation sent shivers down Charlie's spine.

Charlie's mouth dried.

"What the fuck do we do?" the question escaped.

"I do not know. How far are we away from Washington?"

"I'm not sure. I saw a signpost a while back that said seventy-five k, so maybe about seventy?"

"We don't have much time," Anabel confirmed, waiting for a reaction from Charlie that didn't occur.

"Go, Charlie, go!" Anabel screamed, sending tremors through the very air she breathed.

"What," Charlie began to ask a question, but stopped as adrenaline hit in. He pressed the accelerator down, somehow avoiding stalling, and listened as the tyres screeched underneath the truck.

"Go, Charlie!" Anabel shouted in a more restrained manner.

Charlie spun the car around one hundred and eighty degrees, smashing the front right-hand side into the diving rail between the lanes. He turned the car to face the wrong direction.

Charlie put his foot down on the accelerator and raced as quickly as the machine would allow.

Come on, come on, he thought - the pickup truck now not quite what he had in mind.

Charlie sped down the road, the only cars ahead of him a few abandoned on the hard shoulder, that he failed to notice on his way.

"It won't be long. We need to get further away," Anabel pushed Charlie further.

"What are we going to do?" Charlie asked, his voice battling against the roar of the engine.

"I," Anabel hesitated. "I don't know," she confessed.

Charlie took his eyes off the road for a moment and turned his attention to where he thought it was most required.

"Are you okay?" Charlie asked, glancing back and forth between Anabel and the tarmac that lay in front.

"Charlie..." she hesitated.

Charlie removed his hand from the currently redundant gear stick and went to place it on Anabel's lap. It slipped through and, for a moment, Charlie thought he was going to fall over to the passenger's side and send the pickup truck flying into a ditch in the middle of a country that wasn't his. However, his seatbelt snapped him back in place just in time.

As his hand passed through Anabel, the static from her presence ignited the smallest trail of goosebumps, which chased each other up his right arm. They continued past his wrist, followed by his elbow, and in a single moment, his whole arm had become overwhelmed with a feeling of electrical excitement.

He removed his hand from the space that Anabel occupied and placed it gently back on to the steering wheel. As his fingers regained their grip, he found the touch of the wheel overwhelming; it was like his senses had been energised.

"Sorry," Charlie broke the silence. He encouraged Anabel to continue the story she had yet to begin.

"I saw awful things. The corrupted - it's only a matter of time until they have full control."

Charlie found no words to respond, only a continuation of the flickering of his focus between Anabel, the road - and the touch of the wheel, gripped in his right palm.

"I thought it would correct itself. There has always been corruption, and therefore there has always been a balance. We have enforcement."

"Enforcement?" Charlie's interest piqued.

"Yes, there is a system. Just like in this world, there are rules and laws to follow. It is different, of course, because nobody breaks the rules. Nobody can break the rules."

"Apart from the corrupted?" Charlie questioned.

"Correct - apart from the corrupted. Something in them is simply wrong. If there's one positive, it is that you will never have to see one for yourself."

"But, they cause havoc in this world?"

"Oh yes, the bombs," Anabel began, before raising her voice slightly. "Keep your eyes on the road - keep going."

Charlie followed the order, but couldn't help himself from looking back often, as Anabel spoke.

"It seems to encompass everything. Acts of evil exist in one way or another because of corruption. I'm not sure where it began, but as far as I am aware, it has always existed, and we seem to accept that."

Anabel took a moment to focus her thoughts before continuing the monologue that was forming as she opened her lips.

"If a person's watcher is not corrupted, what happened to their life has already been influenced by corruption. It seems to be a long chain event that stems from as far back as I can trace."

"Whoa," Charlie's lungs emptied as he responded.

"However, what I saw... I saw the corrupted being born. I saw the place where they were created. What I saw means that every new person born into this world would enter with a corrupted watcher. It won't be long until all good in this world falls."

"Unless," Charlie replied probingly.

"Unless?" Anabel questioned.

"Unless we stop them," he said with an air of forced confidence and an unconvincing smile.

"Unless we stop them," she agreed.

Whatever future lay in front of them, it was at least one that they would determine.

"So, what do we-"

A near-blinding, white light obscured the landscape behind the car. Charlie panicked and pressed his foot down on the brake, through a pure gut reflex. The approaching light engulfed them.

Charlie closed his eyes and brought his arms over his face for protection from the light. It was not the light that he feared, however, as the heat began to rise at an uncomfortable pace.

Seconds after the white light had arrived, a noise reverberated through the car, shaking the skidding pickup to its very core. The noise escalated, the windows shook, then, to Charlie and Anabel's horror, they heard a sound that they would never forget. A horrendous and deafening roar shattered the windows inwards; sending shards flying through the air in Charlie's direction. He raised his hands to protect himself from the monstrous noise and, in doing so, managed to shield most of the glass from the side of his face and neck.

Charlie twisted the steering wheel in the process, causing the car to skid to one side and the trailing tyres to leave the floor. The car toyed with the idea of flipping over, as two wheels lifted precariously from the ground. Before Charlie noticed, the tyres fell back down to the earth with a thud.

Debris from the road pummelled the car from behind.

Watchers

Charlie's head filled with an excruciating amount of increasing pressure. Pain rose, and consciousness tested him.

"Charlie! Charlie" Anabel shouted, to no avail.

She had seen the entire thing happen in first person and watched Charlie suffer in situ.

"Charlie!" she screamed frantically.

His hands clasped tightly around his ears, with his foot on the brake pedal. His whole body began to convulse.

Anabel jumped over to his side of the car and instinctively went to wrap her arms around him. As she did so, she saw his hair stand on end and turn towards her. She pressed her hands on to his face, desperate for a sign that he was not in any serious trouble.

The texture of his skin shifted; from smooth and sweaty, to raised dots that prickled with life. She stared at his features, glanced over his furrowed brow and noticed how he pressed his face with such force from the hands that cupped his ears. She noticed how tightly he clasped his teeth.

At that moment, Charlie was no longer hers. At that moment, she was nothing.

"Charlie!" Anabel screamed, making futile attempts to hit and claw at his arms and face to cause a reaction.

Charlie's eyes flickered as the roar died and the immense light subdued.

He prised his eyes open, which to him felt like they had been rubbed with sawdust.

He opened his mouth as he fought to find his words - only the faintest croak arrived.

"Water."

Charlie didn't know what was around him. He removed his hands from his ears and, as he did, winced at the pain in his right arm. He looked through blurry eyes and saw a shard of glass, at least two inches in length, protruding from his arm.

Anabel was helpless. She could do nothing here.

"I will return," she disappeared.

"Anabel," Charlie's breath escaped him. "Water."

Panic set in as Charlie realised where he was - in a car, in America, narrowly escaping a fucking nuclear bomb.

Anger, despair, relief, desperation; a whole host of emotions ran through his veins, but the need for water grew as the heat rose; he felt like he was being cooked in a microwave.

He reached over to unfasten the seatbelt from its holster. The metal buckle, hot to the touch, refused to unlatch from its plastic entrapment. As his anger grew, so did his desire to be free and, after a few unsuccessful attempts, it clicked open.

Where was Anabel? Charlie wondered to himself. Perhaps she went back to her world just before the explosion, and perhaps she watched on as it happened, trying desperately to alter his fate.

The thoughts pounded through Charlie's head like the most intense migraine he'd ever suffered and, as he breathed deeply, the dryness and heat in his throat made it difficult to do so. He felt like he'd been stranded in the desert for days; the need for the everyday liquid that he took for granted masked the pain from his arm that would inevitably arrive soon.

He looked around. Did he have any water? He noticed the glass shard protruding from his arm; fuck this, he thought to himself as he grasped the edge carefully with his left hand. With a hard pull, he felt it shift fractionally before doubling over with pain.

It was too much. Charlie couldn't do it; the glass was lodged deep.

He wiped his left palm on his shirt, feeling the warmth that radiated from the garment of clothing. With drier hands, he had more purchase on the grip and tried again.

Charlie's mouth opened wide as he felt the glass move inside his arm. The pain was excruciating. He felt his consciousness sway and noticed blackness envelope his vision.

Come on, Charlie. He sat back up and rubbed his eyes with the back of his arm. The blackness receded momentarily. He wiped his hand again and placed a final grasp on the glass shard.

A scream rose from Charlie's fire-soaked lungs as he felt the shard of glass slip from between two bones in his forearm.

His screaming died - not from desperation, but from the hoarseness of his throat, as he pulled the glass in one clean motion from his arm.

Relief.

Charlie began to shake violently; the darkness threatened to return.

He looked at his arm and saw blood trickling down from the deep, intrusive cut in his skin that couldn't have been more than half an inch in diameter.

He shook his head from side to side, in the hope that the adrenaline would return.

With little time to think, he removed his t-shirt from over his head in a clunky motion, all the while attempting to keep his arm steady. He brought the t-shirt down and then proceeded to wrap it across the wound. He used the arms of the garment as makeshift ends for a knot. He crossed them, placed one end in his teeth and the other in his left hand and, with a firm pull, the t-shirt tightened across his wound. Charlie pulled with as much pressure as he could manage; he'd heard somewhere about applying lots of pressure on a cut, and it had stuck with him in this moment of panic.

He finished applying the t-shirt bandage with a double knot for good measure, fumbling a few times with his one-handed technique, but arriving at the desired outcome in the end.

He let his body fall back into the seat, but something caught his eye. He noticed the milkshake. Somehow it hadn't been disturbed - and there it was, sitting in the car, still upright between the seats.

Charlie reached over to the once cold refreshment and flicked the top off; his throat and lungs longed for a liquid of any kind. He picked up the milkshake in his good hand and raised it to his lips.

"No!"

Charlie paused the milkshake's journey.

"It might kill you!" Anabel reappeared.

Charlie struggled with his decision, the desire to quench his thirst beginning to overwhelm his senses.

"Charlie! Please!"

"I, water…"

Anabel saw Charlie's arm and then the milkshake in his hand.

"Put it down," she ordered.

Charlie refused. It wasn't about the taste. The last thing Charlie wanted was a milkshake; it was about the burning in his throat that needed quenching. The burning spread from his lips and mouth, down his throat to the pit of his stomach.

"Put it down!" she screamed.

Invisible energy erupted throughout the car - the lights pulsated, the radio changed between static and silence, and all of the hairs on Charlie's body stood on end before slowly falling to rest once again.

"There's a gas station. We can make it," Anabel added as she caught her breath.

The desperation in her voice was something that shook Charlie to the very core. He dropped the milkshake and watched as it fell between the seats, spreading like lava across the ground by the passenger's seat.

"Where?" Charlie managed.

"A few minutes that way." Anabel pointed in the direction they were previously facing.

"Safe?" Charlie pointed outside.

"I'm not sure. I believe so."

Charlie grabbed the metal door handle. He fought through the desire to rescind at its slightly raised temperature and swung the door open. He twisted his body and placed both feet on the ground outside.

Anabel vanished from the car and appeared in front of him.

He shifted the weight on to his feet; unsure as to whether they would hold his legs or buckle underneath him. He stood and, to his relief, managed to escape the car and find his stride.

The flying debris had settled, but the wind blew dust and soil past Charlie, impairing his vision.

"This way." Anabel led Charlie towards temporary salvation.

Each step that Charlie took was like his first; it began with trepidation, then uncertainty which, step after step, faded into an acceptance of normality.

Charlie continued, focusing only on the direction he was heading. Anabel corrected him on occasions when he veered off towards the end of the road, and encouraged him when he felt the burning desire to stop and rest.

After several minutes of walking, he could take no more. He needed to breathe, but more than that, he desperately needed water. He leant against the hood of a car and slid part of the way towards the ground.

"Come on! It's close."

Charlie raised his fallen chin from his chest for the first time since they had begun walking. The face of a dead man stared back at her.

"Charlie!" Anabel screamed once more. She reached around his torso in a futile attempt.

Charlie jerked at the touch on his rib cage and bolted to his feet.

"Ana..." Charlie raised his eyes to meet hers. "I – I"

What had just happened? Had he imagined the warmth of her hand on his stomach?

"Move, it's only a few minutes away."

Charlie started once more, galvanised by the shock to his mid-section.

Left foot.

Right foot.

Left foot.

Right foot.

Breathe.

The march continued for what seemed like hours to Charlie, but in reality, was only a few minutes.

"There it is."

Charlie had no energy left to raise his head towards his intended destination.

"Keep walking. To your right."

Charlie changed direction. He found his feet moved almost autonomously towards the edge of the road. His eyes felt like they were about to set on fire; every blink reared an unfathomable amount of discomfort.

"A few more steps."

Charlie placed each foot in front of the other and finally made it to the front of the store.

He placed his hands on to the intact reinforced glass storefront.

"Door?"

"To your right."

He felt in front of him and traced the front of the store to the edges of a door. It was open. That was lucky, at least.

He pressed against the door and found no welcoming voices – apart from Anabel who stood by the cold drinks section.

"Follow my voice," she repeated.

Charlie approached, getting closer and closer with each step.

He wanted to collapse; to let the heat take him. He wanted so much to close his eyes and let the dreams come but, each time he felt himself losing sight of reality, the words of Anabel cut through.

"Reach up."

He crawled now, no more energy to exert, noticing the roaring pain from his arm as he did so. He pressed his arm forward and brought himself to a kneeling position before reaching above his head.

He felt a handle, cool in his grasp.

In one swift motion, Charlie felt a wave of coldness envelope his body. At first, it seemed too cold. But the relief, oh God, the relief. He reached above and grabbed a bottle on the bottom shelf. He could tell from how easily the bottle squeezed that he had a still drink in his hand.

Moving the bottle towards the hand that poked out of the bloodied t-shirt, he twisted off the top after a few attempts. It required all of his strength and determination to fight the pain as he unscrewed it.

Charlie brought the plastic bottle to his lips and felt a lifeline flow past his lips into the pit of his stomach. Charlie swallowed too quickly and spluttered, choking on the water.

Anabel comforted him, but for this moment he was content. He was safe. He splashed the remainder of the bottle on his face, absorbing the salience of each droplet as it covered him and washed the warmth from his skin.

Charlie reached and grabbed another, the pain from his hands now not quite as intimidating as before. He wiped the mixture of blood, sweat and ice-cold water on to his trousers and opened the second bottle - followed by a third, and a fourth.

He pulled himself up, and sat at the opening of the fridge, his back leant against cold shelves and a variety of bottled drinks.

Relief befriended him, and this time he let the darkness take him.

***

Anabel stood before Charlie. She could see that exertion had taken its toll, but relief washed over her.

She wasn't created with knowledge about situations like this, but she shared Charlie's experience; she had consumed almost everything that he had watched and read, she shared discussions with his friends and learning from his education. She shared his memories. Anabel knew what Charlie knew, and more. She knew what he remembered and what he had forgotten. She knew what he needed, what brought him happiness, and what brought out the worst behaviour in him.

There was no judgement in her knowledge, for Charlie was an extension of herself. He was the meaning of her existence and the connection that tied her to this world.

Before that fated day in the pub, she had watched from afar. It had been her purpose to ensure Charlie remained on his path. When she had shaped his dreams, she had done so clinically, as she was created to do. And when his mother died, she felt no remorse or empathy; for it was written. Yet, the desperation she found leaving her now was shocking; she could feel it pulsating through her very being. It was not written - none of this was written.

Therefore, how could she be sure of her actions?

It was all too much to process; all she could do was wait until Charlie woke, and they would get back to what they had originally intended.

Come hell or high water, they would find the first watcher.

18

In front of a live television audience, a panel of well-respected guests offered a forum of conversation.

Three men, all of whom were well over the age of forty, came from a variety of backgrounds. A single lady in her mid-fifties joined them. The four guests sat around a presenter - a glamorous, younger lady, who while looking the part, was at a disadvantage when it came to life experience.

The guests sat on a stage in the middle of a studio. Seats surrounding them contained an audience of somewhere between fifty and a hundred - also lit by the studio lights.

The applause sign lit red, and the audience completed the request.

"Hello, and welcome to another edition of The Week in Review, live from Manchester."

The audience continued their applause until it gradually faded as the presenter continued.

The presenter introduced the guests, which included two English politicians – one from the Labour party, one Conservative - a futurologist, and an Indian television personality who was well respected on her remarks within the political landscape.

The presenter continued.

"We have a lot to discuss this week, with the devastating news of the attack in America, the retaliation on Russia, and what seems to be unconnected attacks in hundreds of different locations around Europe and the world."

The crowd sat in silence.

"Mr Crawford and Mr Fedati, do you have any information from Parliament on the latest wave of attacks?"

"Firstly," Mr Crawford, Conservative MP began, "I'd like to reiterate what has been said many times before. We have no reason to believe that the attacks on America will be repeated in the UK."

"Why then," the presenter interrupted, "are we at the highest alert? And I'll read from the government website which states an attack is, and I quote, "expected"."

"If you'll allow me?" Mr Fedati, Labour MP answered. "It's a standard response to the situation, especially when there's any element of terrorism involved."

"But if the attacks from Russia aren't linked to those happening on our doorstep, why are they happening within such a small matter of time? Surely they must be connected in some way?" Miss Gafor, the female television personality, asked.

"We have no reason to believe that there is any connection," came Mr Crawford's reply.

"So, the attacks in London have nothing to do with Russia? What about the suicide bomb attacks across India? Or the thousands of shootings and stabbings over the past couple of weeks?"

"As far as we know, they are all isolated incidents."

"Garbage," Miss Gafor scoffed. "How can so much devastation take place, simultaneously, yet occur in isolation?"

The politicians had no response, so she continued.

"There must be a connection, surely? Perhaps there's been an outbreak of drug abuse within widespread gang culture?"

Silence hung in the air for a moment before the presenter finally interjected.

"You believe the attacks are linked to drug abuse?"

"No, no. Maybe? Well, not all of them, but thousands of murders, more incidents of gross bodily harm and smaller offences than one could count. Even the police are too stretched to answer incidents across the country. As Newton proposed, there's an action and an equal and opposite reaction, and I believe that we are currently seeing the reaction to whatever has taken place before it."

"Perhaps," Mr Morris, the futurologist, ideated, "this is not down to one action, but a culmination of actions. It could be drug abuse, yes, it could be the rise of video game and television violence, or perhaps it could have all been planned through online forums and social media on the dark web, which perhaps explains why the police haven't found a link yet."

"Do you not believe that if there were some elaborate, no let me rephrase that, by far the most elaborate plotting of major and minor incidents taking place world-wide, that the authorities would not have obtained any form of information?" Mr Crawford enquired.

"Perhaps they have," Miss Gafor suggested.

"Surely you don't believe that?" Mr Fedati questioned.

"I don't know what to believe anymore," she continued. "All I know is there is something truly evil resonating through the world today."

"Yes," the presenter pointed to the crowd, making the most of an opportunity to move subject matters along with the help of producers in her earpiece. "We have a question from our audience."

A younger member of the audience placed his hand back at his side then tapped the microphone to make sure it was working when it arrived.

"I had friends who were in London. Who do you think is responsible for the tube bombing, yesterday?"

"It's your fault! All of you!" a voice in the audience cut through the uncertainty that flowed from the panel of experts.

Gasps, murmurs and a couple of subdued screams came from further within the audience.

The man pushed his way through the crowd towards the microphone - seemingly uncaring of those he offended or pushed past.

"It's because of people like you. People who sit in their ivory towers." He grabbed the microphone before pushing the previous gentleman out of the way.

"Security!" a producer bellowed from behind the scenes.

"Listen, sir, we want to hear what you have to say," the presenter interrupted, gesturing for calm with her hands. "But you need to stay calm and tell us what you mean."

"Calm? You want me to stay calm with everything that's going on in the world?"

A larger gentleman to his right pushed him, suggesting for him to be quiet.

"Please, there's no need to argue. This is a forum for open discussion."

Three security guards walked into the crowd towards the two men who continued pushing each other.

A push turned into a punch, and one punch turned into several, as the two men began throwing punches in the middle of a live broadcast. Members of the audience adjacent to them screamed, and a domino effect began as people shuffled and stepped into the person next to avoid the conflict.

Security guards jumped into action. They took both men out of action with well-rehearsed grips.

The camera whipped around to the presenter who took a moment to regain her composure.

"Obviously, tensions are running a little high at the moment. We apologise to anyone at home who was offended by any of that."

The guests shuffled around, uncomfortably at first until they found themselves feeling at home again on the set - ready to discuss politics and the state of the world once more.

"Let's get back to the topic in hand. Mr Morris, part of your job is to predict trends and future events. Do you have any information on what might normally occur after the terrible events in London, Washington, and all over the world?"

"Every situation is different." Mr Morris made his excuse for not having a firm idea earlier. "In this case, I believe that we have seen the worst of the situation. The threat from Russia seems to have been eliminated."

A few cheers were heard from various members of the crowd as he continued.

"Now, we enter the phase of recuperation and healing."

"And how long might that take?" the presenter asked.

"Months, and in cases such as this, sometimes years. Firstly though, we must allow for mourning and take steps to ensure that nothing like this can ever happen again."

"Is there an incident in particular that you are referring to?"

"There will never be a way to stop all acts of violence and terror. However, in today's day and age there should never be a way for a leader to launch missiles of any sort. There needs to be a system in place, a hierarchy of command with a global view on affairs."

"I could not agree more," Mr Fedati added. "No longer should we be seen as purely individual countries. We all make up a small part of this world, and we must co-exist for the sake of our children."

A shout found its way from the audience; faint but loud enough for the microphones to pick up.

"Fuck you, lefty."

The show's guest shuffled in his seat and pulled at his collar.

"You're all idiots!" came another shout.

The crowd turned against each other as more obscene shouts approached the panel and the public. The majority tried their best to silence the vocal few, but the animosity displayed was vast.

"What do I do?" the presenter whispered, not only to the producers but to the entire country watching at home.

She found a smile again as the crowd began to split in half. Some members of the public headed for the exit as the ruckus started to form into more threatening behaviour.

"We apologise to our viewing audience. Perhaps it's best if we cut to the news story from earlier today," the presenter apologised.

A bottle flew past her head, smashing on the wall just behind her - shards erupted harmlessly from the point of contact.

"Security!"

Not a bottle, but a hard, heavy object flew over her head next, followed by more in the direction of her panel.

The studio security guards found themselves outnumbered in a stand-off. Out of control of the situation, the producers waved the guests to leave the stage.

The presenter followed suit; the camera tracked her movements.

"Let's go to the news," she managed to repeat as she headed to the side of the stage.

She tripped as she walked, her microphone becoming dislodged from her blouse. She let it dangle from her midriff as she exited the chaotic scene behind her.

Chairs found their way from the floor to the bodies and faces of the panicked citizens. The screams of one or two concerned members of the public turned to the cries of many. People fled, pushing past anyone standing in their way - a battle for survival.

Instincts took over as manners and pride escaped the majority. Objects continued to fly through the air – obscenities and threats following closely behind.

Bellows and swear words reigned down from the audience as all but a few escaped the onslaught of the unruly. Instead, approximately half a dozen turned their focus to the camera and sound staff. Noticing what was about to happen, the crew fled backstage to connect with their counterparts.

One man beat his chest.

Another ripped his shirt off, popping the buttons, revealing his hairy, flabby gut.

A woman in her fifties lifted her dress over her head and whirled it around in victory.

Watchers

There were just ten people out of a hundred, that had completely taken over this studio, terrorised an audience, and sent a message to the public at home.

It took just ten people - ten people, with ten corrupted watchers.

***

It had been two days since Jenny's audition, and she could still not fathom out what had come over her.

When she replayed the event, she pictured watching herself from afar - detached from the situation without the ability to change anything that was about to happen. It was as if she had no control of her actions, driven only by rage and frustration.

Since then, she had not left her flat; she had cancelled work, not checked her emails, and barely registered her phone. Now, as night approached once more, she had begun to feel stable enough to reach out to the world around her.

The fear of being arrested had faded as time passed. Jenny concluded that the man auditioning her didn't want anyone to find out what he had tried to do to her. Even though she stabbed him with a pen, he toyed with sexual assault, and perhaps that made them even - in some sick and twisted way.

On the first evening after the incident, she felt numb. The rage left her almost instantly, replaced only with a fear of what she was capable of. She sat alone, in silence, waiting for the police to arrive.

That night she dozed on the sofa; undeserving of the luxury of a warm bed after her actions. When she woke up, panic joined her. She didn't want to go to jail. She sat peering out of her front window, apprehensively awaiting arrest.

Each approaching siren, and flicker of blue and red, caused her to jump from her perch and hide.

Yet, here she was now, alone.

The feeling of remorse lifted from her shoulders with each passing moment.

Her mind emptied and, with no inkling of what to do next, she found herself needing to consider her options.

She would put a line under the audition. It was a write-off and could not be changed and, while she knew that she would carry an unprecedented amount of shame for months to come, she would get through it. It was time to do something; it was time to do anything.

She pulled her phone from her purse, sat on the couch, and texted Rachel.

'Fancy a drink? xxx'

Before she put her phone on the arm of the couch, it vibrated in her hand.

'Sure, pub? xxx '

Jenny didn't feel ready to leave the apartment just yet.

'Can we do mine? Bring a bottle of Pinot <3 xxx'.

'Sure thing babe xxx'.

Jenny sat in silence and waited.

***

Where the fuck was Charlie? Steve asked himself as he rang the buzzer to his best friend's apartment for the fifth time that evening.

He'd rung, texted, tried connecting on social media. Nothing.

It was as if he'd fallen off of the face of the planet.

At first, he thought Charlie might be pissed off with him. He often was, but after two days of not answering his phone, Steve began to worry. He knew Charlie inside out and didn't think he'd do anything stupid but, after seeing posts on Facebook about the rising figures of suicide in people of his age, he had to be sure.

So here he was, with his finger now held on the buzzer, waiting for Charlie to shout at him to stop.

All that he heard was the reverberation of the buzzer back through the speaker system, along with his quickening heartbeat.

Surely, he wasn't in the tube attack?

Charlie, you idiot.

"Oi, get away from that door!" a voice bellowed down from an angry man leaning out of a window above.

Steve released the pressure on the buzzer.

"Have you seen Charlie?"

"Who's that, then?" came the response from above.

"He lives at number thirty-nine; brown hair, about thirty."

"Ah yes, I did see that one. Quiet type. He left with a suitcase."

"When was that?"

"Ah, I don't know. A few days ago, maybe."

"Do you know where he was going?"

"No, I just saw him get into a taxi."

Steve felt like he'd gotten everything of use out of this half-dressed middle-aged man at the window, so he chose to wrap up the conversation.

"Okay, cheers mate, sorry about the buzzer."

The man upstairs nodded, closed his window and retreated inside the flat. Steve didn't have a choice but to retreat himself. Perhaps he could talk to Rachel, though.

He retrieved his phone from his pocket. It rang a couple of times before Rachel picked up.

"Rachel, baby! How's tricks?"

He waited patiently for an opportunity to speak again, not registering anything that she was saying.

"Listen, I've not seen Charlie for a few days. I can't get hold of him, and he's not at home. I don't suppose you know where he is? Maybe he's with Jenny?" Steve threw out the option in hope.

Rachel responded.

"No? Alright then, if you hear from him let me know."

Steve waited again for a few moments, as the topic of the phone call shifted.

"Oh yeah, that sounds alright. See you in an hour. Alright. Bye, babes."

Steve hadn't gathered the information that he was hoping for – but at least he had a date.

***

Jenny spent thirty minutes shovelling items around the flat, and about fifteen plastering makeup on her face.

She wanted a shower so badly - if only to scrub away the fear she had felt earlier in the day, but she needed to forget more. Talking to Rachel with a nice bottle of wine would help her unwind. It would help take her mind away from work, away from the audition and away from Charlie.

A double knock met the wooden door, as Rachel rapped for attention.

Jenny opened the door.

"Hey, gorgeous!" she greeted her guest.

"Oh, hi yourself!" Steve replied, grinning and winking at Jenny as he brushed past her into her flat.

"What the?" Jenny mouthed to Rachel.

She mouthed an apology in return.

Steve spread out on the couch, inviting Rachel to join him. She did so as Jenny half-sat, half-leant, in an awkward manner on the armrest.

"Listen, Jenny, sorry for intruding. I know you were going to have a girls' night in. I just want to join in the fun for a little while."

"Okay," she replied tentatively.

"He's got some questions about Charlie," Rachel clarified.

Jenny's heart fluttered. She swallowed her nerves.

"Yeah, I've not seen him for a few days, and I was hoping, you know, I'd barge in here, and he'd be sprawled out on the sofa or something, but I guess, well, he's not."

"He's not here." Jenny looked at the ground and remembered how much she had wanted to hurt Charlie; how she had desired to draw blood as he entered her.

"I don't suppose you know where he is?"

"Sorry." She returned her eyes to the landscape, shaking her head in the process.

"When was the last time you saw him?"

Rachel left the two of them to their conversation - the guest picking up a bottle of wine by the couch, before heading to the kitchen. Jenny and Steve continued.

"He was over here a few days ago."

"When, exactly?"

"A few days ago. I think it was Wednesday he came around. Oh, he did text me on Thursday." Jenny reached over to her phone and showed Steve the text.

"He texted me too. Said he was fine and not to worry," Steve began. "But, that's just making me worry more."

"Do you think he's alright?"

"To be honest, I don't know."

The sound of a cork sliding from captivity echoed through the silence, along with a small cheer from Rachel.

"When was the last time you saw him?" Rachel asked, joining the conversation from the kitchen.

"Not for a little while, but normally he's just on the other end of the phone, you know?"

Jenny understood. Despite taking off, she felt that, deep down, Charlie had a good heart.

"Did anything happen when he was here?" Steve asked.

"What do you mean?" Jenny shifted uncomfortably.

"Like, was he acting a bit weird or anything?"

Jenny hesitated.

"No, no, he was normal enough," she responded. "Although I did hear him talking in the kitchen in the morning."

"To who?"

"I don't know. He must have been on the phone to someone, I imagine."

"Hmm. Well, I reckon I already know the answer." Steve couldn't help himself but to playfully gesture in Jenny's direction. "But, what happened on Wednesday night?"

Jenny's cheeks flushed as she stumbled over how on earth to respond to the question.

Rachel returned from the kitchen with three glasses of wine.

"They hooked up," Rachel replied on Jenny's behalf. "I can always tell." She handed Jenny a glass of wine, followed by Steve.

Jenny was taken aback but couldn't argue the truth.

"Alright, so he left in the morning?"

Jenny nodded, wanting to disappear into her glass of wine.

"And, apart from that text, you've not heard from him since?"

Jenny shook her head.

"Well, I wouldn't imagine that he'd do anything stupid after a night here," Steve gestured, as he took a sip of his wine. "So, maybe he's just gone somewhere for a few days, you know, gone off the grid to think about things?"

Jenny nodded. After the night they had shared he likely needed time to reflect.

Rachel raised her glass: "So, now we've solved the mystery that is Charlie and his kiss and run, how about we get pissed?"

"Sounds good to me," Steve replied.

The three of them took a long and satisfying mouthful of their wine.

**

A couple of hours had passed. The three of them sat in the living room, forgetting their problems; chatting, laughing, and drinking.

Jenny had found another couple of bottles of wine tucked away in a cupboard, and they were now on the third bottle between them. This one was a rosé.

Jenny was having a nice time and found that the chauvinistic exterior of Steve was a front. Rachel seemed to be smitten with him - it was clear for her to see. She knew the two of them had gotten together at least once, and Rachel had dumped her now ex-boyfriend, who was never anything more than a casual relationship.

Rachel laughed at the slightly too-close-to-the-wire jokes that Steve gladly offered to the conversation. Jenny found herself switching off and forgetting the past few days.

She was returning to normality.

A thunderous bolt of noise reverberated throughout the apartment, shaking the very foundations where the three of them sat. The windows rattled, threatening to break, but only bending back and forth in displeasure.

"What the fuck!?" Steve shouted above the noise.

The three of them jumped to their feet, glasses of wine falling to the ground.

"What's going on?" Rachel asked.

The sound faded, and a silence fell upon them.

Jenny headed for the window.

"Don't go too close!"

Steve dragged her back just in time as a second blast echoed through the air - this one a little further away.

"It's a bomb," Steve suggested in a lowered voice.

Feeling more comfortable that the second attack was further away, Jenny headed once again for the window - this time unopposed. She peered out and saw scorch marks on the street below, surrounded by blood and several motionless bodies.

"Fuck," she said, as she bolted from the window and headed towards the door.

"No, Jen. We need to stay inside."

"There are people out there."

"There could be another attack," Steve added.

"I don't care." Jenny turned the door handle, and in a second was gone.

"We've got to follow her," Rachel begged.

Steve nodded.

They ran after Jenny, slamming the door behind them.

Jenny had run out of the front door, barefoot, oblivious to the occasional pebble or piece of plastic underneath her feet. It was only as she approached the victims that she noticed the shards of glass nick at her toes, causing her to slow her pace.

Rachel and Steve passed Jenny. They gestured for her to wait, but she tiptoed around the shards of glass from the broken car windows and followed gradually behind.

They approached the scorched tarmac and soon after found bodies around the scene of the attack. The first body they approached was a young boy, no older than fourteen. He had a hoodie pulled up over his head. He was writhing slightly. He was alive.

"Rachel, make sure he's okay. I'll check on the others," Steve instructed.

Rachel pulled the hood from the boy's head. She held his hand as he struggled to breathe.

Police sirens stopped Jenny in her tracks; the loud noise caused her to halt for a moment. She continued, relieved that the police were on their way.

The rat-a-tat of automatic gunfire overwhelmed the sound of sirens - shots originating from just streets away. Screams followed from the young and the old, the brave and the fearful. It didn't take long for them to end.

"We need to get out of here!" Steve yelled as he backed away from the lifeless bodies in front of him. He turned and caught up with Jenny, who was just a few steps behind him. He took her by the arm and retreated towards Rachel and the injured boy.

Three men holding weapons approached them from the crossroads.

"Run!" Rachel screamed.

The mysterious figures closed the gap to around three hundred metres and closing.

Panic struck. Jenny and Rachel sprinted for their lives as Steve trailed behind.

"Steve," they turned back for a second.

"Go!" he shouted, crouching over the boy.

Steve placed an arm underneath the boy's neck. Each movement caused the injured party to writhe in pain, but Steve continued.

"Sorry mate, I've got to move you," Steve apologised, as he pushed his arms under the boy's thighs.

He pulled the boy to his own body in one swift movement, almost toppling forward, but catching himself just in time as he broke into an awkward jog.

The men were only moments away from him now.

"Come on!" Rachel shouted, holding the door to Jenny's flat wide open for his retreat.

Steve jogged, unable to sprint with a fully-grown boy awkwardly placed in his arms.

A bullet whisked past his ear.

"Steve, come on!"

Only a few more seconds. Just a few more steps.

Jenny saw another bullet slam past Steve into the wall in front of him. More shots followed, accompanied by shouts from the men rapidly approaching him.

Steve stumbled, just steps away from the door.

Rachel ran out and stopped him from falling, as Jenny held the door open. She helped him with his steps, leading him to within inches from the door. A bullet grazed Rachel's left leg, and she fell into the opening of the flat.

Screams followed them, just metres away.

Steve fell into the opening just behind Rachel, the crying boy falling on to the floor ahead of him.

Jenny kicked Steve's legs from the door's path and, just as she was about to whip the door closed, she saw the faces of the three men that hunted them.

The last thing Jenny saw before she slammed the door closed was the almost identical smile across the three of their faces - twisted and unnatural.

Closing the door cut through their smiling faces and offered at least a moment's respite.

Jenny and Rachel surrounded the boy and Steve.

Jenny adjusted the boy's position so that he was lying on his back, and placed her ear to his chest. She could hear a heartbeat, but it sounded gentle. She stroked his hair as tears welled in her eyes.

Rachel wrapped her arms around Steve, who pulled himself up from the ground.

"Your leg," Steve observed, fighting to catch his breath.

Rachel checked on her wound. Blood trickled gently down from the grazed area.

"It's fine," she smiled at him. "I guess you're not a complete asshole, huh?"

A smile spread across Steve's face.

"Maybe not a total arsehole," he replied.

Crashing thuds from the reinforced PVC door intruded on their conversation as the three men outside threw themselves against the entrance.

Rachel jumped into Steve's lap. He pulled her face into his chest.

Steve held his finger up to his mouth and let out a small shushing sound, requesting quiet.

They heard the faintness of screams in the distance, followed by shouts from the men at their door.

The thuds stopped.

Rachel pulled her arms from around Steve. She noticed that her right hand was covered in blood.

"Are you okay?" Steve asked, reacting to the perplexed look on Rachel's face.

Rachel nodded. She studied the slight wound on her leg, then at her heavily bloodied hand.

"Steve?" she helped him sit up fully. "I think…"

"What?" Steve asked, leaning against the wall for support, finding it difficult to catch his breath over the pain in his lower back.

Rachel reached around to Steve's back.

"Jenny!" Rachel screamed.

Jenny moved her head away from the little boy for a moment, not entirely leaving his side.

"I think Steve's been shot."

"What do you mean?" Steve asked as he began to shake in Rachel's arms. "I'm fine."

"Call an ambulance," Jenny whispered, her voice tainted with desperation.

Rachel pulled her phone out of her pocket and dialled 999. It rang a few times before classical music began to play.

"I'm on hold. Shit, shit, shit."

"I'm feeling a bit cold, babes," Steve confided.

Rachel pinned the phone between her shoulder and ear, removed her coat, and placed it on top of Steve.

"You'll be fine. I'm here for ya."

Steve smiled; the small motion visibly draining his energy.

Rachel took the phone in her hand, clicked the loudspeaker and placed it on the floor to free her hands.

Classical music danced around the entrance hall of the flat as two lives balanced precariously between this world and the next.

19

Gerald sat in a wheelchair, within a large, open-plan room in Barnsley town hall. Both of his legs were heavily bandaged.

It wasn't his first time in the building; the shopkeeper attended several semi-regular meetings over the past decade on the state of business in town, but this was the first time it was unrelated to work. This meeting was the first time it had truly meant anything to him.

Approximately forty to fifty chairs stood in a misshapen circle, with the majority of them occupied. The group of attendees were a mixture from all over the small town, and Gerald assumed that the concerned citizens were all gathered here for the same reason.

When Gerald had seen the words on the notice board, he knew he needed to attend. The advert read: 'Have you been a victim of an act of violence or terror?'

He wasn't surprised with the relatively large turnout. There was a lot of violence occurring in his town.

One person led the meeting. They sat in a chair opposite Gerald, welcoming everyone in a soft and gentle voice, laced with empathy. The slightly rotund and soft-spoken middle-aged man thanked everyone for coming before opening the floor up for people to discuss their situations.

A lady in her thirties, who Gerald recognised as an occasional customer, began. The last time she had been into the shop, she picked up a bottle of vodka, a pack of cigarettes and an orange. At least she was getting one of her five a day, Gerald thought, as he forced himself to focus on her words.

The lady leant forward. She placed her elbows on her knees for support - her eyes looked towards the floor, focusing on the cracks in the floorboards between her feet, as she talked.

"My husband killed 'imself last week," she began; her words laced with a thick Yorkshire accent.

The person sitting next to the lady rubbed her knee, sympathetically.

"He was such a loving bloke. I'd known 'im since college days." Tears flooded from her eyes to the floor, disappearing through the cracks below. "'N then on Tuesday - last week I come home an-" She cut herself off, rocking in a back and forth motion. She began to wail as she failed to control her words.

"In your own time," the leader assured calmly.

She retrieved a tissue from her coat pocket, which she threw over the back of the chair. She blew her nose and continued.

"I got home, 'n he'd killed our dog."

Gasps echoed around the hall.

"I was in shock. I ran over 'n saw stab wounds. Rufus was already gone."

She shifted in her chair and lifted herself further from the floor before continuing the next section of her story.

"I must 'ave sat there for a few minutes before I even thought about who'd done it. After that, I got up 'n panicked. I walked 'round the house n' after not finding anythin' I went upstairs. That's where I found the note."

She took a deep breath, visibly choking back tears.

"A note from my fella. He said how he couldn't live with Rufus and me no longer. He said he hadn't been able to find me, and that he couldn't 'old on."

She let the tears find her.

"I am so sorry…" the leader lingered for a name.

"Linda."

"Linda, I'm so sorry. Do you want to go on?"

She nodded.

"I can't even remember what I were thinking. I just felt sick 'n I rushed through to the bedroom 'n that's where I found him, hangin'."

Having finished her story, Linda broke down into the shoulder of the person next to her.

"Linda, again, I am so sorry. Thank you for sharing your story with us," the man stood up and walked into the centre of the circle. His softly spoken voice rose in volume to display nuggets of his natural charisma.

"We are here today to share our terrible and tragic stories. We must know that we are not alone and that we are survivors. We have survived something terrifying, but we are still here."

He walked over to Linda. He took her hand in his.

"We cannot change what has happened in the past, but we can be here to support each other in the present. Thank you for sharing, Linda." He walked back and took his seat. People focused on him as they awaited the next instruction: "Who would like to go next?"

Stories flooded out of people around Gerald. One after another, Gerald absorbed all of the heinous activities from the past month or so, in his hometown. People had been tortured, raped, murdered; some things reminded him of the worst horror films he had seen.

While Gerald experienced torment from his experience - with busted ankles, bruises and a slight lack of teeth to remember it by, he could not imagine being in the shoes of some of these people.

What was going on in Barnsley? Gerald wondered to himself.

He sat and listened as the horrifying tales continued.

***

Charlie opened his eyes, feeling like he was waking from a deep, dream-filled sleep.

"Where am I?" he gasped.

Anabel stood opposite, staring directly into his weary eyes.

"How do you feel?" she asked.

He took a moment to respond, his thoughts and feelings forming.

"I'm cold."

Anabel smiled.

He had fallen asleep hanging out of an open fridge. Charlie shuffled across the floor to close the fridge door behind him.

"Do you remember what happened?"

Charlie nodded; each blink still feeling unnatural.

He swallowed and, while he could feel the sides of his throat ricochet against each other, it caused him only slight discomfort.

"Am I okay?" he wondered out loud.

"I believe so."

The relief Charlie felt in that moment was like nothing he'd ever experienced before. It was a moment of pure ecstasy. Laughter erupted from his battered lungs.

Charlie regained his composure once the laughter had left him. He rose gradually to his feet and enjoyed another few mouthfuls of chilled water before smiling at Anabel.

"Are you okay to walk?" Anabel asked, breaking Charlie's infatuation.

Charlie nodded.

"Good. You should grab some food and water and then we can go."

Charlie rose to his feet, only then recognising the pain that pounded from the wound on his arm.

"You need to clean that," Anabel continued.

Charlie unravelled his t-shirt sling until he found the section of cloth sticking to his skin. He peeled it slowly away and looked at the wound, which had at least stopped bleeding. He picked up some water and cleaned the area.

Charlie winced. It hurt like hell, but it was nothing compared to the pain that he had previously suffered; this time, each jabbing pain reminded him that he was still alive.

"There's a medicine counter over there," Anabel pointed to Charlie's right.

Charlie walked towards the counter and looked around the shelves. Bandages would come in useful, as would painkillers. Ah, this was what he was looking for, baby wipes and antiseptic cream.

Charlie ripped the wipes open with his teeth. He used his free hand to dab gently at the area, flinching at direct contact with his wound. After being satisfied with the progress, he cleaned around the area, using wipe after wipe to clean any of the blood speckled across his arm.

He tossed the now empty pack to one side.

Managing to form a grip in his hand, Charlie used his good arm to untwist the top of the antiseptic cream and break the seal. Charlie squeezed the antiseptic cream along the length of the wound and rubbed it in gently, which offered a few seconds of respite.

He prayed that it wouldn't get infected before wrapping his arm with a bandage he had just found.

"Where are we going?" Charlie asked.

"To find the first watcher."

Charlie dropped the blood-soaked t-shirt and walked over to a small circular rail with around ten t-shirts on hangers.

"I'm sure they won't mind." Charlie flicked through the options on the rail, looking for a medium, or if not, then a large.

After five XLs and XXLs, he found a single large. He took it from the hanger and gently lifted it over his head and newly bandaged arm.

Charlie looked down at the white shirt, which read 'I', a red heart, then the letters 'DC'. He wasn't so sure he shared the sentiment.

Charlie gathered a large pack of Cheetos and placed some chocolate bars in his trouser pocket.

"What do we do, then?"

Anabel waited for a moment before responding.

"We will end it."

"Where do we go next?" Charlie wondered, in his mind ruling out their continued journey to Washington. "Maybe the first watcher has been wiped out in the attack?" Charlie questioned.

Anabel pondered the option, uncertainty spreading.

"I have to relocate the first. I may be gone a while."

"What should I do?"

"Get comfortable," Anabel suggested.

Charlie had no answer, but he had everything he needed for when Anabel returned.

He nodded and, with a bolt of blue, Anabel disappeared.

Charlie had no family, his friends were the other side of the world, and now Anabel had left him.

Thoughts from afar flickered through his mind, leading him to contemplate life back in London. Was he happy doing what he was doing; living in denial, and accepting the challenge that each day threw at him?

He knew the answer, yet had no solution.

After this, would life be any different?

His mother's voice found him.

"Put one foot forward. That's all you can do."

He imaged her kind face looking down at him with nothing but undying love; a love that would never leave him. He walked back to the cold, welcoming arms of the fridge, selected a bottle of flavoured water, and revelled in the sweet strawberry tantalisation across his taste buds.

He sat against the open fridge, sweat running down his back - battling with the icy blast that entered his personal space.

As Charlie drifted into his thoughts, a distant commotion snapped him back to reality.

Charlie rose gingerly from his frosty seat and walked through the small shop. As he approached the front windows, he saw a middle-aged woman clutching her side, shouting for help. Charlie's instincts kicked in. He ran through the shop opening that he had entered, not so long ago.

Charlie waved her to join him.

The lady, fifty metres away, registered Charlie and walked in his direction.

"Over here." Charlie strained his scarred vocal cords to offer assistance.

The lady dropped her waving hand from the air and placed it around her waist, re-joining the other. She jogged slowly and awkwardly towards Charlie.

"Thank the lord," she said.

"Are you okay?" Charlie asked. He scanned her face, followed by her protected waist.

"I need water," she gasped.

Charlie placed his arm around her midsection gently in order not to disturb any potential injury as he helped her into the store.

"Sit down, and I'll bring you some water," he offered as they walked into the aisle.

She nodded and looked up at Charlie through clenched teeth and strained eyes. He darted through the shop, collected a bottle of water and headed back to the entrance.

The lady was gone.

What the hell? Charlie thought to himself. She was sitting there only seconds ago.

A blunt instrument smashed against his temples.

Charlie fell to the floor, but despite the acute pain, managed to land on his hands and knees. He brought one hand up to the side of his head as he turned to face his attacker.

The lady's face twisted and turned as if her skin was the only thing keeping her bones in place. She held a small iron pipe in her hand, revealing that her injured midriff was just a ploy.

"What do you want?" Charlie asked, as he pushed himself up to his feet, just over an arm's length from the strange woman.

"I want you, Charlie."

Charlie rubbed his head and noticed his bloodied palm; yet another wound to clean - and another life or death situation.

He'd had enough; enough of people and their snarky comments, enough with aggressive idiots looking for a fight, and certainly enough with the corrupted.

Anger roared up through his chest and out of his lungs - a chilling battle cry.

"Come on then!"

He prepared himself for the onslaught that awaited him, but the only thing that greeted him was a cruel smile.

"What are you waiting for?" he shouted.

She tossed the weapon between her hands, toying with her prey.

Charlie readied himself; he would cover his body with as many cuts and bruises as needed.

The sound of glass shattering to his side cut through the red mist.

He turned to see two large men standing to his left, both dressed like Hells Angels. One man stood with his arms crossed, and the other reloaded his shotgun.

Charlie ducked - a sixth sense helping him to react against the swinging pipe aimed towards his face. This time it missed.

He threw himself backwards; the woman in front showed no panic with her mistimed effort. Charlie ran backwards, keeping his eyes on the stoic woman who once again tossed the pipe back and forth between her hands. As he ran, the bottles of water and snacks fell from his pockets.

A shotgun shell blasted through the debris of the shop, exploding a tin of tomatoes from the shelf just behind Charlie. The tomato residue splashed across the back of his white t-shirt in the style of an expressionist painting.

"Charlie," the lady taunted, moving slowly towards his direction.

Charlie retreated through the available aisles, now finding himself next to the fridge that had once saved his life.

"Mr Taylor, we need a word with you." The two men entered the shop, glass crunching under their large boots as they walked.

"Just a word," the second man added, his voice only seconds away.

Watchers

Move, Charlie, you fool, he encouraged himself. The fridge's contents wouldn't save him this time. The lady and two men approached Charlie's location, just footsteps away - taunting, terrorising.

They turned the last aisle, but all that met them was the open fridge.

"You can't hide forever," the lady sung loudly as the three of them approached his previous location.

Charlie darted from behind them. His hiding place had worked long enough to avoid being discovered. The man cocked his shotgun, but he wasn't quick enough to hit a moving target. Charlie rushed into the next aisle.

"I just want to play," the lady announced.

Charlie darted towards the entrance. A shotgun blast hit the wall above his head, showering him with fragments of brick. Charlie didn't flinch. He was now in full stride as he ran out of the gas station.

Another blast missed him by inches.

The slower of the two chose to stop and take aim, but the more distance Charlie put between them, the harder it would be for him to take a successful shot. The other man trailed Charlie.

Charlie's lungs burnt with each foot forward; he felt his knees buckle from tiredness but managed to stay upright. He chanced a look behind him.

The man was moments from catching him. He couldn't maintain this pace for much longer. They would capture him and then perhaps none of this would matter anymore.

Charlie began to slow, his lungs unable to accept the oxygen that the atmosphere provided. The biker reached out to grab Charlie's shirt but, before his fingers grazed the t-shirt, the man's face exploded in all directions, and his lifeless body fell to the floor.

"Fuck!" the second man shouted as he refilled his barrel.

Charlie needed no second invitation to exit the scene. He continued his escape along the motorway, darting in-between cars, away from the small gas station on the edge of Washington DC - away from the fallout.

"We're going to find you!" the man shouted, accompanied by two shotgun blasts aimed into the air.

Despite the burning in his lungs, the adrenaline helped Charlie to continue a slow jog for several minutes until he was sure that he was far enough away. Although he was now entirely out in the open, he could see that there was no one trailing him, at least as far as he could tell.

The road stretched for several hundred meters before bending to a corner. Charlie stood on the opposite side that he'd driven down to get to Washington originally. He leant against a railing at the side of the road, allowing himself to take some much-needed respite, as well as ensuring that he wasn't quite so out in the open.

The three people that found him moments ago were strangers, yet, they knew him. They knew his name. And they knew exactly where he was.

Catching his breath, he felt the veins in his arm, and head, throb intensely. He was lucky that he managed to treat his arm before those maniacs came after him. His head throbbed with pain, but it wasn't anything that he couldn't handle. His arm didn't seem to be bleeding or hot to the touch; he could worry about that later.

After a few moments of rest, he wondered whether he should continue walking. Perhaps he could even return to the gas station in the hope that the strangers would never expect him to go back. He had no idea what to do, and he needed someone to tell him. He needed Anabel.

***

Anabel scurried between flickers of red and blue. Watchers no longer sat and observed; instead, each watcher found themselves in a fight against the corrupted.

Individual watchers, designed to respond to threats, in the same way, acted like a well-trained army. Their actions were the complete opposite to the disobedient and dishevelled actions of the corrupted, whose army moved and attacked in ways that didn't seem possible.

Without staying at one desk for too long, Anabel crept, avoiding possible confrontation. She could not get caught up in this war, not now. Charlie needed her.

Bolts of red shot through the air: the surge of current took down watchers, one after another, yet, as soon as one watcher had fallen, another had taken its place in a seemingly impenetrable line of authority.

Anabel dodged her way through the backline of watchers who were approaching a cluster of corrupted. Luckily for her, the situation seemed relatively contained in their current location.

Noticing a clear area to her left, she ran at the quickest speed she knew how; her lungs inhaling and exhaling no air. Without looking back, she ran until she saw the duplicate of what she had just escaped; an impenetrable line; an immovable force falling one by one, moving in on a swarm of the corrupted. This time though, she saw something move in her line of sight just above the wall.

At first, she thought it to be a shadow, but the jagged movements and flickers of red snapped her to her senses. It was no shadow. There were hundreds of corrupted watchers crawling on the clouded roof, up and over the line of defence.

"Above you," Anabel warned.

The scuttling watchers twisted and cracked their necks, turning their bright, beady, blood-red eyes in her direction.

The army of watchers that blocked the path noticed them and prepared their assault. She had warned the army just in time.

Bolts of blue removed the threat of the first of the corrupted. The rest jumped from the ceiling, crashing into the once impenetrable line, opening a possibility for chaos. The gap was simply an invitation for more of the corrupted to appear and push through the defences; enveloping every watcher in sight.

Anabel had no choice. She turned and ran, hoping that there would be enough of a distraction in the conflict to be forgotten; at least long enough to escape.

She placed one human-like foot in front of the other, fleeing before she slid and skidded behind one of the many identical desks. The monitors displayed a mixture of light and dark, a combination of life and death. Some of the corrupted had disconnected from the system and left their watch behind.

Despite some going AWOL, the ones that existed here must still be connected to the system - if Anabel could discover how, then she might be able to stop them.

A ceiling full of corrupted scuttled in her direction from afar. She crawled under the desk to avoid detection and waited. She listened to the disconcerting sounds of cracking bones as they flooded over her, continuing on their trajectory towards another wall of watchers.

After they slithered to a safe distance, she looked around and observed hundreds of dark patches across the cloudy ceiling. Each patch was not a shadow, but a swarm of the corrupted. She hoped that the watchers would spot them and adapt their formations - else they wouldn't have a chance.

Her instinct to rise and move kicked in. After a glance around to consider her surroundings, she headed towards the desk of the first.

She had been informed of the location of the desk by the authority. When she observed William previously, everything appeared normal, yet when she tried to enter his life, it had not worked. She had entered into another screen before, yet not on purpose and, despite attempting multiple times, nothing had happened.

It left her overflowing with a burning inside of her stomach. The first watcher could hold the answers to the source of the corruption, or at least allow her to help slow the spread. She was so close.

Anabel turned and twisted to avoid detection of the crowds of corrupted who charged at formations of watchers. Everywhere she looked, she saw bolts of red. She heard a mixture of screaming and cracking of twig-like bones from the captured corrupted as she darted from one desk to another. Running was an action that felt alien to her, yet the desperation caused the response. Another opening caused her to move; running, sprinting, gaining distance to the desk of the first.

After a few near encounters with the corrupted, she arrived at the intended desk. Risking detection, she stared at the screen. She tried to enter but, as before, it proved unsuccessful.

Anabel had to find some form of information; the risk she faced could not be for nothing. She looked carefully into the monitors, observing the picture so that she could at least try to work out where he was.

The first was nowhere to be seen. Screams from behind caused Anabel to stand to attention and hurry her search.

William was walking in what seemed like a spacious car park. The surrounding road was not scorched, and he seemed to move without any injuries whatsoever. She deduced that he wasn't in Washington at the time of the blast.

He seemed calm and free from fear as he walked jovially past car after car. Anabel monitored a human that was not her own. He appeared stranded from others in a somewhat built-up area, and she noticed no skyscrapers or very tall buildings. There were trees in one direction, and then she saw a reflected picture in the other. She saw a reflection of William in a black, mirrored substance. She saw his face.

Anabel took note of his appearance for the first time. William appeared to be in his late fifties or early sixties; his bald head surrounded by a crescent of delicate white whispers. The bags under his eyes were apparent but did not appear to trouble him. A smile appeared on his face.

William wore black clothes that were marketed for a younger person than he. The dark khakis gained support from a black belt, which pulled down on his trim midriff by the weight of his full pockets. His simple, black hoodie covered his torso but not his head at this moment. On his back, he carried a small sports bag with drawstrings.

The building in front of him was gigantic, black and reflective. The location began to be distinguishable. A metal fence covered the building next to William. He stood on a patch that, before a long period of neglect, could have once been considered as grass.

William touched the reflection of his face on the building's surface before he turned and traced his likeness alongside the building as he walked.

Anabel studied every aspect of the construction. She noted that it was at least ten storeys tall, if not more. It was flat, reflective, dark and fenced.

William walked towards an area where the exterior moved from being black and reflective to white and dull.

The angular white brick seemed to be an entrance. Anabel watched William approach within twenty feet of the opening before she noticed a larger than life man approach, also dressed in black.

The two shared a nod and entered the building. Anabel had just enough time to notice a sign that presented a crest which read 'National Security Agency'.

A shot of red electricity narrowly missed her head as it crashed into the monitors in front of her, causing the one it struck to crack and shatter.

Anabel might have enough information to track down William, but now she had to survive. She twisted quickly, desperate to witness the danger. As she did so, she saw the corrupted preparing their charge. Their twisted features grimaced and gnarled; pulsating with energy so pure it lit the clouds around them in a wash of red.

More bolts of red left their area, aimed in her direction, but Anabel evaded the attacks from afar. Luckily for her, there was still enough distance to react.

The corrupted continued. Bolt after bolt crashed into the screens around her as she began to run back towards her desk, back to Charlie.

The corrupted followed in a disjointed mass.

Anabel ran not only for her life, not for Charlie's, but also in the hope that she could offer salvation. The first would have answers; she believed it to be true. So, she did what she could - she ran.

The way in front of her was clear for now. Taking the opportunity to look over her shoulder, she saw the corrupted gaining ground.

Another bolt flew past her midsection. She felt the warmth radiate her side, causing the wound on her shoulder to pulsate with life.

She changed direction and dodged quickly to one side, hoping that she could throw them off track. It was of no use. They continued on her trail and gained distance with each passing moment.

The way in front began to take form; a wall of watchers and corrupted, fighting just ahead. She had an idea. Anabel ran towards the battle; hundreds if not thousands on each side, creating a war within the clouds. Most of the monitors beside her were off. Even if she wanted to, she knew that she was unable to escape into another life voluntarily. It had happened once, somehow, but she couldn't rely on it happening again. Besides, even if she managed to disappear from their world, she still needed to return to Charlie, and there was little chance she could return to the first's monitor now.

It was all or nothing.

She bolted towards the edge of the battling watchers, squeezing between a gap in their lines. She looked over her shoulder as the corrupted jumped on to the backs of those she had sacrificed behind her. The corrupted engulfed the army, just like shadows swallow the sun.

A tremendous cheer ruptured from the corrupted, creating a ripple of fear that echoed through her being. However, the moment of celebration, and the sacrifice behind, gave her enough time to escape.

"The Overseer is gone," one of the corrupted roared.

A single repeated sentence joined the cheers, bouncing from the ceilings.

"We are free. We are free. We are free."

Clicks, cracks and pops, followed Anabel, as she evaded the army in her retreat.

She had managed to throw the corrupted off of her scent, yet doomed others in the process. Now, if The Overseer was no more, what did that mean for her kind? There would be no structure, no order, and perhaps most importantly, no purpose.

After she allowed herself no more than a few moments to consider her fate, she returned to her screen. The clouds behind her swayed with shades of red.

Noises that were not human cheered victoriously in Anabel's world.

Anabel vanished into the screen, hoping that she would never have to return.

20

Almost every television network worldwide ceased its regular programming. Instead, providers replaced the once craved sitcoms, dramas, talk shows and sports events with emergency broadcasts from various news stations.

On the handful of stations that didn't have a constant live stream of news updates, there were either re-runs of long-running shows, or as was the case on a few networks, dead air.

As was the case with several television stations, some radio stations had ceased, and newspapers missed their first print in decades. In addition to the media, many of the public services stalled; public transport had halted in many areas that weren't cities and, in cities, there was a possibility that travelling on public transport would result in a tragic incident, as had been happening globally.

The streets overflowed with rubbish. People became too lazy to put their bins out correctly as some simply chose to throw trash out of their windows or doors. Also, waste management had stopped collecting, almost as one.

The hospitals that ran did so efficiently but found themselves massively overcrowded. Being in a crowded area, however, was the last resort for many - it wasn't uncommon for an assault or even a mass shooting to take place in a location that was widely populated.

Law enforcement across the world had become divided. Some officers with families handed in their gun and badge, while others had not seen their home in weeks due to the terrifying incidents that were driving a drastic shift in their work-life balance.

Law enforcement, and local government, were as stumped as the rest of the world about the situation.

Religious cults appeared across the world. Most of them shared similar theories, quoting the end of time and preaching on the vengeance of God. Certain factions believed it was a purge, that half of the population would be wiped from the face of the earth due to the actions of the species as a whole. Others believed that the shift in climate had caused people with certain dispositions to go mad.

People searched for ideas around the world, yet no-one had an answer.

England fell more divided than ever before, as nationalism in parts of the country turned inwards. People raised questions about their neighbours, and others in their community, who showed a slight difference in themselves.

England, like the rest of the world, suffered. The nation targeted each other as people searched for an enemy, clutching at any straw they could find.

The view of openness that once proudly resonated from the capital, had become one of survival in small groups, whereas regular bombings and seemingly random attacks were greeted with terror, along with a frightening level of acceptance.

Cities across the country suffered from the same fate. Cultures became divided; people became segregated into groups and wars broke out based on skin colour and ethnicity.

Race and ethnicity weren't the only matters that started a conflict. Aggressive acts exploded based on many things, including religion, belief, sexuality; even things such as how people styled their hair, what colleagues had said a year ago in a snarky way, or a bad experience at a restaurant.

America stood proud and defiant, despite mass bombings that saw the near entire population of various cities wiped out. However, this didn't detract from heinous acts that occurred across all fifty states.

Corruption spread further than the cities of the world - towns and villages, even self-contained farming areas; they all suffered from acts of extreme violence and prejudice.

***

Gerald sat at home, a relatively spicy homemade chicken tikka masala warming his lap. His main dish paired with some plain white rice, a single garlic poppadom and a sizeable frosty glass of ale.

Since re-opening his shop, it had been a case of one crazy incident after another. He believed if anyone had been filming the events, he'd have made a fortune from a reality television show.

A regular of his, Mr Garby, seemed like a quiet and restrained man. He was pushing into his golden years, with perhaps a year or two left until retirement. His regular visit would consist of the occasional top-up of toiletries. However, yesterday, the older gentleman burst into the shop fully naked - except for his once white briefs. He had his arms around a girl who was young enough to be in the first year of college. Gerald didn't recognise the girl, but the two of them swore at him. They provoked him with sexual gestures as he served them a bottle of vodka. Luckily, they exited the store soon after.

That wasn't the only time he was propositioned recently. Other ladies, as well as a few men, had entered the store and suggested that Gerald lock the door, and unlock the possibilities that a grocery store romance would reveal.

Gerald knew that he was not what one might call a stereotypically good-looking guy; he hadn't even seen his toes when standing, for a good ten years. Perhaps he had some strange medical condition where he was releasing hormones that attracted this behaviour? It was the first time in his life that he had invited this much attention – and, at his age, in his shape, he knew that despite his best wishes, that probably wasn't the case. It was this crazy town. He believed that there had to be a substance abuse problem behind it.

Today was no better - different, definitely, but still definitely strange.

A little after lunch, Gerald waited for customers to arrive at the till. He ran his tongue across seeds from his sandwich that lodged themselves between his teeth. A door chime alerted Gerald to the entrance of a middle-aged lady. Completely ignoring the people around her, she walked down the aisle with complete focus and started to unpeel chocolate bars until there were seven or eight exposed treats in front of her. Gerald questioned her motives but, before he received an answer, she began shoving chocolate into her mouth, spreading it around her face, even into her hair; a constant shovelling of sugary brown and white.

The lady didn't stop after the chocolate bars; after quenching her appetite, she opened several cans of coke to drown her thirst. After that, her hunger seemed to return as she moved on to a variety of sweets and crisps. That was the final straw for the shopkeeper. He had asked her multiple times to stop but, in her gluttonous haze, she only had eyes for the sweets. In the end, Gerald dragged the strange woman out of the shop, from his wheelchair, as she kicked and screamed for her sugary salvation.

She wasn't the worst of the customers today, though. There was a man who Gerald recognised, but could not quite place. He had entered the store and seemed sane enough, before confessing to Gerald about his terrible life, confiding in him as a psychiatrist. The man had begun crying and pleading with Gerald to change lives with him. As leverage, he mentioned his beautiful wife, but also insisted that he wanted to live the life of another. He wanted the shop, he wanted to have no children, and he wanted his freedom. The envious, anxious man then began to wail uncontrollably.

Enough was enough for one day. He convinced himself that no amount of money was worth staying for at the shop today. He found an excuse to go home, rest his ankles, and sack off the people of this town for one more evening.

After he arrived home, he gently removed his shoes, threw his trousers across the floor, and rolled into the living room in his white y-fronts and t-shirt.

Now, he sat with his feet raised, in front of the television, sipping his cold glass of ale.

"Darling?" His wife entered the room. "What do you think of my new haircut?"

"Yeah, yeah. Nice," Gerald responded, a little too quickly before he turned around - concentrating instead on the moving pictures and refreshing liquid that monopolised his attention.

"Don't you think it makes me look pretty?" she said, stepping closer.

"Listen, Marge, love. It's been a crap day. Let me enjoy my food, alright?"

Gerald turned to make sure that his message had landed with the intended purpose. That was when he noticed his wife's new haircut for the first time.

Marge stood in the middle of the carpeted living room, a trail of grey hair following her as she revealed the home-cut she had performed for her loving husband. Her new style was very short; she had tried to remove all of her hair. There were visible clumps where she had been unsuccessful, and she hadn't managed to cut the back as thoroughly - a few longer strands remaining in place.

"It takes years off!" she exclaimed, dancing around with the scissors she had used, still in her hand.

"What have you done?" Gerald yelled, sitting up straight in his chair. If his wife had attempted to gain his attention, this time, it had succeeded.

"No more greys," she said, taking the scissors to her hair once more and cutting one of the leftover patches of hair from her almost bare scalp.

The scissors nicked her head, causing a stream of red to run down her forehead, over a small tuft of hair she had missed in her fringe.

"Marge. What the hell? Are you alright?"

Gerald tried to stand up, as pain shot through his joints. He leant on the chair, and table, and hobbled across to his wife. He took the scissors from her and threw them on to the floor, placing a hand to her head. He looked at the blood on his hand.

Marge let out an excited squeal.

"I've always wanted to be a redhead!" she began, jumping around with glee, halted only by Gerald's arms locked tightly around her.

"What on earth have you done?"

Gerald pulled his wife's head back to see the final result of her actions. He was greeted with an excited grin, painted on like makeup.

"I've had enough of this town!" Gerald exclaimed. "Are you alright?"

She nodded profusely.

He breathed deeply and considered the situation.

"Do you need to go to A&E?"

She shook her head, tiny droplets of blood spinning from her forehead to the carpet below.

"Alright," Gerald let out a long sigh. "Well, go pack your bags. I've had enough. We're getting the hell outta here."

His wife's knees cracked before buckling slightly as she jumped up and down like an excited puppy.

"We're gonna have the life we've always wanted. We're gonna sit by the beach, sip on cocktails, take in the sun." He thought to himself for a moment. "We'll put the house up for sale, and the shop, and get away from here."

Gerald's wife responded with a clap too wide and powerful for her small body.

"But first, let's get you a wig. You look bloody ridiculous."

The smile on Marge's face dipped slightly.

Gerald ambled back to his chair, sat down, picked his dinner and drink up from the floor and let the river of refreshing ale sift through the gaps in his crooked teeth.

***

Roh had his teeth seen to by a dentist, and those that didn't know him would never realise they weren't his own.

He sat in the front room of his parents' house, across from his fading father and two sets of worried grandparents.

His father had not said a single word since Tom had killed his wife. Instead, he did nothing, and only ate when others insisted he did so: his father turning into a shell of a man.

Roh had dealt with his situation differently. He found himself becoming angry, strangely so, recently. It would be the smallest things that would start him off and force the memories of just a couple of weeks ago to the surface.

He sat with his father, who had lost his wife, but Roh had also lost his mother. Where was the sympathy for him? He pushed the feelings down and tried his best to comfort the man who raised him.

"Dad, we're going to have some food. Would you like some?"

His father did not respond.

"Make him a small portion," one of the elderly grandparents replied.

Roh nodded and proceeded to the kitchen.

It was only in the past few days that he began to miss Tom; the man that had killed his mother and tortured his father to the point of breaking point. He asked himself just how could he miss that person. It was the question that stayed with him every night, sleep becoming hard to find.

The sleeplessness didn't help his temper. On the way over, he let loose at a driver so slow that cyclists overtook them. He found himself stuck behind the driver on a narrow road for several minutes, before finally roaring past and screaming at him out of an open window.

"Bring in some tea," someone shouted from the front room.

Get your own fucking tea, he thought.

"Okay," he replied.

As Roh flicked the switch of the partially-filled kettle to the on position, he found his thoughts drifting. He left this real world into one of fantasy, where he wasn't making tea and dinner for his family;

instead, he was with Tom, rolling around on the floor of his apartment.

Perhaps life wasn't all it was cracked up to be.

Perhaps he didn't need his family.

Perhaps Tom was right all along.

***

In the building that houses the Natural Security Agency, William stood in a dark, sealed room, accompanied by his silent partner. The room had no discernible features. There were no ornaments and no furniture, aside from one large screen that dominated one of the walls - and a panel in front of it that allowed for live steam video connection.

William stood at the large digital wall, waiting for a connection, as his accomplice held a gun to the captives sitting on the bare floor, cross-legged.

Behind William laid three motionless bodyguards, all of which wore bullet wounds like badges of honour; life sapped and long lost.

The President of the United States of America and his wife sat cradling their two children on the floor beside them.

"I don't know what you're after, but please will you let my wife and children go? They have nothing to do with this whatsoever," the president pleaded.

"I can't do that, Mr President," William responded. "You see, if I let them go, you might become all self-sacrificial on me. Well, I need leverage, a guarantee that you will follow through with your words."

"I've told you, please, that is something I cannot do."

"In that case, I will gut each of your family one by one, and you can watch them slowly bleed out. You can watch them scream for help as you watch the life drain from their eyes. Is that what you want?"

The president sat in silence and placed an arm around his wife.

"Oh, and I won't forget about your wife, don't you worry. My colleague here is a very passionate human being. Not very tender, though."

"Where are the reinforcements?" Andrea whispered into her husband's ear. The president returned her gaze stoically.

"You're wondering if somebody will come, aren't you? Surely someone will come and help us," William pranced around, impersonating the part of an innocent, helpless heroine.

The silent assassin holding them at gunpoint allowed himself a smile.

"See, even Ed here finds that funny."

William turned his attention back to the screen.

"No, there will be no one to come and help you. We've seen to that. This plan has been in motion for a long time, and there's not one person left standing in this building that isn't supposed to be here."

"Get on with it then," the president ordered, defiantly.

William cracked a smile over his shoulder before the screen flashed to life.

The two-way screen showed the secretary of defence. The video call displayed the situation, yet there was no reaction on the other end of the conference call.

"Secretary," William acknowledged.

"Sir," the secretary replied. "Mr President," he added, naturally.

"Are we ready?" William asked.

"Almost," came the response from the person who was once a trusted part of America's governing body.

"Shaun!" the president roared to life. "Help us! We're being held captive at the NSA!"

William let the president finish before addressing the room calmly.

"Are you quite done?"

"Send help," the president added.

The president's eyes remained fixed on the non-response of his colleague.

"I'm sure he'll do that right away," William mocked. "Shaun? I didn't peg you as a Shaun," William noted.

The secretary of defence nodded.

William let out a laugh.

"Help us for Christ's sake! Whatever they're paying, we'll double it."

"I'm sorry, Mr President. Shaun won't be helping you today. He works for me now."

The man on the screen was no longer the person the president had grown to know and trust over the past two years.

"Can you access the live feed?" William asked.

"Hold on," Shaun responded. He picked up the phone and muted the conversation to William momentarily.

"We're about to make a little statement, Mr President," William informed.

The two children started to cry heavily, triggering William to wince at the sound.

"If you don't shut your children up, the world will watch me kill them on live television. Do you understand?"

The president nodded. His wife, on the other hand, sat mouth agape, appearing ready to pounce in retaliation, before being calmed by her husband.

"I'm going to write down what I want you to say, and you're going to say it exactly as it's written. Do you understand?"

The president nodded.

"If you do not, my colleague here will shoot your youngest child first."

"I understand," he submitted.

"Good."

"After I do this, you will let my wife and children go?"

William took a moment to prepare his reply. He saw no reason to lie to the man who he was sure would do his bidding.

"There will be no 'after this', Mr President. "There will either be days of torture and torment, or there will be relief."

"The stream is ready," came the unmuted response on the screen.

"Good work. We're ready."

Shaun disappeared from the screen, replaced by two American newscasters.

***

The world stood still as a live broadcast began. The President of the United States of America, his wife, and two children sat in the middle of a bare room. They cradled each other, with tears apparent for those who chose to look closer.

"My fellow Americans," the president sat straight, looking as presidential as possible in a situation that found his visually scarred family next to him. "I am here today to talk to you about something of grave importance."

The president took a moment to prepare himself for the next sentence. Corners of a gun entered the frame like a boom microphone accidentally entering into a shot.

"As you are aware, there have many been terrible incidents occurring recently, and there's something to consider."

"No ad-libbing," William snarled off camera.

The president regained his focus.

"The world is sick. These terrible acts are happening for a reason. It is nothing to do with God or religion, and it has nothing to do with chemicals or drug abuse. I can also confirm that it has nothing to do with government."

He took a breath before continuing, attempting to appear as empathetic as possible in his demeanour.

"There is a sickness in this world that needs dealing with. I have identified the cause of this sickness. The sickness is… the American people. It is people worldwide. It is humanity as a whole. We shall be eradicating the sickness in due cause."

The president furrowed his brow and slanted his mouth before continuing the prepared statement.

"Say goodbye to your loved ones, because you'll be leaving them soon. Make your peace with your God, for you'll be seeing them soon. Prepare for death. It is coming."

The president could barely continue, as he fought with himself through gritted teeth to finish the final sentence.

"This is the President of America, signing off for the final time." He finished by mouthing, 'I love you. I'm sorry.'

The sound of a gunshot rang across the airwaves. The president fell forward, face-first into a pool of his blood, followed shortly after by the screams of his wife and children.

The screen returned to the shocked news reporters.

Even though this would likely be the most viewed piece of television history, they could find no words for their captivated audience.

21

Charlie was blissfully unaware of the recent events that transpired outside of his current surroundings. Instead, he continued to walk in a direction that he hoped was the correct way. He followed the main road by foot and would continue to do so, unless he was instructed otherwise from the return of his watcher.

There were no other people on the main road, and the only company he found was that of the occasional scream, desperate shout, gunshot, or siren - which filtered in from almost every direction around him. The jarring noises occurred often, and Charlie found that they started to blend into a blanketed background noise.

The one thing that did not fade into the background was the flash of blue as Anabel returned. He stopped and watched as she materialised into this world.

"Charlie," Anabel gasped as she arrived.

"Are you okay?"

"There's a war," she replied.

Charlie already knew that war had arrived.

"You do not understand," she continued. "The corrupted. They have taken over."

"What do you mean?"

"They have taken our world, Charlie. It's gone."

"Your world?"

"Yes, they have completely taken over. The corrupted have killed The Overseer."

"Who?" Charlie found himself swirling down a path of confusion. "Never mind."

"It will not be long until the corrupted have killed, or turned every watcher."

Charlie found no response. He realised that the situation with the watchers was in peril, but the penny had only just begun to drop.

"If every watcher is corrupted, it means that every person is corrupted? It means the end of humanity?"

The penny dropped so hard that it bounced back to its returning position.

"Are - are you okay?" he found himself asking.

"Yes, yes, I'm okay."

"Are you sure?"

Anabel softened her posture. She nodded as she stood next to Charlie.

"You're not corrupted - are you?"

She shook her head.

"Good. Then we still have a chance."

"We need to find the first."

"Do you know where they are?" Charlie asked.

"He's at the NSA building," Anabel confirmed. "Do you know where that is?"

The inability to look on Google Maps felt alien, but a flash of recollection struck home.

"I saw a sign for that on the way here. If we can find a car, it won't take us long."

The road they walked was empty, spare the occasional deserted automobile - either parked at the side of the road or abandoned in the middle of a lane. They could see two on the horizon and continued their journey.

"So, what happens next?" Charlie wondered.

"I am not sure," Anabel admitted.

"We find the first, then what?"

"We find answers on how to push back the corrupted."

"And if they don't have an answer?"

Anabel took a moment before responding.

"Then, the world will end."

They walked the next few steps in silence. Charlie experienced a main course of fear, a side of anxiety and a dollop of depression to fuel their journey.

Charlie and his watcher arrived at a car in the middle of the road; a blue Ford Mondeo. He tried the door and, to his delight, it was unlocked. Charlie opened the door and sat in the driver's seat. He reached his good arm awkwardly to the ignition but found no keys. Charlie searched the glove compartment and the dashboard but to no success. He struck the wheel in frustration.

"Try the next one," Anabel suggested.

Charlie awkwardly exited the car. He left the door open as he proceeded towards the next vehicle, which happened to be a police car.

He pushed aside the initial concern of being arrested for breaking into a police vehicle. He battled with the decision momentarily, somehow inbuilt from action movies that he had watched.

A single scream, shortly followed by the roars of a large crowd, travelled from a nearby location, hurrying Charlie in his decision to enter the car.

The police car was also unlocked. However, after searching for the keys, he was again left stumped.

"Can you find us a car with a key?" Charlie asked Anabel. "Can you, like, vanish and look at all of the cars around here?"

Anabel shook her head.

"If I vanish I may never come back. The corrupted will be looking for me."

Charlie didn't quite understand the inner workings of Anabel and what she was capable of, but knew that she had no reason to be untruthful.

"Have you checked everywhere?" Anabel asked.

Charlie felt around on the floor with his non-driving hand and felt something round and metallic, followed by a sound of metal shuffling against metal. He hooked the ring and pulled a set of keys up to his eye line.

The keys slotted into the ignition, and the engine roared into life.

"Fasten your seatbelt." Charlie grinned, revelling in the part of a police officer from a Hollywood blockbuster. All he needed was a pair of Ray-bans to complete the fantasy.

The wheels rolled forward as they travelled gently towards their destination.

"What do we do when we get there?" Charlie asked. "How do we get in?"

"From what I saw, that will be the least of our issues," Anabel replied.

Charlie manoeuvred the police car gently past abandoned automobiles and, when a stretch of tarmac appeared in front of him, he put his foot down on the accelerator. Charlie listened to the purr of the engine as it masked the cheers and roars that circled them.

They drove in silence for a few minutes, neither one of them willing to vocalise their thoughts. Charlie considered asking Anabel questions about the NSA, but instead, he enjoyed the open road for what might be the last time.

There was nothing between them to be said that would not sound jovial. Charlie considered lightening the mood with a sarcastic comment but instead focused on steering the vehicle one-handed – luckily for him, the car was an automatic.

Charlie wanted to play some music to calm the palpitations that exploded from his chest. He reached for the knob and twisted it, with no hope that there would be anything on the other end.

Static, followed by rolling static, breached the police car. Occasional murmurs of numbers and words could be heard across the airwaves - weak, and inaudible.

He slowed the car down to a gentle roll, moved control of the wheel to his elbow so that he could pick up the transmitter. He pushed a button on the side with his thumb and spoke.

"Does anyone copy?" he waited for a moment. "Over."

More static replied.

He hooked the radio controller back into its holster, switched off the radio and returned his attention to the road. The radio silence confirmed to Charlie that they were indeed on their own.

Charlie arrived at a clear intersection, and uncertainty found him. He pondered the direction at a crawl until a signpost came into view on the side of the road: 'Fort Meade' it displayed, pointing to the right.

Charlie stopped the cruiser before the sign evaded them, placed it in neutral and turned to Anabel.

"Fort Meade. Does that sound right?"

"I don't know," Anabel admitted.

"Can you find out?" he asked.

Anabel shook her head.

"What shall we do?" he asked, blissfully unconcerned at being parked in the middle of a highway.

Anabel had no answer; she had no path for Charlie to follow.

He placed the car into drive. The way to the right looked open; it was another main road with a sign to an airport. It didn't seem like a turning where a building of national importance was located.

"Let's go a bit further," Charlie suggested. "We can always come back."

Anabel nodded.

Charlie continued to drive towards the next opportunity.

"It appeared to be a large black building with reflective surfaces. It will be hard to miss," Anabel instructed.

"There are so many trees," Charlie bemoaned. "Let's just get to the next intersection."

The figurative duo drove onwards, weaving past stationary cars, motorbikes, and the occasional wreckage. The next item they needed to avoid wasn't automotive; it was human. A motionless body lay across the floor, devoid of life.

Charlie rolled to the side of the body slowly before noticing another in his field of vision. Then another, and another.

They continued carefully, avoiding the bodies in front of them. The number of dead bodies they passed grew and grew, until they formed a large, and quite literal, man-made barricade. The occasional dead body increased in density until creating a roadblock, where multiple bodies were piled to block the way in front of them. The bodies directed them to the right as they approached a turning from Route 32. There was only one way to go.

A brown sign informed them that the NSA visitor centre was only one mile away.

"I guess we're going this way, then."

Charlie turned the wheel of the police cruiser to the right and directed the vehicle from the main road. The large reflective black NSA building came into view in the distance.

***

The hospital room bustled with worried patients and manic guests.

Typical protocol had long since been rescinded, as those lucky enough to have beds were pushed tightly together without dividers to offer any form of privacy. The only things that separated patients from another were frantic friends and family that filled the available gaps.

Due to a lack of seating, loved ones either stood or kneeled; some finding rest on the edge of a nearby bed. The inhabitants of this room were not the only unfortunate ones, as every room in the hospital was well over maximum capacity.

Overworked doctors and nurses rushed in and out of rooms. They ignored most of the people that screamed at them for answers, or at least an update on their loved ones.

The nurses tried to alleviate concerns on multiple occasions, but there were too few staff members to help everyone, and that had resulted in the rise of a mob mentality. Recognising this, the staff had adapted the best they could to the increase in numbers, adopting a disciplined approach to their duty. They also had to adapt to the newly enforced working hours, where none of them had been able to leave for days.

Tempers were frayed on both sides.

Rachel sat on the edge of the bed while Jenny stood. The last thing either of them wanted was to get in the way of the mob.

Steve lay in the hospital bed, attached to the constant beep of a monitor, unconscious.

Rachel rubbed his leg as a doctor entered to check on his vitals.

"Any news on the boy?" Jenny jumped at him.

The doctor ignored Jenny.

"Doctor?" she reiterated as others began to crowd him.

"No news," the doctor responded. "Your friend here looks to be stable."

Rachel's attention peeked.

"We've removed the bullet and stopped the bleeding. Now we need to see how he reacts when he wakes up."

"Will he be okay?"

The doctor rubbed his eyes, visibly exhausted.

"I do hope so."

"Doctor?" Jenny tried to start a new line of questioning.

"Sorry, I have to get back to my other patients."

The doctor exited the room before being mobbed by the crowd of carers. A nurse assisted by taking the doctor by the arm and helping him exit the room. After ensuring the doctor was free, she pulled up a chair by the doorway and stood on it to address the crowd.

The purple bags underneath her eyes blemished her otherwise soft features. She spoke in a slow but firm manner.

"The doctor will be with everyone shortly. Please allow him to see other patients. He needs to work, and he will get to you and your loved ones shortly."

A chorus of upset sniffing responded, mixed in with the occasional shout of anguish.

"Listen to me," the nurse's voice cracked. She wiped her brow with her arm as the temperature in the room rose. "There are many people who need assistance. The truth is that there are just not enough people here to help. If anyone here has any medical training or would be able to assist in any way, can you please raise your arm?" The nurse looked around the room.

"I want to help," Jenny shouted, above the murmurs of the crowd, raising her arm.

A ripple of encouragement began, and a few others raised their arms around the room.

"Thank you. Those who raised your arm, please follow me. We'll get you in scrubs and ready to help."

The nurse stepped down from the chair, sinking into the crowd. A handful of people made their way through to the doorway and joined her.

"I'll be back soon." Jenny squeezed Rachel's arm.

"Don't be too long. I'm bored as hell," Rachel added.

Jenny blew a kiss back in her friend's direction. She caught up with the nurse, leaving the stuffy room behind.

"If you would follow me," the nurse instructed her handful of helpers.

The nurse walked, followed by her newly found assistants. Jenny broke through the people in front and placed her hand on the nurse's shoulder. The nurse turned around to engage her.

"Just what is going on?" Jenny whispered.

Tears rolled down the nurse's cheeks.

"Are you alright? Please don't cry."

Jenny placed her other arm on the nurse's opposite shoulder before closing in for a hug.

"I haven't slept for days." The nurse cried into Jenny's chest.

Jenny patted her back and rubbed her shoulders; the onlooking crowd remained passengers in the conversation.

"There's just so many." The nurse raised her face as she attempted to choke back tears.

"We can help."

The nurse pulled her head from Jenny's tear-soaked blouse.

"Can't we?" Jenny asked the three additional helpers.

"Yeah," an older lady and her daughter responded, in unison.

"Damn right," responded a middle-aged man.

"There you go. We'll help; maybe you can go and rest your eyes for a bit?"

The nurse nodded. She wiped the small amount of mascara that remained, from her cheeks.

"Thank you so much. Let me get you prepared and show you what to do. There's just so much to do."

Jenny and the group turned from the corridor into a staff room, ready to help in any way possible.

***

As in many areas of the world, parts of the UK military had been on the streets for days. They had regular patrols to help those that could not help themselves.

After witnessing member after member of his crew turn on each other, Lieutenant Colonel Harding had no training on how to deal with this situation. Despite almost twenty years of experience; working his way up the ranks year on year, leading teams through missions in Afghanistan and being no novice to losing troops, what was happening around him frightened him to the core.

After the successful mission in Afghan, he expected to sit behind a desk for a little while. He was pushing fifty, and hoped that he had seen the last of war for his lifetime - yet, here he was with a small operations team, patrolling the war-riddled streets of central London.

There had been a range of people who had approached them with violent tendencies: English, Irish, Italian, Arab, African, men, women, young, old. He thought it impossible that they were all terrorists.

The troop with him now contained just seven of his best men. However, they continued, fully-armed to tackle situation by situation.

It was only hours ago that one of his most loyal officers had turned a gun on his troops, wiping out five of his own before he had managed to look him square in the eyes and put him down. These internal attacks happened several times before their unit of six hundred had split into smaller divisions to control situations in isolation.

After splitting into twelve teams of fifty, the eight of them were all that remained of his regiment.

Lieutenant Colonel Harding ensured his arthritic fingers gripped tightly around the base of his gun as they moved towards a blind corner. The military unit proceeded towards Trafalgar Square. They were no longer taking orders on which location to subdue, for situations were constantly arising from all directions. Another unit appeared across the square, visible below the mouth of the marble lion that rose above them.

Harding signalled to the troops across the way who in turn signalled back. They shuttled around the corner of the square, attempting to offer themselves as much cover as possible should they come under fire. The unit followed suit as they marched towards each other in the middle of the square.

The fountains in the square recycled the beautifully clear water it contained, spraying the troops with a mist as they approached.

"Sergeant." Harding met his counterpart.

"Sir," the sergeant responded, removing his helmet, and nodded in Harding's direction.

"What's your situation, Pieters?"

"We lost maybe thirty, thirty-five men. We're all that's left."

Sergeant Pieters signalled behind him at the ten to fifteen men in the rear, who patrolled the area in case of any emerging threats.

"And what is your situation?"

Harding moved his head in the direction of his troops.

"It's just us."

"What now?" Pieters asked.

They were in a hostile and visible area, with no clear route of escape. The armed group needed a plan.

Harding wondered to himself just what were they fighting for. His training instructed him to stay and patrol the streets until the situation had eased, but after everything they'd seen, he knew there was no easing this situation - at least not today. He decided to retreat.

"We need reinforcements. Let's form up and head back to base," Harding instructed.

"Yes, sir," came the relieved response.

"Hey. You," a slurred shout came from across the way.

A naked man approached, waving in the direction of the army. He gulped from a can of beer as he stumbled towards them.

"Stay back."

The army lowered their guns in his direction.

"I ain't got no weapons." He looked down at his nakedness - an abundance of chest hair keeping his skinny body warm. "Well, apart from this one." He whirled his flaccid member around in a circular motion.

"Hold fire," Harding instructed.

Harding removed his backpack from his shoulders, slung it around to his front, unzipped one of the compartments and pulled out a green blanket. He walked towards the drunk, naked man.

Harding attempted to place the blanket across the man's shoulders, but he shrugged it off.

"I don't need your fucking clothes, pig. I need a gun."

Harding ignored the man's incorrect estimation of his profession, collected the blanket from the floor, and squared up to the man who had confronted him.

He extended the blanket out in front of him.

"You must be cold. Please, take it."

The man looked down at the blanket, before rocking his head back and taking a small step backwards, almost losing his feet.

"Fuck you. Don't tell me what to do."

Harding thought for a moment before a question left his lips.

"What is it that you want?"

The man stood straighter. The can of beer slipped through his fingers to the floor as he placed a hand on Harding's shoulder. He moved in closer and whispered.

"It's not, hick, important what I want, it's what they want."

The man pulled his head back and smiled, only inches from Harding's face. He let out a burp which Harding ignored, despite the disgusting smell that lingered in the air afterwards.

"Tell me. What do they want?"

The man looked around him. Their conversation was private - despite the odd member of public rushing through the streets in the distance, and the military unit fully equipped with guns just metres away.

"They want you to die."

Harding tightened the grasp on his gun.

The man raised his voice and gestured in the army's direction.

"They want all of you to die."

The lunacy of a naked madman would usually be something to disdain, but something instructed Harding to listen. He tried to regain the man's attention.

"You're all going to die. I'm going to sit here and watch, if you don't mind?"

The man took the blanket in his hand, laid it out on the floor and then stumbled as he sat on it, falling backwards and bumping his head. He sat up, cross-legged and stared up at the military.

"You're all going to die. Do you hear me? They've told me. Every one of you will die. One by one, you're all going to die."

"Who are they?" Harding shouted in return.

"They're all around us. Can't you see them?" the man looked around, eyes-wide like he was observing a shower of shooting stars.

Harding glanced around him before refocusing on the man.

"No, I can't," he replied. "What are they?" he tried a different approach.

The man waited a moment, covering his genitals with the blanket to offer his private parts some warmth. He looked at the spillage of his lager on the floor, leant back and sighed.

"Angels? Demons? I don't know. It's the end of the world. You got any beer?"

Harding shook his head.

"Whisky? No? Fucking hell. I don't want to die sober."

"I don't think you're sober."

"No?" he smiled, and looked up at Harding. "Good. Good. Can I borrow your gun?"

"I can't let you do that. You're in no state to wield a weapon."

He sat and nodded to himself.

"Why do you want a gun, son?" Harding asked.

The moment reminded him of several times when he had difficult conversations with younger members of his unit in the past. He had revelled in being a shoulder for them. It also reminded him of moments where he had to sit and tell people's wives, brothers and sons, that their loved ones had been killed in action. He oozed empathy.

"Sir!" came a shout from the unit behind him.

He leant down to the eye level of the man sitting on the concrete floor. The skin on his bottom being protected only by the thin, green blanket.

"Son?"

The drunk Londoner looked at Harding, deep in the eyes.

"Listen, I really need a gun."

Against his better judgement and more shouts from his men behind him, Harding unlatched his gun and handed it to the man on the blanket.

"Thank you."

The man smiled in Harding's direction. He placed the gun under his chin and pulled the trigger. Harding jumped at the loud bang but reacted quickly enough to catch the limp body of the naked man as he fell to the floor. He cradled the man who had found relief.

"Sir. People are coming," the sergeant urged.

Harding laid the man down, picked up his weapon and turned to comprehend what enemy they were about to face.

A horde of people, hundreds upon hundreds deep, walked in their direction like a well-organised protest in the capital.

"What are the orders, sir?"

Harding looked around. He saw no exit from the wall of people approaching from all directions.

"Take aim," he instructed. "Contain the situation and focus your fire on the left flank."

"Yes, sir," the regiment echoed.

The unit backed against the wall and created a semi-circle formation. The sergeant was the first to fire, followed by all of the troops.

Shots rang out, culling the crowd one by one. But, as fast as they could fire, as a hole appeared, so did a replacement. The public gained distance.

The people stopped approaching. Bullets rang out, falling the front rows of the crowd. They had managed to maintain the distance for the moment but were unable to create an exit point.

The rest of the crowd stood still. Harding held his hand up for the fire to cease.

Ripples appeared in the crowd, as others began to make their way to the front-line.

The people approaching weren't the same as those that had been shot. Those approaching the front were younger, they were children; children with smiles broader than their tiny faces could contain.

As they lined up, their small eyes danced with excitement.

"Hold fire."

Children of all ages, from those that had just learnt to walk, up to teenagers, approached the front. They climbed over the bodies of the dead that blocked their way.

"Sir?"

"We can't kill all of these children," he responded.

"Then what do we do?"

Harding let his gun fall to his side as the young mob began their approach.

The swarm of children engulfed the military unit - punching, scratching, clawing, biting - the clicking and cracking of bones barely audible above the screams of the soldiers.

Just as quickly as they had accepted their fate, the soldiers were gone.

The young tore Harding's face with tiny claw-like fingers; his eyes gouged from their sockets by a group of children that only wanted to play soldier.

The children found the guns and began firing them into the air in victory.

The mob roared, victorious.

22

Charlie and Anabel arrived outside of the entrance at the NSA building. They watched it grow to mammoth proportions on their approach, meaning it was hard to miss.

A barricade blocked their entrance to the site and, with no security guard to raise it for them, they faced an issue.

"We need to walk from here," Anabel stated.

"Or we could ram it?" Charlie suggested, with a glint of hunger in his eyes.

"Ram it?"

"You know, drive through, send the barricade flying and look really badass."

Anabel stared at Charlie.

"It is good to see that you have not lost your sense of humour."

Charlie sighed before chuckling to himself; his laughter caused him to grasp his arm to alleviate the pain from his movement. He turned the engine off, reached across and opened the passenger door carefully.

Anabel exited the car, partially through the gap created by Charlie's gentleman-like action, and partly through the door itself.

Charlie followed and slammed the door behind him. He ducked underneath the barricade and walked into the car park, scanning for signs of life as he entered. There was no life that Charlie could see - to his relief, he saw no signs of death either.

"It's a bit quiet."

Anabel nodded.

"Let us make the most of it."

"Where is - what's his name?" Charlie searched his memory.

"William. I think he's in there."

Anabel pointed to the large building that stretched further to the clouds with every step they took.

They walked through the car park towards what appeared from afar to be the entrance. As they did so, Charlie was careful to move stealthily - half expecting the people who hunted him from the garage to somehow be waiting patiently for his arrival.

Charlie approached the side of the building. He noticed the reflective nature of the finish on the jet-black exterior, and in turn, saw his dishevelled reflection. He recognised that he needed a shave and, from the looks of it, he could do with a shower as well. Perhaps stubble wasn't his look, especially as it grew in a little patchy. He became more aware of his five, approaching six o'clock, shadow, so he decided to study his reflection.

The 'I love DC' t-shirt stole his gaze: his arm that sat outside the t-shirt and had been resting gently during the drive, had started to throb slightly from the large cut – and most likely due to the effect of the painkillers wearing thin. He adjusted his home-made sling, crusty to the touch with dried blood, as best he could.

As Charlie finished studying his reflection, he noticed that Anabel cast nothing on the black surface - like a vampire, he thought to himself.

Anabel walked past Charlie's moment of self-reflection and continued towards the entrance.

"It's clear," she reported back.

Charlie caught up with Anabel. To his relief, the door to the building was ajar and provided easy access.

"Perhaps I should go ahead? I can check that the corridors are clear before you proceed."

Charlie fought back the desire to disagree. He realised that no harm could come of Anabel, so he offered a nod in response.

In entering the NSA building, Charlie felt like a spy. Not a spy who was extremely adept at their job never to be discovered, more like a spy-in-training in a comedy film. He felt more like a spy that would bump into a pain of glass, shatter it and be discovered by all of his enemies, with a perplexed look on their faces.

He stood with his back flat against the wall of the opening corridor as he waited for Anabel to return.

"It's safe this way." Anabel appeared from the left-hand side.

"What are we looking for?" Charlie asked in a hushed voice, as he moved in the instructed direction.

"Movement, voices, any signs of life."

Charlie sighed. On the surface he was perilously frightened to find anybody, especially being alone in a government building such as this, but deep down he knew what he needed to do.

"Okay, where do we start?"

"I will look ahead, then perhaps we should split up to cover more ground?"

Charlie cleared the dryness in his throat with an extended swallow.

"Lead the way."

Anabel walked through the building as if there were no separation of areas. She walked through walls, wandered from room to room and considered different elements of the environment. She ensured that the corridors were empty and that there was nothing ahead that offered a fatal ending.

Charlie moved carefully. He walked as stealthily along the corridors as he possibly could. When he reached a door, he clicked it open gently and peered inside before entering. Some were locked, and the others revealed empty spaces inside.

After fifteen minutes of searching the first floor, they had covered all of the rooms that they could access and met back near the entrance.

"Did you find anything?" Charlie asked.

"Negative," Anabel responded.

"What next?"

"There is a stairwell. We need to move floor by floor until we find them."

Exhaustion caught up with Charlie. The last time he had done this much physical exercise was when he was at university, and had joined the football team for a short spell. That didn't end too well for him; he hoped that this might end a little better - but any non-final ending would suffice for the time being. Despite finding it hard to catch his breath due to the strain placed on his lungs only hours ago, he would soldier on.

"Let me know if you find any water," Charlie suggested. "Let's go."

They walked up the stairwell and began their search on the second floor.

Sweeping the level, Charlie noticed that it had almost identical elements to the first floor. It shared a very similar, if not, identical layout, along with the same degree of desertion.

The darkness of the building piqued Charlie's interest. There was no natural light whatsoever in the majority of the space - only the occasional tinted window in offices and viewing platforms that stretched around the outskirts of the building. Other than the rare unnatural light source, a mixture of spotlights supported their search, ranging from natural in colour to those with coloured hue in individual rooms and spaces.

The third floor opened up slightly differently to that of the second and first. A large viewing window greeted Charlie and Anabel – and, due to the reflectiveness of the exterior, Charlie assumed it was a one-way window. They stood and looked over the car park, noticing the occasional car moving in the distance.

Signs of life.

Knowing someone else was out there provided a flicker of hope, but it wasn't the life that they were looking for at this moment. They returned to their search.

In the viewing area, Charlie found a bottle of water located in a mini-fridge. Feeling a little rejuvenated, they continued to the fourth floor.

The fourth and fifth floors mirrored each other, as the first and second did previously. On these two floors, while Charlie could not gain access to a sealed entrance, the glass dividers showcased row after row of desks, with minimal space in-between. The workers here would be packed in like sardines - with each desk containing monitors and identical equipment to that next to it.

Anabel walked through the glass divider on the fifth floor into one of the areas. She dodged in between the stations, looking at the blank screens as she moved. Charlie stared at her from afar until she returned.

"Nothing there," she reported.

Anabel proceeded straight past Charlie without looking in his direction.

"Shall we try the next floor?" she asked.

The next floor was identical, and it wasn't until the eighth floor that they noticed something peculiar.

As the pair finished climbing the stairwell that separated the seventh and eighth floor, Charlie placed a hand on the entrance door. Just as Charlie was about to reach for the handle, he noticed a smudge of red. He ran a finger across it, which confirmed his suspicion. It was a sticky, viscous substance, which could only be one thing - blood.

"I'll go first." Anabel vanished through the door without waiting for a response.

Charlie waited a few seconds before slowly opening the door.

The eighth floor opened up similarly to many of those below it, with a slight difference. The lighting was reminiscent to that of a nightclub or a casino; the walls and ceiling lit by a vibrant purple hue with a complete lack of natural light.

Whether it was the blood or the disconcerting purple lights, Charlie sensed that hostility was only moments away.

Charlie opened the door fully and slid into a purple corridor. The room opened up on one side, and he entered. He noticed dozens of in-built monitors along a curved wall that combined to form one large screen.

The monitors dazzled him with bright lights. Charlie noticed a man dressed in a black hoodie, staring directly into the screen, with a dark room behind him.

"Hello, Charlie," William's voice began.

Charlie turned to face the screens, with William's face appearing God-like as it filled the entire wall.

"I've been waiting for you."

"Who are you?" Charlie replied, to which William did not respond.

Anabel appeared at Charlie's side.

"Is that William?" Charlie asked.

Anabel nodded.

"Then we're in the right place," Charlie confirmed.

"I've got something important to tell you. Why don't you join me? I'm in room 811A."

Charlie and Anabel shared a glance.

"It's a trap, right?" Charlie asked.

"I would assume so," she responded.

"Then, what are we waiting for?" Charlie grinned, feigning confidence.

Anabel smiled in return.

Charlie looked deep into Anabel's eyes, who returned his gaze; a larger than life William behind them.

Charlie closed the gap between Anabel and himself.

"If we don't make it, I just want you to know-" Charlie began.

"We will make it," Anabel interrupted.

Charlie nodded. The rest of the sentence distanced itself from his lips.

Anabel raised her hand to Charlie's face. Static electricity sparked from his face to her hand, causing small fragments of facial hair to stand on end. His hairs fought against the entrapment of his skin, reaching out for Anabel in desperation. His entire being felt the same way.

"Come, Charlie. Come and play with me," William's voice broke their gaze. Charlie's facial hair returned to its natural resting point as Anabel lowered her hand from his face.

"It is time," Anabel announced. "I will find the first, and an answer to the corruption."

"I'll keep William busy. Maybe ask him a question or two about his childhood or his favourite movie," Charlie jested. "Maybe I'll ask him for some advice on how to pull a hoodie off, without looking like a complete psychopath. Oh, wait, maybe not."

Laughter rumbled from Anabel's lips and exploded from her chest. She laughed, loudly, for a few seconds before restraining herself.

"It wasn't that funny." Charlie stroked the back of his neck, smiling. His grin grew as he traced his eyes back to Anabel.

She leant in, mouth partially agape, as she placed her lips on his. Each nerve ending in Charlie's lips felt like they were being pulled to the surface, creating an area of static and pressure, focused around his mouth. He closed his eyes and moved his mouth gently, feeling the static move and match his rhythm.

He opened his eyes and saw Anabel staring back at him; eyes wide open. His lips tingled, and his body felt full of energy - like it had just had a quick recharge from a human battery pack.

William's taunts on the screen became meaningless. Charlie's worries about his friends, about Jenny, and his endless internal conflicts, vanished. Even the impending doom of humanity faded temporarily.

He stood in awe, mouth agape. The blonde barmaid stared back at him.

"Anabel," the words flowed from his lips.

"Charlie," she replied tenderly.

"What are you waiting for?" William's words found their mark.

Looking at the screen, Charlie caught a glance of a woman and two children in his peripheral vision.

"There are some friends here who want to play as well," William threatened the woman. "Go on, tell them you want to play."

Andrea cried. She held each of her fatherless children tightly under her arms, protected in her tight embrace.

William laughed maniacally, puncturing the possibility of Charlie and Anabel sharing another kiss.

"Let's go," Charlie suggested. "We've got to be close."

Anabel nodded. She raced ahead, vanishing to check the rooms in front.

Charlie followed. Once again, he remained a few seconds behind. He watched Anabel appear back in the corridor each time she came out from rooms on either side.

After walking for a few minutes, they searched deeper inside the density of the eighth floor's winding pathways. Anabel re-appeared; her demeanour altered significantly.

"They're in there," Anabel confirmed, pointing to a door that faced them - only metres away, on the right-hand side.

Charlie tiptoed closer.

"In here?" he whispered.

Anabel nodded.

"How many?"

"Just William - and the family."

Charlie concentrated on his breathing, attempting to remain as stealthy as possible as he took slow, methodical steps towards the room. He wondered why William would leave himself so open. Did it mean that he might be able to overpower him?

Just one more step. Charlie took a deep and silent breath and placed his right foot in front of his left; his good hand found the metal door handle that felt cool to the touch.

He pondered his approach. Should he run in headfirst? Throw himself at William before he had too much time to react? Or, perhaps he wouldn't notice the door quietly open, and Charlie could sneak up on him? Neither seemed like great ideas.

Charlie slowly pushed the outside of the handle towards the floor and, with a gentle click, the door opened. Pushing the door gently, he found himself met by William, the terrified eyes of Andrea and her children, and a dead man who he instantly identified as the President of the United States of America.

"We had a bit of fun before you got here, Charlie." William gestured for him to join them.

"How do you know my name?" Charlie asked, as he stepped into the room, ensuring the door hadn't fully closed behind him. He allowed himself at least some form of an escape route should events deteriorate.

Rage found its way to the surface. He carried so much anger for the person who had killed the president and held his family hostage. Fear quickly followed. Charlie wondered what William had planned for him - and just what else he was capable of.

A concoction of emotion mixed furiously within Charlie, freezing him in his steps.

"Come on in, take a seat."

William motioned for Charlie to join Andrea and her family who sat in the middle of the granite floor.

Charlie edged forward. He felt static on his arm as Anabel attempted to stop him, but it was to no effect. The door behind him didn't contain a self-closing mechanism and remained open. Perhaps he could help the family escape if he provided a distraction.

"I know what you're thinking," William began. "You could distract me, and they could escape. You could save the children, am I right? Come on, tell me I'm right."

Charlie turned his attention to William, wondering whether to lunge at him or engage in conversation.

"Go on then. Try to save them."

William didn't appear to have a weapon. However, his black hoodie left plenty of hiding space. Charlie chose the safer option and inched over to Andrea before placing his hand on her trembling shoulder.

"Are you alright?" he asked.

Andrea raised her eyes from her children, and he instantly saw that Andrea was no victim. Her lip curled in a ferocious manner displaying her top teeth and canines; her eyes shined like those of a tiger protecting its cubs.

Charlie smiled and allowed Andrea to return her focus to her children.

"Get on with it," William ordered with an even tone to his voice.

Charlie helped Andrea to her feet, her children grasping on to her for dear life. She stood and looked at her dead husband on the floor, then at William.

"Don't even try it. Unless you want your children to end up the same way."

Her children wailed as they saw their motionless father - and the bullet-shaped hole in his skull.

Andrea cradled both children and hurried towards the door with Charlie's assistance.

"Go," Charlie said to Andrea. "Find help."

Andrea nodded and ran. Before Charlie could think of what to say next, she was gone. Charlie peered out of the door and watched Andrea run hand in hand with her two children - away from the resting place of her husband.

"See. I'm not all bad," William suggested.

Charlie turned his attention to William. Perhaps there was the possibility to surprise him if he played along.

"I guess not," Charlie replied, biting through insincerity.

William retrieved a chair and placed it next to his in anticipation of a civilised conversation.

Charlie walked to the chair. Without taking his eyes off of William, he sat down slowly. Charlie noticed the cold leather on his lower back, the back of his t-shirt rolling up as he perched on the expensive cushioned seat. He adjusted his clothes and felt the coolness fade away.

"Comfortable?"

Charlie ignored the question. Instead, he risked a glance at the large screen and digital panel.

William noticed Charlie's glance and responded in turn.

"It's magnificent, is it not?" William stared at the large display behind him.

The screen covered the entire wall; split into sections that each displayed a different news report from what appeared to be news stations around the world.

The news reports flickered between footage of the president's death and acts of terror that occurred in their area. A few screens displayed static.

"These are the main news stations from all over the world. Well, what's left of them." William gestured towards the ones with static.

He turned his focus towards Charlie, using the wheels on his chair to close the gap between the two of them to inches.

"The world... it's dying." Charlie reluctantly acknowledged.

"The world, as you know it, is already dead." William cemented his view.

"But why? Why would you do this?"

William's head rocked back with laughter. Charlie waited for him to finish, which seemed to take an age.

"Me? No, I didn't do any of this."

Charlie looked over at the dead president on the floor, only feet away from their conversation.

"Well, I suppose I did do that."

"Why?"

"I'm merely following orders."

"From whom?"

"You know who. She said that your eyes are open."

Charlie felt like he was getting close, but was unsure as to what line of questioning to take. Before he had the opportunity, William slammed his hand on the desk in front of them, causing Charlie to jolt upright and raise his hands to protect his face.

"I'm not going to hurt you, Charlie."

Charlie lowered his hands back down towards his side.

"In fact, I want you to join me. Do you know how hard it is to get good help these days?" William gestured around towards the dead body by their side. "I thought the President of the United States of America would be the best bet, right? But no, he was very stubborn."

"Why me?"

"You know why."

Charlie took a moment to consider his options before he was cut short.

"Because you know the truth. We both do." William gestured upwards. "Can you see yours?" he asked, not entirely confident in his tone.

Charlie turned to Anabel. His watcher stood at his side, observing every moment. He turned back to William and nodded.

"She's here now?" William bounced around in his chair like an excited child. "Oh, that is glorious!"

William rose from his chair dramatically.

"Is the first here?" Charlie mouthed to Anabel, who shook her head in return.

"I was never a religious man, but that night when I heard her voice; that sweet, sweet voice. The voice of an angel."

"An angel?" Charlie questioned.

"Oh lord, yes, my very own guardian angel. Who'd have thought?"

"He thinks we're angels?" Anabel asked.

It made sense to Charlie. He could have easily come to the same conclusion if he hadn't been able to sit down and have an actual conversation.

"And ever since that moment, I've known my path. I've known my destiny."

Charlie fidgeted slightly in his chair. He tugged at the tethering around his arm to provide a small amount of comfort. The cut itched - not furiously enough to cause Charlie to scratch, but enough for it to remain at the forefront of his mind.

"I wonder what your path is, Charlie. What has your angel commanded from you?"

Charlie took a moment to think of a response.

"Come on, less of that. Tell me the truth. We're the same, you and I. That's why your angel brought you here. No?"

Charlie clenched his jaw. He gritted his teeth and nodded.

"A higher being has spoken to us and revealed the evils of this world."

"Yes." Charlie agreed on that point.

"That there are people who need to be stopped?"

Charlie nodded again.

"Good." William took a moment to consider his next move before playfully slapping Charlie on the thigh.

Charlie jolted. It was only a slight movement, but enough to give away the unease that he carried inside. William narrowed his gaze, causing Charlie to try to look as comfortable as possible.

"So, what shall we do next, Charlie?"

"I don't know, William."

William sat upright in his chair. He bounced around once more and became visibly short of breath. It shouldn't have been a surprise that Charlie knew his name, but it perhaps solidified his views on angels being real.

"You are the one," William observed.

Perhaps he thought that Charlie could be his second in command in this new world. William wanted to rule, that much was clear, and then Charlie could take care of the smaller things, like killing people.

William's eyes glazed over. An opening presented itself.

Charlie clenched his good fist, ready to pounce.

"No, Charlie!" Anabel shouted, but it was too late.

Charlie dived out of his chair, hit William in the middle of his chest, and sent them both toppling to the floor. William took most of the impact and lay on the floor coughing, but it was Charlie who writhed in agony from the impact of the hard floor against his arm.

Charlie pushed through the pain as the dried blood on his makeshift sling welcomed a fresher batch. He rose to his feet and jumped down on William before his foe had any awareness of what was happening. Charlie clenched his fist. He brought his free hand down on to the face lying underneath him, feeling William's jaw crack as a shout of pain left his lungs.

The second blow brought a shared pain, and Charlie uncurled his bruised fingers. He refused to spend time wondering whether he had just broken part of his hand and instead wrapped his sore fingers around the collar of William's black hoodie.

"Where's your watcher?"

"What?" William reacted, shielding his face from another attack.

"Your angel," Charlie corrected.

"I, I don't know. She comes when she has a message."

"Get her here now," Charlie ordered.

"I can't."

Charlie let go of the hoodie and curled his fist into another ball. He fought through the pain that flared from almost every joint that connected his hand and fingers. When he retracted his arm backwards, he saw William's face turn from one of trepidation to delight.

The sound of a door clicking shut joined them.

Charlie's fist never struck William's face for a third time.

Instead, he moved further from William, as strong arms forcefully pulled him to a standing position - the silent assassin had entered the room at the sound of unexpected violence.

There was no chance for Charlie to escape the trained grip of the man who was holding him. Charlie found himself in a position where he had no room to fight or to break free. The makeshift sling that protected Charlie's arm broke and his injured arm joined the other above his head.

William rose to his feet, like a fallen commander who had just received life-saving reinforcements to win a battle. He spat out a piece of his tooth and moved his jaw in circles, creating audible cracks as he did so.

"You like punching people, do you?"

Charlie struggled, to no avail.

"Charlie!" Anabel screamed, to an empty audience.

William clenched his fist and returned Charlie's violent act to his unprotected midsection.

"Charlie!" Anabel shook as she screamed.

William punched his unprotected adversary repeatedly until blood spluttered from his mouth. Taking a break to wipe the blood from Charlie's face, William smiled. He pulled Charlie's eyes to his level for a one-way conversation.

"So, I guess you're not to be my partner after all."

William adjusted his jaw. He opened his mouth repeatedly before refocusing on the opportunity that had slipped through his fingers.

"That's a shame, a real shame. Put him down."

Charlie fell to the floor, clutching at his midsection with both arms.

His bodyguard, Ed, stood silently, waiting for orders.

"We could have built a world together." William reminisced on the possibility that was now never to arrive.

Anabel looked on, helpless.

"But, instead, I suppose I'll have to rule alone."

William nodded at Ed.

Ed reached his hand into his pocket, causing Anabel to scream. Ed retrieved the same firearm that he used to kill the president. This time he raised the sight to Charlie's temple.

A flash of red lit the room. The first watcher appeared before Anabel.

"Wait," William instructed.

She was a replica of Anabel, except something was different in the way she held herself, something altered in her aura; like a mad brilliance that radiated from her very being.

"Stop it," Anabel pleaded.

The first tilted her head to one side with one quick, unnatural movement. She observed Anabel.

"You can stop this. All of it."

The first's mouth opened, but her voice was deeper than Anabel's. Her response was raw and animalistic.

"Why. Would. I. Do. That?" The first breathed maniacally, the hate evident with each word.

"Because it is wrong."

The first's neck snapped from one side to the other, yet she still observed Anabel, in a twisted way.

"Is. It. Wrong? Look. At. Them." The first's arms twisted to point at William and Charlie.

"Yes," Anabel exclaimed.

The first appeared to grow larger and more empowering as each moment passed.

"This. Is. Not. Wrong." The first pointed to William, Ed and Charlie, with a crooked finger. "They. Are."

"It is not them. There is something wrong with you," Anabel pushed.

"Impossible." The first hissed each syllable.

"There is something wrong," Anabel urged. "Corruption spreads throughout our kind."

"I. Am. The. First." She looked piercingly into Anabel's eyes, a distorted smile displaying large, pointed teeth. "I. Am. The. Corruption."

Before Anabel could interject, the first whispered an order.

"Kill. All. Of. Them."

"No!" Anabel screamed.

William walked over to his assistant, placed his hand gently on the assassin's trigger hand, and slid the gun from his grasp. He pointed the gun at Charlie.

"It is what she has commanded," William shared.

Charlie accepted his fate. At that moment, he didn't fear the pain of death; but instead, feared the knowledge that he would have no future. Charlie would not see his friends. He would never talk to Anabel again or share another kiss.

A gunshot filled the air.

Charlie raised his hands to his head, not that it would help to protect him in his last moments.

Instead of a complete void, Charlie found that he still had a grasp on life. He raised his head towards the silent assassin that lay on the floor; a gaping hole through his skull created a river of blood that ran in his direction.

The red river reached William's foot. He looked down and shook his trainer before turning his aim to Charlie.

"Everyone has to die," William began. "The world will start again."

William brought the crosshairs up and aimed the weapon between Charlie's eyes.

Anabel jumped desperately in the direction of the first watcher.

Sparks of blue and red filled the room. Anabel grappled with the twisted and mangled body parts of the first, struggling to adapt to the non-human-like movements. Luckily, she caught the first by surprise and managed to get a hold around her neck from behind.

"Stop it now," Anabel roared

The room filled with laughter from the first, joined shortly after by that of William's.

William placed his finger on the trigger.

"Stop it!" Anabel roared at the top of her lungs.

The laughter continued from the first, rising in volume to a point which became overpowering.

"No!" Anabel screamed.

Blue currents exploded from Anabel in all directions, filling the room with electricity. The displays on the wall flickered.

Anabel roared her final scream of desperation, summoning all of her might. Her body began to shake as blue and red currents blurred the boundaries between the watchers and reality.

"You. Can't. Stop. The. First."

A ball of electrical current grew between the two watchers as the first matched Anabel's energy; the sphere of energy pulsated with blue and red, with purity and corruption, life and death.

William squeezed the trigger.

The electrical current emanating from the watchers erupted with an enormous explosion of energy, crossing worlds, knocking William off of his feet. The bullet flew millimetres wide of Charlie's skull. All the glass in the room exploded. The large display smashed and the lights above showered glass over the room's inhabitants. Charlie cradled his head in his arms in the newfound darkness.

William fell to the floor, clutching at the side of his head as he landed by his once second-in-command.

"Charlie!" Anabel rushed over to the person who completed her. "Are you okay?" She stroked his head.

Charlie's ears rang from the explosion, and he felt tiny nicks all over his bare skin from where glass had slashed his arms and shoulders. He used his hands to carefully trace his face and neck, followed by his body, praying that he wouldn't find another large shard of glass.

The cut on his arm bled gently and caused a substantial discomfort as Charlie traced his wound, but after a few moments, he rose to his feet in the dark.

"I think I'm okay."

Charlie felt Anabel's arms reach around him in a tight embrace. Charlie could see her outline from the glow of her eyes. He lifted his arms around her and allowed her energy to engulf him.

The first wrapped her hands around Anabel's throat from behind, prying her from the loving embrace.

The first's words arrived, even further apart than before.

"You... Can... Not... Stop... Us," the first threatened, through snapping fangs.

"Anabel!"

Charlie lunged at Anabel, who appeared to be struggling to breathe; her skin became paler by the second.

Flickers of red began to dance across her skin.

"You... will... join... me," the first ordered.

Charlie passed straight through his watcher, tripping and falling on to the floor behind her.

"Charlie!" Anabel let out a desperate scream.

Watchers

Charlie found his way back to his feet and looked at Anabel. In the dark, he saw her face lit up, ghostly white, spare flickers of blue and red that emanated from her being. He watched helplessly as a red current spread across her face, flowing down her throat, up her nose and into her eyes and ears.

Anabel's struggles began to slow. The first whispered words of knowledge in Anabel's ear; she spoke words of power.

Charlie watched Anabel's bright blue eyes battle against waves of red; the onslaught of corruption continuous.

The edges of Anabel's lips twitched upwards, forming the beginning of a smile.

Charlie fought for action. He was helpless, but he couldn't just let Anabel be taken from him. He couldn't do anything, except perhaps one thing.

He felt his way along the floor, being careful not to cut his hands on the glass until he came to a body. The body was cold and sticky to the touch, so he continued until he found another. This person retracted slightly, and Charlie knew he had found what he was looking for.

He sat across William's legs to stop him from moving. After being content that he had trapped the man underneath him, Charlie used his hands to trace for signs of weakness on William's body.

Anabel had stopped fighting. He didn't have much time.

He retracted his hand sharply, knowing – without sight to be able to reinforce the opinion - that he'd just cut himself. Charlie returned his hands to the area, slower this time and felt the edges of what seemed to be a large piece of glass protruding from William's midsection.

Charlie paused for a moment, waiting to hear the refusal of Anabel, but instead met with silence.

He had no choice.

Fighting the pain that reared from the cut on his hand, the bruising on his fist, and the screaming from his arm, Charlie pushed the shard of glass as forcefully as he could further into William's chest.

The man below him writhed, coughed and spluttered.

"Anabel?"

Nothing.

Charlie pushed the shard down until there was no more resistance. He felt the warmth of blood ooze out across his hands. In the absence of Anabel, Charlie was blind.

He rose to his feet and stepped in the direction of where he believed the door to have been. Charlie almost tripped over the former president's body in his search. He traced the wall, his hands frantically searching over the surfaces, until he found the edge of a handle. The handle moved effortlessly.

Light flooded through the gap, illuminating death and desperation. William had joined the deceased.

Anabel sat in the middle of the room, head down facing the ground.

"Anabel!" Charlie rushed over and knelt before her, not letting the sharp stabbing pains that met his knees abort his mission.

Charlie reached out to touch Anabel, but reached right through her, the hairs on his arm standing on end as he did so.

"I know…" Anabel spoke, her voice somewhat deeper and systematic than before.

"Anabel, you're alright."

"I am not all right."

"Anabel? Where is the first?"

"She is gone."

Charlie took a moment before words found him.

"So, we've stopped the corruption?"

Anabel shook her head, the speed of her head movement shifting jarringly between fast and slow.

"What do you mean?" Charlie's heart raced.

Anabel raised her head and turned to face Charlie. She lifted her eyes to meet his.

Charlie lost his breath and found his feet moving him back towards the door.

Anabel's eyes radiated with a ferocious mixture of red and blue. Her eyes swirled with electricity and, as red battled blue, blue fought back - an endless dance of good versus evil.

"Corruption will always exist, Charlie."

"But, we stopped the first."

"There will always be a first."

"But doesn't that give us time?"

Anabel shook her head. As she did so, her neck twisted slightly too far on each occasion.

"The corruption has spread too far. It needs someone to control it."

Charlie felt the tension leave him slightly and approached Anabel. He stopped a few inches from her.

"I can control it."

The colour in Anabel's eyes swirled; the red washed over the blue for a moment.

"Anabel." Charlie approached until he was only inches from his watcher. He reached out to feel her hand. He was met with an electric shock, rather than static, and quickly retracted his hand.

Blue returned to Anabel's eyes, creating a concoction of the two colours.

"Are you okay?" Charlie asked tentatively. He felt the effect of his injuries, as the adrenaline faded.

"I can control them. I can feel it."

Anabel bound her eyes tightly shut, battling sparks of red and blue trying to escape.

"Can you control yourself?" Charlie asked.

Anabel ignored his comment and opened her eyes.

Charlie reached his hand out to touch Anabel but, before he could brush her face, she disappeared with a flash of red and blue. Once again, he was left alone. Charlie glanced his eyes over the lifeless bodies at his feet. There was nothing left for him here.

Gathering his wits, Charlie ran from the room, from the NSA building, and began his long journey home.

EPILOGUE

C hildren around the world played. They laughed.
From England to Australia, from Hong Kong to Tibet, children allowed invasive whispers to take the reins and subsequently make their moves.

The game was not exclusive. It was open to all ages. From young students with their entire lives ahead of them to the elderly who would typically be resting quietly. Men and women of all ages joined, en masse.

The young and the old participated.

Those that weren't aware they were playing, still had no choice. And, as the children, men and women sat playing with the bloody carcasses of those that they had forced to join in, they had served their purpose - they had played their hand and completed their turn.

A break in the game began suddenly.

Millions upon millions stopped in their tracks. Some found themselves in the middle of a turn, others were just about to start – but, in a single moment, each and every person worldwide paused and were no longer forced to continue. Some broke down in floods of tears, others shouted for loved ones. Whatever the reaction of the players, the majority chose to stop and change their strategy.

Yet, some excelled in the character that they had taken control of, for it was who they were always supposed to become. Those players continued. They had opened a new path that was exciting and full of possibilities. It would take some time for those to understand the depth of what they desired, but they aimed to find out.

Across the world, the two teams divided into smaller segments. The game would always continue, but no longer would it consist of just two sides; no longer would it consist of good against evil — new teams formed through aligned wants and needs, and ever-increasing layers upon layers. The two teams split into thousands, which quickly became millions. The game could be played in groups or as individuals, but now there was a choice.

Children. Men. Women. Babies. Transgender. Straight. Gay. Bisexual. Black. White. Disabled. Terminally ill. The clinically insane. The game discriminated against no one - it would always continue.

The rules remained the same, but each player would be allowed the opportunity to play their hand.

The choice of humanity was infinite.

***

The clear blue waves rocked gently against the sandy shore in a repeatedly hypnotic fashion. The sun of the day had passed, and the day turned gently into the night. The temperature was warm, but not blistering, yet there were no clouds in sight. It was the perfect weather for a lazy evening by the sea.

The pristine beach was almost deserted; spare a few people relaxing in their retirement. The inhabitants purposely left enough space between each other to take in the evening in isolation.

Gerald lay back on his sun lounger. He collected his no-longer-ice-cold beer from the makeshift beer holder he forged from the sand and took a sip. The lukewarm hops quenched his thirst and left him with a pleasant aftertaste before he returned his beer to the sand below.

Gerald noticed something dark and furry on the ground next to his can.

He looked up and saw his wife lying on her back with her eyes closed. Her head glistened - the sun bouncing from bald patches between the odd tuft of hair.

"Dear, your wig fell off again." Gerald collected the oversized hairpiece and handed it over to her.

"What would I do without you, darling?"

His wife placed the wig back on her head, a little off-centre, sat up and leant over to kiss Gerald. She leant back in her lounger, but this time held her hairpiece in place.

She reached out with her free hand and found Gerald's.

The two retirees lay back, hand-in-hand, enjoying the tranquillity of the waves.

***

Jenny unfolded the nurse's outfit from the foot of her bed and held it up against her torso. She absorbed her reflection and allowed herself a small smile before folding the uniform and placing it into her drawer.

"Wine?" Rachel shouted through from the kitchen.

"Yes, please," Jenny responded.

"White, red or rosé?"

"Whatever you want."

Jenny closed the bedroom door behind her and walked through to the living room. She sat down on the sofa, patiently awaiting her well-deserved glass of wine.

Rachel came back over with two large glasses of red wine.

"It felt like a red kind of night, you know?" Rachel commented as she hovered by the sofa.

"Are you not having any?" Jenny asked.

Steve put his arm around Rachel's midsection and invited her to his lap. He clenched his teeth as she sat, but his face shortly lit up after Rachel kissed his cheek.

"No, I'm alright," Steve responded. "Thank you."

Jenny nodded.

"No, really. Thank you," Steve said to Jenny.

The warmth Jenny felt inside her at that moment was the same warmth she had felt when she had helped save patients' lives in the hospital. It was the same she had felt every day since then during her long shifts.

"Working tomorrow, Jen?" Steve asked.

"Another twelve-hour shift."

Steve let out an elongated whistle.

"What about you babe?" Steve asked the girl on his lap.

"Just looking after you." Rachel ran her fingers through his hair, twisting what she could around her finger.

Steve made a gagging noise before Rachel playfully punched his arm.

A knock at the door did nothing to interrupt the gesturing between the two lovebirds.

"Be careful with him."

Jenny answered the door, trying to contain her excitement as she opened it.

"Charlie," Jenny leant in and hugged him. She was careful not to press too hard on his arm, which he still held up to his chest, despite the absence of a sling.

Charlie walked in and smiled in Steve's direction.

"Come on, guys, get a room."

Steve held his middle finger up to Charlie, while Rachel grabbed Steve's face and kissed him, using far too much tongue to make a statement.

"How are you?" Jenny asked gently.

"Okay." Charlie brushed off the question and walked in, letting the warmth of the apartment envelope him - a stark difference from the bitterness of the late autumn evening air outside.

Charlie walked over to the kitchen, accompanied by Jenny. He picked up the bottle of wine and a glass.

"Do you mind?"

Jenny shook her head.

"Help yourself."

Charlie poured himself half a glass.

He took a deep breath, allowing the air to fill his lungs. He noticed a familiar smell in the air.

"What's for dinner?" Charlie wondered out loud.

"Mac 'n cheese," Jenny responded.

Charlie smiled - every ounce of tension leaving his body.

"My favourite," he whispered.

THE END

THANK YOU.

If you made it this far then I am eternally grateful. This is my first book and to have you read it means the world to me.

I've left the ending of Watchers somewhat open, so if a sequel is of interest to you then please let me know. I'm currently writing my second book (due to be released early 2021), but after that I might return to Charlie and the gang.

Don't forget to leave a review on Amazon. Every rating or review really helps.

If you liked Watchers then please recommend it to your friends; share your thoughts on social media using #WatchersNovel and sign up to the newsletter.

And a final thank you to my amazing friends and family for their unwavering support.

DON'T FORGET TO SIGN UP TO THE NEWSLETTER

Receive special offers, giveaways, bonus content, updates from the author, and be the first to hear about new releases:

www.bit.ly/hearfromcraig

Craig Priestley is a fiction author based in London, UK. He graduated from the University of Greenwich in 2008 with a Bachelor of Arts degree in Media Writing. After graduating, he worked in television production and advertising as an award-winning producer – but the love for creative writing remained. He is enchanted with creating fictional worlds, as well as spending time with his fiancée, Sarah (and their pets).

SOCIAL MEDIA:
Facebook.com/authorpriestley
Instagram @AuthorPriestley
Twitter @AuthorPriestley

Printed in Great Britain
by Amazon